'I have to le

'Leave!' His remark jolted her back into reality. 'You cannot leave in this weather. You will be dead within half an hour! And you are in no condition to travel,' she added, seeing the perspiration on his brow and the fever in his eyes.

'Neither is the rest of the army,' Tristan said bitterly.

'Even Bonaparte cannot expect dead men to fight for him!'

Dear Reader

We welcome new author Marie-Louise Hall to the list—
she has treated us to a look at Napoleon's retreat from
Moscow, and a tempestuous love story for Tristan and
Angèle! After two excellent Regencies, Paula Marshall
has moved to fifteenth-century Tuscany in her new story.
Piero is a wonderful hero, and the blossoming of Bianca
is a delight! Despite a six-month gap, Paula has not been
idle, and there are excellent books by her scheduled for
next year—look out for them.

The Editor

Marie-Louise Hall was born in Wiltshire. She studied
history at the University of London, where she met her
husband. After several years they moved to rural
Aberdeenshire. As she is domestically incompetent, her
ambition since marriage has been to find time to write.
Recently her husband suggested she leave the housework
to him, and now she spends every spare minute at the
typewriter. She also works for her husband's oil industry
consultancy, looks after her young son, three cats, and
three delinquent donkeys.

THE CAPTAIN'S ANGEL

Marie-Louise Hall

First published in Great Britain 1992
by Mills & Boon Limited

© Marie-Louise Hall 1992

Australian copyright 1992
Philippine copyright 1992
This edition 1992

ISBN 0 263 77921 1

Masquerade is a trademark published by
Mills & Boon Limited, Eton House,
18–24 Paradise Road, Richmond, Surrey, TW9 1SR.

Set in 10 on 11 pt Linotron Plantin
04-9211-83251

Typeset in Great Britain by Centracet, Cambridge
Made and printed in Great Britain

CHAPTER ONE

'IT IS not far now. Not far.' Angèle spoke aloud, to reassure herself as much as the three shaggy cream ponies that drew her sleigh. The blizzard was worsening by the minute. Huddling deeper into her soft white sheepskin coat, so that only her blue-green eyes showed between its high collar and the Cossack cap pulled low on her brow, she raised her whip and flicked it expertly above the ponies' heads. The ponies responded, increasing their pace through the ever-deepening snow.

Would André and his men still be harassing what was left of Napoleon Bonaparte's army? she wondered. Or was he even now on his way back to the dacha? At least one thing was certain: he would not be able to pursue her during this storm. The snow was falling in smaller flakes now, whipped by a biting wind. The tracks left by her sleigh were covered within seconds, and it was impossible to see any further than the tips of the lead ponies' ears. But safety from pursuit had its price. Even her sturdy little Siberian ponies were beginning to falter in the face of the storm. Surely she must reach the lodge soon?

Gritty particles of snow stung her eyes as she raised her head. Nothing except the swirling, flurrying snow. Soon it would be nightfall and if she had not reached shelter before dark. . . It was best not to think of that or of wolves. She blinked, trying to clear her eyes of the snow; was that a more solid shape in the whiteness? A moment later she uttered a heartfelt prayer of relief as the ponies came to an abrupt halt before the long, low shape of the Perenskovs' hunting lodge.

The deserted wooden building was divided into two,

one half a barn, the other the living accommodation. The windows were dark and there was no sign of life, but as she clambered down from the sleigh she could not rid herself of the uneasy sensation that she was being watched. But it was ridiculous. The Perenskovs were in St Petersburg with Tsar Alexander, and no serf in his right mind would be out in the forest in such weather.

The ponies pushed forward eagerly and their weight sent the barn door swinging inward, away from the drift of snow that had built up against the outside. The interior was forbidding and almost pitch black, but the ponies showed no sign of unease as they dragged the sleigh in after them. Reassured by their lack of anxiety, she followed.

Discarding her outer gloves, Angèle began to unharness the ponies. Servants had always done this for her, and the task took all of her attention. After what seemed like an eternity the ponies were free to snatch mouthfuls of hay from the pile stacked against one wall. As soon as they were cool she would bring them water to drink. But in the meantime she needed warmth and refreshment. There was a connecting door from the barn into the living quarters, but it seemed to be bolted from the inside. Wearily she replaced her gloves and prepared to step out into the storm again, without noticing the exhausted black horse that stood, head down, in the darkest corner of the barn.

Captain Tristan Beaumaris watched the Cossack arrive through one of the windows. His chapped lips curved in a wry smile. It seemed as if the luck that had brought him through such battles as Marengo, Austerlitz and Borodino was about to run out. The devil's luck, his men called it, half envious and half admiring.

Out of long habit he assessed the odds. His pistols were empty and he had no more ammunition. He was cold, damnably cold. His body was stiff and sluggish, protesting at every movement. The wound in his shoulder meant that his right arm was almost useless. The fellow must have seen his horse in the barn by now. He shook his head and a lock of untidy black hair fell forward on his forehead. This was a fight he was unlikely to walk away from. But it would be better to die fighting than be flayed alive while a Cossack dragged you behind his horse over the frozen ground. Awkwardly he drew his sword with his left hand and waited.

'*Sacrebleu!*' He swore beneath his breath as he watched the snow-blurred figure heave the barn door shut. Could it be that the fellow had not noticed his horse? There was no sign of wariness about the man who trudged towards the door of the lodge and he had not drawn a weapon. Any soldier deserved to die for such carelessness. Smiling grimly, he moved silently to the door. Now he had one element in his favour—surprise. If he struck first he might just have a chance.

Angèle pushed at the door of the lodge with all her strength, expecting the hinges to be frozen solid. To her surprise, it gave immediately, and she went sprawling into the dim interior.

The fall saved her life. The savage swinging blow that the man aimed at her hissed over her head, and there was a dull clunk as the heavy sword sank itself into the door-jamb.

Sick with terror, she scrambled to her feet, backing away from the tall figure. A French soldier clad in a tattered green cloak—that much she saw in her first horrified glance. Everything she had been told about the men who served Napoleon came flooding back into her mind. They were coarse, brutish, mercenary men, ill-educated and uncouth. Men who lived only for killing and war. As if in a nightmare from which she could not wake, she heard him swear violently in French as he wrenched the sword free of the wood and turned towards her. He was going to kill her; she saw it in the way he moved and in the harsh line of his mouth.

She should stop him. Tell him she was French by birth, not Russian. She must say something, anything. But her tongue seemed thick and swollen, refusing to frame the words. Her brain was paralysed with fear, and her heart slowed painfully as she stared at him helplessly. She was tall for a woman, but he towered over her by a head and shoulders. Gaunt-featured and black-browed. Ridiculously she noticed that his thick, unruly black hair needed cutting and he was badly in need of a shave. Then her eyes collided with his, and her blood seemed to turn to ice in her veins. His eyes were the coldest she had ever seen, frosted silver like winter moonlight on snow.

Holy mother! He's only a boy. Beaumaris swore inwardly as he raised his sword again. All he could see of the Cossack was the pair of large, intensely blue-green eyes that peeped out from between the high fur collar of his coat and the fur hat pulled low on his brow. He knew better than to show sentiment to any Cossack, no matter how young. But the fear in the boy's turquoise eyes touched a part of him that years of campaigning had never quite succeeded in hardening. He could still remember the initial terror that had gripped him in his first real fight. A fair fight was one thing, murder was another. But there was no alternative. Neither he nor the army, if he should ever find it again, were in any condition to take prisoners. And he could not allow the lad to raise the alarm. If he restrained him and left him in the lodge he might freeze or starve to death. No. Better to make a clean end to it one way or the other. These Cossack lads were weaned with swords in their hands. If the boy would fight, the odds were probably in his favour. Surely the lad had noticed how awkwardly he had used his sword with his left hand?

'What's wrong with you, Russian? Why don't you fight, damn you?' Beaumaris shouted in halting, heavily accented Russian. 'Arm yourself!' He gestured towards a pair of sabres hanging on the wood-panelled wall.

Angèle found herself obeying his command instinctively. For some reason that she did not understand, he had not killed her yet. Discarding her overmittens, she reached up and took down one of the swords. It was so heavy that she needed both hands to lift its point from the floor. The blade wavered from side to side in her hands, and her legs were trembling so much that she couldn't move a step.

'Fight me! I never thought I'd find a Cossack who's as lily-livered as a damn Bourbonist,' Beaumaris goaded, lapsing into French, wanting to get it over with. His wound had reopened and he could feel the hot blood trickling down his arm. Soon he would be too weak to fight.

In desperation Angèle threw herself forward. 'Life is more important than honour,' Katja had said when she had tried to dissuade her from leaving the dacha. Now she understood what the old woman had meant. It was not so easy to resign yourself to death. She wanted to survive.

She had made a clumsy thrust, aiming her blade at his head. He blocked it effortlessly with a force that sent an agonising pain through her arms and shoulders. But somehow she held on to the sabre and swung again, bracing herself for the shattering impact.

It was the worst swordsmanship Beaumaris had ever seen. It puzzled him. Cossacks learnt how to handle arms from the moment they could walk. This one was fighting like a. . .woman! Momentarily taken aback, he stared at the slight figure, who was preparing to swing at him again. By Mars! It was a woman! He would stake his life on those turquoise eyes being feminine. The devil was still riding on his side after all.

Angèle struggled to raise her blade again. To the tortured muscles in her arms it felt as if it were made of lead instead of steel. It meandered wildly in her hands. He was not even bothering to defend himself. He was laughing at her. He could have killed her a hundred times over during the last few seconds. Sobbing for breath, she swung at him with all her strength. He sidestepped with contemptuous ease. Her sabre crashed into the wall and spun out of her numb fingers.

Her instinct was to run for the open door, but before she could move a step she felt his blade touch her throat, pricking her flesh. It was cold, as cold as his steel-grey eyes, she thought irrelevantly. Would death be cold? *I don't want to die*! She wanted to scream, to plead, but fear choked her. The muscles in his shoulder bunched and tensed and for an anguished second her eyes collided with his. There was no rage, hatred or bloodlust in the grey depths as she had expected, just glittering silver sparks of. . .

'No!'

The word came out as a hoarse whisper, a pallid echo of the scream of protest in her mind. Her heart stopped as his blade flashed across her face. But, instead of the killing stroke she expected, he had flicked her hat from her head. Released from the confines of her hat, the thick glossy braid of her hair tumbled heavily to her waist. Unable to grasp that she was still alive, she stared at him in disbelief. He was smiling. A slow, lazy smile that filled her with dread.

When had he realised she was a woman? she wondered with a new fear forming in the pit of her stomach. 'Rapists, murderers! And they call themselves officers and gentlemen.' Her mother's assessment of Bonaparte's army echoed in her head. She shrank back against the wooden wall, her arms wrapped tightly across her body like an inadequate shield. It was then that she felt the hard shape of the knife in her sleeve. Katja had made a special sheath and stitched it into her coat. A knife against a sword. It was hopeless, but she had to try.

Beaumaris's breath caught in his throat as he returned her stare. Such hair! As if someone had added a tint of bronze to molten gold. Titian himself would have struggled to put that colour on canvas. But her face was pale and cold as marble as she looked at him disdainfully. An ice maiden, he thought as he studied her features. She was not pretty in the common pert way. But there was an almost classical perfection about her wide brow, fine straight nose and planed cheekbones that reminded him of Roman statues he had seen years ago during the Italian campaign. But then he changed his mind as his eyes touched on her mouth. It was a sensual mouth, full, with an almost imperceptible but irresistible pout to the lower lip. He'd wager there was fire beneath the icy exterior, a fire to match the hint of red in her hair.

As for her eyes. . .they flared in response to his gaze, flashing like a kingfisher's wing caught by the sun. Her sudden intake of breath gave him a split-second of warning. It was enough. He dropped his sword and caught her wrist in a punishing grip as the knife skidded off one of the metal buttons of his cloak.

'*Cochon*! Let go of me or I will kill you!' Angèle lashed out furiously with her free hand as she shouted in French.

'I do not think so.' He laughed dismissively as he increased the pressure on her wrist until the knife dropped from her nerveless fingers.

It was useless, she thought with rising panic. His body was like steel beneath the shabby clothes. For all the effect her struggles were having, she might as well have aimed her blows at the wall behind her. Yet she could not stop, nor stem the insults that came to her tongue.

'Your French is excellent, *mademoiselle*,' he said drily, holding her effortlessly at arm's length. 'Where did you learn it? In the barrack-room?'

She ceased struggling abruptly. The dry, sardonic enquiry extinguished her panic as if he had dashed a

bucket of icy water into her face. André's insinuations
and insults had been bad enough to bear. And now this
Bonapartist *parvenu* had dared to speak to her as if she
were his inferior!

'The barrack-room! How dare you?' she spat at him
between ragged breaths that tore at her ribs.

'I dare because you are at my mercy, *mademoiselle*,' he
answered with a faint smile as he read the murder in her
eyes. He had heard that Russian ladies were high-spirited
and enjoyed a much more robust upbringing than their
contemporaries in England and France, and this girl was
proof of it. She was unmistakably frightened, but she
had neither given in to a fit of the vapours, nor was there
a hint of tears in the clear, defiant depths of her iridescent
eyes.

'And now perhaps we can behave like reasonable
people. If you do exactly as I say, I will not harm you.'

'Never!' Angèle spat at him. The way he had just
looked at her had confirmed her worst fears. 'I will die
rather than give in to you!'

'I do not make war on women,' he replied tersely,
releasing her wrist. 'And I have never found it necessary
to resort to rape.'

'Then what do you want of me?' she asked, her
surprise mirrored in her eyes. To her knowledge, not a
single Russian man, woman or even child had shown any
mercy to the frozen and starving French soldiers, and
she had not expected any in return.

'Simply your co-operation, not your body.' He smiled
cynically. 'I see I have fallen short of your expectations
of a French officer.' His black brows slanted sardonically. 'If I have disappointed you in any way, please
accept my apologies.'

For a moment she was speechless. His arrogance took
her breath away. He had spoken to her as if he thought
her a. . . Her mind shied away from a word that had
never passed her lips. For the first time she realised the

full implication of the risks she was taking in travelling alone. Even if she succeeded in reaching her real father in England, if the details of her flight ever became known she would be ostracised by polite society. All men would feel free to address her in such a fashion, to look at her in such a way. . . Her hands itched to strike him, but she would not give him the satisfaction of making her lose her temper again. The barrack-room remark still rankled.

'You are exactly what I expected of a Bonapartist, sir!' she retorted icily. 'You might pass for an officer, but never for a gentleman!'

'And you, *mademoiselle*, are scarcely the model of a respectable young lady,' he responded scathingly as his eyes travelled from the crown of her head to her feet. 'Or is masquerading as a Cossack and travelling unchaperoned the latest fashion in Russian society?'

She knew he could see nothing of her figure beneath the long sheepskin coat, but his insolent gaze seemed to strip her naked. Her nails dug into the palms of her hands as she fought to control her temper. 'If you insult me again,' she grated through tight lips, 'I. . . I will. . .'

'Kill me.' His black brows lifted again, mocking her. 'Your conversation is becoming repetitive. Perhaps you are a little tired. Please sit down.'

'Why should I?' she fumed.

'Because I do not consider it polite to sit in the presence of a. . .lady.' He somehow managed to give the last word an entirely different meaning from its usual interpretation.

She flinched from his intonation. What had she done? she wondered miserably. Katja had been right—it was madness to travel alone; fear of André must have fuddled her wits.

'And if I do not rest soon, *mademoiselle*, I will fall down.'

The matter-of-factness of his statement broke through

the bleak chaos of her thoughts. She stared at him, wondering how she had not noticed the spreading dark stain on his right shoulder, or the greyness of his skin beneath the weather-tanned veneer. He was wounded, losing blood. Without another word she crossed the room to the chair he had indicated and sat down.

She was utterly confused. He was wounded, desperate. But he had behaved with a kind of chivalry that she would never have expected from one of Bonaparte's officers. He had given her the chance to arm herself, despite believing her to be an enemy. An enemy who would have shown him no mercy in return.

He slumped, head bowed, into a chair on the opposite side of the table.

Covertly, through the screen of her lowered lashes, she studied him. He had an undeniably attractive face beneath the black stubble and grime, though it was a little too harsh to be strictly handsome. The aristocratic nose was a shade too long, and the sardonic mouth a fraction too wide. The straight black brows were unequivocal, like the clear-cut bones above his hollowed cheeks and the aggressive line of his jaw. With a jolt she realised that he was not more than ten years her senior. The exhaustion on his face and the sunken shadows beneath his eyes had made him look older. He was, after all, a fugitive like herself, alone and hunted in an inhospitable land. . .and unlike her he was wounded and in pain.

His head came up suddenly, surprising her. She had no time to disguise the sudden pity in her eyes. His own eyes darkened to the colour of gunmetal. He was angry. As if she had somehow insulted him. With an obvious effort he drew himself up in his chair, and involuntarily her hand lifted in a helpless gesture as she saw the pain slice across his face.

'As you can see, I am hardly in a condition to indulge in rape, loot and pillage.' His mouth curved ironically.

'Fortunately for you, if I'd had the use of my right hand I should not have fumbled the first stroke and you would not be sitting here now.'

'Then I am heartily grateful to you for only frightening me half to death instead of decapitating me!' she retorted as sharply as she could manage. Having allowed herself to think of him as a man, rather than one of Bonaparte's followers, she found that instead of anger and fear she felt only sympathy for him. He was swaying in his chair and she had little doubt that it was only masculine pride that kept him upright. Not that he would thank her if she offered assistance, she guessed. He did not look the sort of man who would readily admit to weakness.

He laughed raggedly. 'Then perhaps you will be so good as to tell me where I am? I became a little disorientated in the storm.'

'This is the Perenskovs' hunting lodge; it is about forty miles east of the Berezina River.'

For a moment he regarded her steadily, as if assessing whether or not she was telling the truth. Then he nodded. 'Thank you, *mademoiselle*. I shall not press you for any other information—I do not expect you to aid your country's enemies willingly. But, since I have not harmed you, I ask in return that you make no effort to raise the alarm until morning.'

'It would not be possible tonight even if I wished to,' she admitted freely. 'Can you not hear the wind? Only the devil himself would try to travel tonight.'

'Yes. . .you are probably right.' He gave her a wry half-smile.

It was on the tip of Angèle's tongue to tell him that she was not Russian but French. But the impulse vanished as he got slowly to his feet, and walked painfully across the room to where he had left his sword. With her heart in her mouth she watched him bend painfully and pick it up with his left hand. She averted her eyes as he made a clumsy attempt to replace it in its battered scabbard on his left side. There was something about seeing such a powerful man so helpless that aroused her sympathy.

'Let me.' Somehow, without being aware of it, she had crossed the room and was at his side. Involuntarily she glanced up into his taut, dark face as she slid the heavy steel blade into its leather and gilt scabbard. Without meaning to, she met his gaze. The shock was mutual. She heard his breath catch at the same moment that her heart stopped and skipped a beat. 'So it is you.' The sense of recognition, of inevitability was so intense, so unexpected that she froze, as startled as if he had reached out and caressed her. Then it was gone as quickly as it had come. His eyes were shuttered and chill, making them perfect strangers again.

'Thank you, *mademoiselle*. You are a model prisoner.' A faint knowing smile lifted the corners of his mouth as he regarded her steadily. 'But if you will excuse me. . .' He hesitated, and glanced down at his sword.

It was only then that she realised her hand was still resting on the sword hilt, as if she was reluctant to break the contact. A rush of colour came to her face as she snatched her hand away. Minutes ago she would gladly have murdered him, but now. . .her body would not obey her mind. She could not move away. Her friend Irina had often spoken of the physical magnetism that some men possessed, but she had never experienced it until now. It left her totally bemused, unable to think clearly.

His eyes came back to her face, speculative, almost amused, mocking her.

'Now I know which direction to take, I have to leave,' he said drily.

'Leave!' His remark jerked her back to reality. 'You cannot leave in this weather. You will be dead within half an hour! And you are in no condition to travel,' she added, seeing the perspiration on his brow and the fever in his eyes.

'Neither is the rest of the army,' he said bitterly, with
the ghost of a smile. 'I have no choice. My place is with
the Emperor. It is my duty.'

'Even Bonaparte cannot expect dead men to fight for
him!' she exploded, wondering why she was arguing
with him. What difference did it make to her if he was
foolish enough to want to freeze or bleed to death?

'It is not just the Emperor. . .' His eyes were steely as
he emphasised the title, warning her that he did not
accept such insulting references to his master lightly. 'I
have a duty to my men to try and get them out of this
hellish country. I have fought alongside many of them
for seventeen years. They are my friends.'

'Don't you see you will never reach them?' She
stamped her booted foot in frustration.

'But I have to try.' He stepped past her to the door as
he spoke. 'Perhaps you would be so kind as to look after
my horse. She won't move another step today. But with
a little food you'll find her a willing enough beast. I call
her Montespan. . .because she's a black witch. . .'

The blast of icy wind and snow from the open door
took away the rest of his words.

'You are mad!' she shouted above the howl of the
wind.

'Just as well—there is nothing sane about war, *mademoiselle*.' He laughed as he turned up the deep collar of his
dark green cloak. Then betrayingly he winced and
clutched at his wounded shoulder.

He was delirious, she thought; it was the only possible
reason for such madness.

'For heaven's sake! Do you know nothing of the cold?'
She had to do something. Ridiculously, knowing it
would make little difference, she caught up her fur hat
from the floor and thrust it into his hands. 'At least wear
this.'

He took the hat and put it on. '*Merci*.'

He gave her a quizzical smile as he thanked her. A

smile that tied a knot in her stomach as she glimpsed the
man he might have been in other circumstances. Suddenly she found she did not care that he was a
Bonapartist. She knew only that his death would be an
utter waste. For, as night drew in, the temperature
would drop. Dressed as he was, without shelter, he
would freeze to death—if he lasted that long, she
thought, looking at the pallor of his skin and the feverish
glitter in his eyes. This, then, she thought bitterly, was
the reality that lay beneath all the shining talk of
chivalry, honour and righteous causes. The unnecessary
death of a man. He was staring at her as if reading the
bleakness she felt in her face.

'While there is life there is hope, *mademoiselle. Au
revoir. . .*'

He spoke so softly that she was not sure that she had
heard him correctly, but before she could reply he had
stepped out into the snow.

What made her stay at the open door, she did not
know. Her teeth chattered from the cold as she watched
him stumble on into the storm. The flurries of snow
made his tall figure blurred and indistinct, and then it
disappeared completely.

He had collapsed. By screwing up her eyes against the
icy flakes she could just discern his still, dark shape on
the ground. Without hesitation she turned, snatched up
a fur from the bed and wrapped it around her head and
face, and then plunged out into the freezing air. The
man in the snow was the enemy of everything she had
been raised to believe was right. The tattered green
uniform was familiar throughout Europe. He was no
unwilling conscript, but an officer of the Chasseurs of
the Garde Impériale, Bonaparte's most loyal and devoted
bodyguard. But it was not in her nature to abandon him
to his fate, no more than she had been able to abandon a
bird to the stable cat at her stepfather's dacha.

The cold made her heart and lungs ache agonisingly.

She tripped and fell twice in the deep, powdery snow as she plunged towards his recumbent figure.

'Idiot! Imbecile!' she swore beneath her breath as she reached him, uncertain if she was cursing him for his rashness or herself for her own stupidity in attempting to save him. He was unconscious, a dead weight. She could not possibly carry him. But by catching him under the shoulders she could drag him a few feet at a time. When she reached the door of the lodge she felt as if her heart would burst, and her breath was coming in painful ragged gasps. She moved him through the door with one last effort and slammed it shut. Exhausted, she slumped to the floor beside his long figure, sobbing for breath. Every muscle and sinew in her body had been stretched to breaking-point. She felt as if she would never move again. But she could not rest. If she did not act quickly he would die. She was sure of it.

There were healing herbs and ointments in her luggage, packed by the ever-practical Katja. The thought became action as she stumbled breathlessly to the connecting door that led into the barn and threw aside the bolts, careless of the damage to her knuckles.

Moments later, clutching the little leather satchel of herbs, she returned and knelt down beside him. Putting her arm beneath his good shoulder, she hauled him to the low wooden-framed bed and rolled him on to it.

He was frozen. His heavy cloak and wadded coat were sodden, and the close-fitting green uniform beneath was stiff with ice and snow. It was little wonder the French army was freezing to death, she thought as her fingers fumbled and fought with the unfamiliar masculine fastenings. The long full tunics, thick pleated trousers and sheepskin coats that the Cossacks wore were infinitely warmer. And far easier to put on and off. She used a Russian oath learned from her stepfather as she wrestled with the copper buttons and gilt frogging that fastened the dark green dolman jacket and skin-tight breeches.

At last she managed to peel off the jacket and breeches, leaving him clad only in his blood-soaked shirt. Very gently she eased the shirt away from his body.

His nakedness neither shocked nor frightened her. The remoteness of the dacha had meant that they could not rely upon a doctor. Katja, her stepfather's housekeeper, was a skilled healer, and Angèle had become her willing apprentice. She had learnt how to make remedies from herbs, to set bones, even how to stitch wounds with a boiled needle and thread. Her mother had been appalled that her daughter should sully her hands with such work. But on this one issue Angèle had defied her mother. Healing others had been the only means she had of assuaging some of the guilt she felt about Yashi's death.

The wound in his right shoulder did not look as grave as she had anticipated; the extreme cold had slowed the flow of blood, but she feared that the bleeding would become heavier as he became warmer. Quickly she tore some strips from the shirt and, using the rest as a pad, bound it as tightly as she could. She studied him with an expert eye, assessing the factors that were in favour of his survival and those against.

Aside from his wound, he looked exceptionally fit. There was great strength in his broad shoulders, his stomach flat and taut, his thighs well muscled. He could have been the model for the bronze of Mars that her mother had brought with her from France to Russia, except that instead of polished bronze there was flesh, marred here and there by old scars. But he was exhausted, weak from loss of blood, and cold. Cold—that was his greatest enemy. For all his muscle and sinew, he was as vulnerable to the cold as a child. Hastily she wrapped him in the fox, wolf and sable coverlets, trying to preserve what spark of warmth was left in his body.

He needed heat, quickly. She looked around her. The

lodge was much as she remembered it from the visit she had made years before. In addition to the bed, chairs and table, there was a cupboard and some rough shelves on which stood cooking and eating utensils, including a large copper samovar. A profusion of furs was scattered on the wooden floor in place of rugs, and a large iron stove dominated one wall of the room. To her joy, there was a supply of ready-cut wood and kindling beside the stove. A moment later she found a tinder-box on one of the shelves. Within minutes the stove was alight, filling the small room with the smell of woodsmoke. Hastily she took an iron pan down, and, going to the door, she filled it with snow and set it on the stove to heat while she searched in her satchel for the necessary herbs.

An hour later Angèle gently smeared a soothing ointment on to his chapped lips. There was something distinctly intimate about tracing the shape of his mobile, sensual mouth with her fingertip and she was relieved when the task was finished. But, as she stared down at his long, rangy form, she frowned. She had cleaned and dressed his wound, and staunched the renewed bleeding with packs of snow, but his body was still as pale and cold as ice. He was not even shivering. That was a bad sign. Neither the gradually increasing warmth from the stove nor the furs seemed to be making much difference. There was but one remedy for exposure left, and she couldn't do that with a stranger, a man. . .could she? But Katja had said that if a fit and healthy person got into bed naked with the victim and held them until they were warm, they could be revived. . .

She glanced down at his face. He was still as death; his eyes were closed, the lashes startlingly long and black against the pallor of his cheeks. As she looked she could not help remembering the glimpse of vitality and life there had been in his face when he had laughed. No, she could not let him die while there was a chance of saving him. The decision made, she began to pull off her boots.

The lodge was still far from warm, and she shivered as she took off her Cossack tunic, trousers, shirt and stockings. Her skin goose-pimpled as she reached her *chemisette*. She decided to keep it on, judging that the fine silk fabric would do little to impede the warmth from her body reaching his, but the semblance of modesty it afforded would do much for her courage.

Nevertheless, her heart thumped painfully beneath her ribs as she crept cautiously beneath the furs. He was lying on his left side, with his back to her. She gasped aloud as her breasts, stomach and legs came into contact with his frozen flesh. The cold bit through her *chemisette* as if it were non-existent. Instinctively she recoiled. But then, gritting her teeth, she forced herself to lie against him, putting her arm around his waist, and bending her legs behind his so that her body fitted against his.

It was like embracing a block of ice rather than a human body. At first she could not control her own shivering, or the chattering of her teeth. It seemed an eternity before her own body felt warm again, and then almost imperceptibly she felt an answering warmth in the lean, hard body next to her. It was working. Light-headed with exhaustion and relief, she relaxed a little, letting her head rest against his bare shoulders. It was strange, she thought with a detachment borne of fatigue, twelve hours ago she would not have willingly compromised her reputation by receiving a man alone in her drawing-room, and now. . .now she could scarcely believe her own conduct. . . But what else could she have done? He had spared her life; she owed him his. . . As soon as she was certain he was warm she would get up and dress, and no one except her would ever know.

How long she had dozed she did not know, but his agonised shout woke her instantly. Hastily she fumbled at the side of the bed for the tinder-box and candlestick she had placed there earlier. As the candle flared she saw he was struggling to throw aside the heavy covers, flailing like a drowning man.

'Stop it. Please!' She grabbed at his arms and held them down with all her strength. 'You will open your wound again.'

He fell back on the folded fur she had given him as a pillow, his eyes wide with horror, as if he could see something she could not. She wanted to calm him, to reassure him, but she did not even know his name. What gave her the idea to sing an old French lullaby her mother had taught her she didn't know, but it was effective. Within seconds his eyes had closed again and his breathing was more regular.

At least he was warm now, Angèle thought. Too warm. There was perspiration on his forehead. He had a fever. Carefully she slid out of bed and, wrapping a fox-fur coverlet around her, poured a cup of hot water from the pan on the stove and made an infusion of herbs.

'Can you drink this?' she asked gently, slipping an arm beneath his shoulders. 'It will make you feel better.'

'Blanche? Is that you?' He smiled sleepily without opening his eyes. 'Was I dreaming again?'

'Yes. It's me. And you were dreaming,' Angèle lied soothingly as she slid an arm beneath his shoulders and lifted him so that she could feed him sips of the liquid. He swallowed it without protest and slumped back, trapping her arm beneath his shoulders. Frightened of disturbing him, she remained immobile for several minutes after he had finished the draught. The candle-light emphasised the planes and hollows of his face, and with inexplicable certainty she knew that even if she lived to be old, which did not look likely at this moment, his would be one face she would never forget.

His weight was heavy against her arm, and very gently she tried to ease away from him. But he stirred instantly.

'Blanche! Don't leave me!" His anxiety was obvious and he began to toss and turn feverishly.

'I am here,' she lied to reassure him.

'Come to bed. . . I am cold. . .'

'Very well,' she agreed hastily, wanting to lull him back into a quiet sleep. He made a murmur of contentment as she slid back beneath the furs.

'*Je t'aime, Blanche.*' He found her hand beneath the covers and squeezed it. '*Et tu?*'

'*Oui, je t'aime,*' she whispered quickly. Never had she expected to say those words for the first time in her life in such circumstances. But the lie had worked, she thought as she heard him sigh and settle into sleep.

Harmless as the falsehood was, it depressed her as she lay awake, listening to his even breathing. She had never shared a man's bed before, nor was she likely to again, she thought in a rare moment of self-pity. Even if she reached England, a twenty-four-year-old woman of uncertain parentage and dubious background was unlikely to be deluged with offers in England's prim society. Whoever Blanche was, Angèle envied her with all her heart. Lying here beside this stranger who held her hand so tightly, even in his sleep, she had glimpsed what it might be like to be loved and cherished by such a man. And for some reason it had made her feel frightened, more alone than she had ever been in her life. From outside came the unmistakable howl of a grey wolf, threading eerily through the screaming wind. A sound as dismal and desolate as her thoughts. Instinctively she clutched tighter at the hand that held hers, holding on to it as if it were a talisman against disaster.

CHAPTER TWO

BEAUMARIS awoke slowly. It was oddly quiet and it took him a moment to realise that the wind had dropped. He should get up, he thought, and make haste to find the army while there was a lull in the weather. But he could not bring himself to move. He was conscious only of the delicious sensual warmth that surrounded his body. How many days or months was it since he had felt warm? It seemed like years since the army had left the smouldering ruins of Moscow. He stretched slowly, and then jolted fully awake as his hand touched the soft, unmistakably feminine body lying beside him in the nest of furs.

He sat up abruptly. The lodge was dark, since the snow had covered the windows completely during the night. But the guttering light from a candle stub beside the bed told him that his sense of touch had not deceived him. A woman. What in the name of Mars was he doing in bed with a near-naked woman?

He looked at her again, disbelieving his own eyes. Recollection came suddenly. The Cossack girl. . .of course. But what had happened after the fight. . .what was she doing in his bed? Perhaps the whole thing had been a delirium brought on by exhaustion. He could think of no other rational explanation. At any moment he would awake to the sound of swords clashing, the cries of wounded men and the never-ending squeal of protesting wood and metal as the guns and wagons were hauled across the frozen wastes. He shut his eyes and then opened them again.

She was still there, lying like a child with one slender arm flung out across the black sable she had used as a pillow. There was no trace of the hauteur he remembered in her sleep-flushed face, just a beguiling softness, almost an innocence. He found himself mesmerised by the silky texture of her ivory skin, luminous against the velvety black fur. And as for her hair. . .it had come loose from its severe braid and spilled out across the sable and her white shoulders, a rippling, cascading mass of gold and bronze. She stirred slightly, and as she moved he caught the scent of lilies of the valley from her skin. By the gods, she was lovely! Ivory, rose and gold. But how in heaven's name had she come to be sharing a bed with him? She was a Russian, his enemy. . . He reached out and shook her roughly, trying to ignore the disturbing sensation he felt as his fingers touched her silken flesh.

'André!' Angèle cried out as he touched her, jerking away from the contact and sitting up before she was fully awake. Her eyes were panicky, and then as she focused on his face she smiled with relief. Her first thought was that he was alive, and she was glad.

'I'm afraid not, *mademoiselle*. I am Captain Tristan Beaumaris of the Chasseurs of the Garde Impériale,' Beaumaris introduced himself sarcastically. So much for her air of innocence. What kind of woman was she to flaunt her charms so blatantly? And who in the devil's name was André? Her lover? Of course! What other reason could there be for her to be travelling in such a clandestine manner? In spite of himself, he felt a stab of envy as his eyes skimmed over the scrap of pink silk that did nothing to disguise her full taut breasts, her willow-slim waist and the beginnings of the tempting curve of her hips. Whatever her scheme, she was a clever little coquette, he decided. In different circumstances, he'd have been hard-pressed to resist such an invitation. And he'd long since thought himself immune to every feminine wile. Blanche had used every one in the book and invented more besides.

His mouth curved cynically as he saw her sudden intake of breath and hasty wrapping of her arms across her body, as if she had only just become aware of her *déshabillé*.

'Allow me.' He picked up the black sable and handed it to her, but made no effort to avert his eyes as she wrapped it around her body.

'I did not mean you to see me like this. . .' Her voice faltered. This was terrible. A disaster. She had meant to get up early and dress before he woke. From his face, she could see all too clearly what he took her for. 'I. . . you. . .' Scarlet with embarrassment, she began to explain.

'What do you want from me, *mademoiselle*?' he cut in derisively. 'Do you seek to detain me until your lover arrives? I did not think that anything a Russian would do to defeat an invader could surprise me any more, but. . .' his black brows rose '. . . I was mistaken.'

'Do you think that I would offer myself to one of Bonaparte's officers?' she gasped, white with shock and rage. 'Perhaps your brain, if you have one, which I doubt, was damaged along with your shoulder!'

'Such indignation, *mademoiselle*,' he drawled lazily. 'It is almost convincing.'

Only modesty prevented her from striking him. He was insufferable. 'I wish I had left you to die in the snow!' she hissed furiously.

'What are you talking about?' The mockery faded a little from his voice.

'You! Do you remember nothing of yesterday? Like the imbecile that you are, you insisted on going out into the storm again. I had to drag you back here like a sack of grain!'

For a moment he stared at her suspiciously, and then a memory trickled back into his mind. She had been standing beside him at the door, and she had given him her hat. . .

'Why should you help me?' he asked sharply. 'You are my enemy, a Russian.'

'I am not. I am as French as you are. I was born in Paris,' Angèle retorted impatiently.

'French!' He stared at her in disbelief. 'What in God's name is a Frenchwoman doing in the middle of Russia, disguised as a Cossack? Surely you are not a *vivandière*!'

'I am not!' Angèle snapped. First he accused her of secret assignations with lovers, and now he was suggesting that she was one of the girls who supplied the French army with extra rations and other less respectable services.

'No, I did not think so.' He groaned and shook his head and then sank back on the furs, puzzled by the contradictions between her manner and her actions.

'Your wound, is it hurting you?' she asked anxiously, forgetting her outrage instantly.

'No. . .' he smiled wrily '. . .but my brain is; please explain simply, *mademoiselle*, I am finding it a little difficult to concentrate.'

She blushed pink again as she saw the direction of his gaze. The sable had slipped from her shoulders, revealing the translucent silk that covered her breasts. Mortified, she drew the fur hastily up to her chin.

'Thank you,' he said with suspicious gravity.

She made the mistake of giving him a sharp look and found her gaze locked with his. His eyes were glittering with ill suppressed merriment. For an endless moment she found herself in danger of laughing with him at the incongruity of their situation. Abruptly she looked away.

'So, tell me what a young Frenchwoman is doing in the midst of this God-forsaken country,' he said softly after a silence that was almost tangible.

'Trying to leave it,' she answered shortly, fighting the impulse to look at him again.

'Then we have more in common than a shared bed.'

'I doubt that I should have anything in common with a Frenchman who supports the Corsican ogre,' she retorted haughtily, unnerved suddenly by his easy familiarity. Unlike her, he did not seem in the least disconcerted by their situation and she felt at a complete disadvantage.

'You are a Bourbonist.' To her annoyance, he began to laugh helplessly, bracing his wounded shoulder with his hand.

'I fail to see what is so amusing about supporting the legitimate claimant to the French throne, sir!' she said tartly, wondering if he was becoming feverish again.

'I am sorry, *mademoiselle*,' he managed to apologise through his laughter, 'it just seems a little ironic that my rescuer should be a devotee of King Louis—God help me if my regiment ever finds out! I am sorry,' seeing her set face, he sobered, although his silver eyes still danced with suppressed amusement '. . .you were telling me how you came to be here; please go on.'

'My mother was French. She was forced to marry my stepfather, Count Kerenski, when her family discovered she had been having an affair and was. . .' Angèle hesitated, not wanting to confide her personal affairs to a stranger, but a glance at his face told her he would not be convinced by anything less than the truth '. . .with child.' She looked at him challengingly, watching his face for the shuttered look that had crossed the faces of so many of those whom she had thought friends, until they learnt the truth about her parentage.

'In Napoleon's France we judge people on their merit, not their pedigree,' he said quietly.

The barb was tempered by the unexpected sympathy in his eyes as they met hers. Abruptly she turned her head and looked away, unconsciously twisting a stray strand of amber hair between her fingers. During the years at the dacha she had perfected the ability to hide her emotions. But now this stranger had pierced her guard as easily as he had outfought her with his sword.

Beaumaris glanced at her averted face curiously. That she was an illegitimate child he believed—the hurt in her eyes had been all too genuine—but as for the rest of the tale about the mother and the stepfather, he was not sure. . .

'You were saying, *mademoiselle?*' he prompted softly, wondering if she was playing for time in order to invent a convincing tale.

'My stepfather knew about my mother's condition when he married her. He went ahead with the match because of the wealth my mother stood to inherit. Then the revolution came, my mother's estates were lost. . .' She paused, struggling to keep the hurt out of her voice. 'My stepfather was deeply disappointed, so he kept my mother and myself at the dacha, so that no one would know he had sacrificed his pride for nothing. I have lived there all my life.'

'Why run away now?' Beaumaris queried. 'Surely your mother will be concerned for you?'

'She died three months ago,' Angèle answered flatly. 'She made me promise to try and leave. She was concerned. . .' She stopped, unable to bring herself to talk about André. 'She asked me to leave Russia and go to my real father. When my stepfather's Cossacks went in pursuit of your army I took the opportunity to escape. The blizzard forced me to seek shelter, and you know the rest. . .'

'So you are fleeing from your stepfather?'

'No. . . Yes,' she corrected herself hastily.

'I see.' Beaumaris smiled. More likely she was fleeing from a wealthy but elderly lover to join André, he decided cynically. 'Then we are both fugitives, *mademoiselle.*'

'Yes,' she answered shortly, annoyed by the hint of mockery in his smile and the scepticism in his eyes. He knew there was something she was not telling him.

'You will be pursued?' He was suddenly abrupt, as his eyes went instinctively to the door.

'I think it is likely,' she answered curtly, trying to

edge out of the bed without revealing any more of her nakedness than was humanly possible. 'But there is no immediate danger while the blizzard lasts. The storm will cover my tracks, and it will be at least another day before my stepfather's men return to the dacha.'

'Wait!' he demanded as his eyes followed her movement towards the edge of the bed. 'I can understand that you might have shared my bed for warmth, but why. . . in a state of undress?'

'It is simple,' Angèle replied, meeting his cynical gaze with clear, angry eyes. 'You were suffering from the cold and I could think of no other way to revive you. I thought you would die.'

'I see.' A flicker of doubt flashed through Beaumaris's mind. Supposing she was telling the truth after all? His hand went to the dressing on his shoulder. 'You did that for a stranger. . .and I have you to thank for this?'

'It was nothing.' Determined that he should not have the opportunity to laugh at her again, Angèle answered with an assurance that she was far from feeling.

So he had been right in the first place, Beaumaris thought with a slight sense of disappointment. She was used to sharing a man's bed. But her performance would not have been out of place at the Comédie Française. He found himself intrigued and could not resist teasing her. 'So I am indebted to you for my life,' he said, smiling at her.

'You owe me nothing. You could have killed me and you chose not to. We are even, Captain,' Angèle answered, swinging her long legs out of the bed, deciding that sooner or later she would have to brave his eyes.

'I am very glad I didn't.' As ever, there was a hint of mockery in his voice.

It pricked at her senses like a persistent thorn, and she glared at him over her shoulder. He was so insolent, so arrogant! He was not even attempting to disguise the direction of his gaze, letting his eyes linger on the smooth expanse of her thigh where the fur parted.

'If you are a gentleman you will close your eyes while I dress,' she snapped, pulling the edges of the fur more tightly together. 'Or is that too much to expect of one of General Bonaparte's officers?' The scathing emphasis she had placed on the last three words had the desired effect. His eyes flashed like polished steel, but he said nothing and lowered his black lashes.

The sudden moan he made brought her spinning round to face him again. His eyes were shut and his mouth was taut as if he was in pain.

'Are you all right?' she asked anxiously.

'I am feeling a little chilled, *mademoiselle*,' he answered faintly.

'Has your wound opened again? Let me see.' She bent over him.

'No,' he drawled, his hawkish mouth curving at the corners. 'But I was hoping you might come back to bed.'

She gasped, shocked to the depths of her being, and would have pulled away, but he had caught her hand. 'Let go of me! You are. . .' She struggled to find an appropriate word.

'Incorrigible?' He grinned boyishly. 'You aren't the first woman to tell me that.'

'I never assumed I was,' she retorted, remembering Blanche. 'I do not understand how you can attempt to indulge in. . .jokes, Captain Beaumaris. You would be better employed in praying! Do you know what your chances are of getting out of Russia alive?'

'Can you think of a better reason for making the most of the time I have left?' he countered levelly. The amusement faded from his eyes, leaving them the colour of dull steel. 'And are your chances so much better?'

'I can pass for a Russian, I have warm clothing, supplies and a sleigh!'

'And you are a beautiful young woman, travelling

alone between two armies. . . I am sorry, *mademoiselle*, but the best thing you could do is forget your romantic notions about finding your natural father and go back to your "stepfather's" dacha. I am sure he will be delighted to see you again. That way you may live to see next spring.'

'When I require your advice I will ask for it! Do you think I should choose winter to travel if I had any choice?' she flared furiously. 'André. . .' She stopped— he had no right to explanations. Despite her lack of experience, she had understood his implication clearly enough. He had as good as said he did not believe a word of her story, and seemed to think she was running from some sort of sordid liaison. . .and he was half right, she conceded.

'Ah, André,' Beaumaris drawled. 'You forgot to include him in your little *story*. What role have you assigned him—an unwelcome suitor perhaps?'

'Marriage is not what my cousin André had in mind,' she fired back at him, her free hand going to the bruises André's fingers had left on her shoulder.

'He did that to you?'

Her breath stopped in her throat as he released her hand and reached out to brush aside a tress of her hair. He touched the purpling marks with a tenderness that sent a tremor through her body.

'You need not be frightened of me, *mademoiselle*.' He withdrew his hand abruptly, misinterpreting her shiver for revulsion. 'I prefer my women to be willing.'

'Then I'm never likely to be in danger,' she replied furiously, snatching up the sable and wrapping it about her again before backing away from the bed.

'Little wonder if your cousin always treats his women so roughly,' he drawled indifferently.

'I am no one's woman! Least of all André's.' She jerked the words out, shocked beyond measure that he

had assumed her to be André's mistress. 'And no
gentleman should mention such matters in front of a. . .'

'Lady?' He raised one cynical brow, reminding her
that she had forfeited the right to be treated as such
when she had left the dacha alone.

She was silent, having no defence except the unmistakable despair that shadowed her face. Society judged a
woman by her conduct, not her motives.

'I did not mean to add insult to injury. . .' Beaumaris
apologised, surprised to find that her sudden vulner-
ability had made him question his judgement again. 'I
should like to meet your "cousin" André. . .in certain
circumstances.'

Angèle followed his gaze to where his sword was
propped against the wall and felt a lump rise in her
throat. The new protective note in his voice had touched
her far more than his disdain. She had become used to
fending for herself since childhood. There had never
been anyone to protect her. Katja was only a servant and
had lacked the power to do so. Her fragile, beautiful
mother had been too preoccupied with her own misfortunes. As for her stepfather, he had never been able to
look at her without seeing the rival he had hated. Now
this stranger, one of Bonaparte's officers who did not
even consider her a lady, wanted to defend her. She did
not know whether she wanted to laugh or cry.

'I have to get dressed,' she said tersely, not wanting
him to see how his unexpected kindness had affected
her.

'Do you trust me to close my eyes, or would you
rather blindfold me?' he asked provocatively.

She did not deign to answer, but picked up her clothes
from the back of a chair and placed herself on the other
side of the enormous iron stove.

She washed as quickly as possible in the warm water
that had simmered on the stove all night. Then she
pulled on her clothes. The fine wool shirt, with its

brightly embroidered collar and cuffs, was full and loose, coming down almost to her knees, as did the high-necked blue wool over-tunic. Feeling much more assured, she stepped into the gathered Cossack trousers and fastened them about her waist. Since the trousers were very full and loose in the leg, she was able to leave her woollen stockings until last, judging that it was preferable to cover as much of herself as she could in the shortest possible time.

More than once, as she risked a wary glimpse around the corner of the stove, she saw his dark lashes flicker. But his eyelids remained lowered.

She relaxed a little and stepped out from behind the stove to sit on a chair, so that she could pull on her soft wool stockings.

'It's a pity we are not in Paris.'

His sudden comment startled her and she paused in her task of rolling her stocking over her rounded knee.

'Why?' she asked with a naïveté she instantly regretted.

'Because there is a little shop on the rue de Sèvres that makes the most exquisite silk stockings in the world. I can think of no others that would be worthy of your legs.'

'Does your word mean nothing to you?' she seethed, flushing scarlet as she hastily pulled down the leg of her trousers and stepped into her fur-lined boots. How dared he compliment her in such a way?

'I don't recall giving it.' He grinned devilishly. 'And there are some temptations that I have no desire to resist!'

Not trusting herself to reply, she turned her back to him as she belted in the waist of her full tunic. Rummaging in the bag she had brought in from the sleigh, she pulled out her silver hairbrush and began to brush her hair in angry, sweeping strokes. It crackled and floated

down her back, almost to her hips, a swaying, silken
cloak of bronze and gold.

'You have beautiful hair. Don't ever cut it. So many
women in Paris have cut their hair since Josephine set
the fashion.' There was an almost wistful note in his
voice that made her stop in mid-stroke and turn to face
him.

'Did Blanche cut her hair?' The question came unbidden to her lips and she could not imagine what had
possessed her to ask it.

'Blanche!' He glared at her in astonishment. 'How the
hell do you know about Blanche?'

His reaction startled her. There was a cold fury in his
eyes that she did not understand.

'I am sorry. You mentioned her name last night
when you were feverish,' she said ashamedly. 'I
shouldn't——'

'No. You shouldn't,' he grated bitterly.

Perhaps he could not bear to be reminded of the
woman he loved when he was so far from home, she
thought as she parted her hair and braided it in the
awkward silence. Aware of his eyes on her, she coiled
the thick plaits around her head with jerky, nervous
movements. Then she crammed her Cossack hat on her
head and pulled on her sheepskin coat.

'Where are you going?' he asked.

'To see to the ponies and fetch more wood from the
barn for the stove,' she answered without looking at him.
There was a new tension between them that had nothing
to do with their political differences or mutual suspicion.
A tension that she did not understand.

'Let me help you.' He started to get out of the bed.

'Imbecile! I did not ruin my reputation so that you
can bleed to death,' she scathed. 'Or is it that you still
don't trust me? Relax. André will not know I am missing
yet, and no one will venture out today if they can avoid
it. Listen to the wind—already it is increasing again.

You can get up and wash, then you will go straight back to bed. When I have finished with the ponies and the stove I will make you some breakfast.'

With a sigh Beaumaris leaned back on the piled furs. He had never met a woman with quite so many bewildering contradictions. One moment a haughty little Bourbon lily, whom he would have judged incapable of fastening her own shoes, the next a highly competent and practical young woman.

Angèle was halfway through the connecting door into the barn when he called her back.

'Wait, *mademoiselle!*'

'What is it?' she asked impatiently.

'Your name—what is it?'

'Angèle. . . Kerenski.' Deliberately she used her step-father's name. She would not give any Bonapartist the satisfaction of boasting that he had spent a night in the bed of a de la Rochère.

'Angèle.' He repeated her name softly, and in spite of herself she liked the way he said it. But then she noticed the upward tilt of his black brows, and the tell-tale silver lights that glittered around the pupils of his eyes.

'I do not recall giving you permission to use my name, and fail to see what is so amusing about it,' she said hotly, her eyes blue and brilliant as she met his gaze.

There was not the slightest hint of apology on his face as he replied, 'I was just thinking that dressed like that you're the most unlikely ministering angel I've ever met. . .'

'Perhaps you are too used to the fallen variety,' she broke in, disconcerted by the way his tone made her heart quicken and slow.

'Probably,' he agreed with annoyingly cheerful unconcern as she threw back the bolts on the door that led into the barn.

'Angèle!'

Exasperated, she sighed and half turned back towards

him. 'What now, Captain Beaumaris? I have not the time for idle chatter.'

'And, I was going to add, the most beautiful.' He smiled at her, a slow, knowing smile that sent her blood racing and pulse hammering.

She fled, slamming the door shut behind her, taking refuge in the welcome gloom of the barn. She did not know which was worse—that he should flirt with her as if she were a coquette, or that she should react to his compliments in such a way. He is a Bonapartist, she reminded herself. The enemy of everything she had been raised to believe in. A Bonapartist. She repeated the words silently as if they were a charm that would shield her from danger as she hurried through the task of tending the ponies. For she was in danger. Not from him. She could believe all too easily that he had never needed to force a woman. The danger came from within herself.

She was breathless and rosy-cheeked when she came back into the living quarters, having gone outside to sweep some of the snow from the windows to give them light.

'How is my horse?' he asked as she shut the door that led into the living quarters.

'Better for shelter and a stomach full of oats. Which is more than you will be if you persist in disobeying my instructions,' she added impatiently, seeing that he was clad only in the breeches she had left hanging up to dry and was engaged in loading logs into the stove.

'My shoulder is much improved,' he reassured her. 'You must have magic in your fingers, *mademoiselle*.'

'And you must have sawdust in your brain!' she replied shortly, averting her eyes from his bare torso. Now that he was evidently much recovered, she did not find it so easy to regard his nakedness with detachment.

'If you will not stay in bed, at least be seated until you have had some food.'

'Your wish is my command.' He made an insolent bow and seated himself at the table.

She glared at him. 'You are not even dressed; do you want to catch your death of cold?'

'Only if you promise me the same cure.' He grinned wickedly.

'I most certainly will not!' she answered, her eyes flashing from sapphire to emerald. She was furious with herself for leaving herself open to such an obvious reply. 'But we must do something about your clothes,' she added firmly, changing the subject. 'Your uniform is so threadbare that it might as well be made of muslin.'

Then inspiration struck. Why had she not thought of it before? She flung open a large cupboard beside the bed. As she had hoped, there was an assortment of male garments that belonged to Count Perenskov. It was fortunate that Perenskov was also above average height, she thought as she selected the warmest tunic and trousers she could find, a thick woollen shirt, a sable-lined coat, gloves, wool stockings and best of all a pair of soft leather fur-lined half-boots.

'Here!' Unceremoniously she dumped the clothes on the table in front of him. 'Put these on!'

'I'll look like a damned Cossack!' he complained.

'I should have thought that an advantage in the circumstances.'

'Perhaps.' He glanced at her with a new respect in his eyes and picked up the clothes without further demur.

While he dressed she took off her coat and hat, washed her hands and began to sort through the selection of food she and Katja had packed in such haste. There were bottles of rowan and cherry vodka, smoked ham, smoked fish, cheese, polinka, coffee, tea, a net of lemons, some of Katja's cherry-preserve tarts and fresh bread, as well as more basic provisions such as flour, oatmeal and eggs.

But whatever had possessed her to include jars of caviare and a bottle of Russian champagne from her stepfather's cellar?

A few minutes later she had set out bread, caviare with wedges of lemon, cheese, ham and Katja's tarts. She was about to light the samovar when she remembered her mother saying that all Frenchmen were addicted to coffee. She placed a small pan of water on the stove and added some ground coffee. Within a minute or two its unmistakable aroma had filled the lodge.

'You are indeed an angel, *mademoiselle*! I cannot remember when I last saw real food, and as for coffee. . .'

Angèle started as his voice came from over her shoulder. He was standing so close behind her that she could feel his breath on the fine down at the back of her neck. His nearness was overwhelming, making every inch of her flesh prickle with an unfamiliar anticipation. Her blood seemed slow and heavy in her veins, as if time itself had slowed. She had to force herself to move away, but as she did her shoulder brushed against his chest, a fleeting, trivial contact that took her breath away. She dared not raise her head and meet the gaze she could feel on her face.

'Then please sit down and eat.' To her relief, her voice was calm and steady as she stepped past him. But the sudden rapid beat of her heart did not decrease until she had placed the table between them.

'Thank you.' Beaumaris smiled at her easily, but his eyes were speculative, grey as smoke, as he studied her carefully composed face. 'But not before I have drunk a toast.' He grinned and picked up the bottle of champagne and took two enamelled goblets down from the dresser.

'This is hardly a time for celebration!' she protested,

astonished by the resilience of his mind and body and the speed of his recovery.

'I cannot think of a better time,' he said, suddenly sombre. 'You said yourself that we are safe today; we cannot travel because of the blizzard, but neither will we be pursued. I have fought my way across Europe and back again. And I have learnt to take my pleasure where and when I find it. Any soldier who lives for tomorrow rather than today is a fool.'

He poured the bubbling, pale straw-coloured liquid into the goblets and held one out to her. 'Here's to today and the devil take tomorrow.'

He touched his goblet to hers and drained it.

'Today,' she echoed, taking a sip of the champagne. 'You are right; it is better to concentrate on the present.'

'I am glad something I have said meets with your approval.' He grinned at her provokingly.

'Perhaps it is the first sensible thing you have said since I met you,' she retorted.

He laughed. '*Touché*. Now let us stop fencing for a while and eat.'

She managed a tense smile of assent as he pulled out the chair for her and then seated himself on the opposite side of the table.

She had never dined alone with a man before in such intimate circumstances. But oddly, as they began to eat, she found herself more at ease. She smiled suddenly.

'What are you thinking about?' Beaumaris asked, thinking that when she smiled there were few women in Paris to rival her.

'Nothing,' Angèle said, colouring.

'Nothing?' He raised sceptical brows.

'It was just that. . .' She faltered; it would sound so rude.

'Just what?' His mouth curved invitingly. 'I assure you, I am not easily shocked.'

'I was just thinking that not even my mother could

have found fault with your table manners,' she confessed in a rush.

'Is that all?' Beaumaris laughed. 'Do you really think it is only the royalists who know which fork to use? Or that it is vulgar to say *un cadeau* rather than *un présent*, or that Bordeaux should always be referred to as *vin de Bordeaux*? Do I pass, *mademoiselle*?' he asked lightly.

Angèle stared down at her plate in embarrassment. He had put her in her place with a good humour that she did not deserve.

'I am sorry,' she apologised instantly.

'For what? Discovering that I do not fit your preconceptions? Perhaps you do not quite fit mine either. Your mother, for example; you speak as if she considered herself a doyenne of society.'

'She was of noble birth,' Angèle said, more than a little shamefaced. 'She was a royal ward; she grew up at Versailles and became a lady-in-waiting to Marie Antoinette before. . .'

'Before her indiscretion,' Beaumaris supplied.

'Yes.' Angèle nodded.

Beaumaris was puzzled as he studied her delicate face. He would swear she was telling the truth about her mother; could it be the rest of her tale was true? 'Tell me,' he said abruptly, 'where did the daughter of an aristocrat learn to dress a wound?'

'My stepfather's housekeeper, Katja,' Angèle explained briefly. 'I used to assist her; she has great skill at healing.'

'You must have been an apt pupil,' Beaumaris said with feeling, flexing his shoulder.

'It is a little soon for you to judge that.' Embarrassed by his praise, she changed the subject. 'But I have been talking too much of myself. What of you, Captain? I am sure a soldier's history must be more interesting than mine.'

'That is an invitation you should never have given an

old soldier, unless you wish to be bored to death,' he warned with a grin.

But he proved to be an acute and witty raconteur. She found herself laughing aloud as he described the consternation of an English officer who had followed his hounds straight into the French lines in Spain.

'Fox-hunting in the midst of a war!' she exclaimed. 'I have heard the English are devoted to the sport, but that is taking things too far!'

'Not to an Englishman. I saw some of his companions try to stop him, but he refused to call off his hounds and followed them straight into our patrol. We returned him and his hounds under a flag of truce the next day, of course.'

'You let him go!'

'It would not have been sporting to do otherwise. Besides which, I liked him. Our countries may be at war, but in other circumstances I should have been glad to count him as a friend.' He sighed. 'I cannot say the same of any of your Cossack friends, I am afraid. . .'

'No.' She dropped her gaze to the table. 'How did you come to be in the Perenskovs' hunting lodge?'

Beaumaris sighed and leant back in his chair. His eyes became chill, making her wish that she had not asked.

'I was riding escort to the Emperor,' he began slowly. 'A troop of Cossacks came on us suddenly out of the woods. We were taken completely by surprise. They damn nearly reached the Emperor—one got to within twenty feet. I was wounded while driving him off. The others managed to get the Emperor away safely, but several of us were taken prisoner. The ordinary Hussars they killed. Not cleanly; they tied them behind their horses and dragged them over the ice. . .shredding their clothes and then their skin. . . They only spared me because I was an officer and they thought I might have useful information about the Emperor's route.'

Angèle paled, sickened by the sudden nightmare

image of the man opposite her lying bloodied and
battered in the snow. To think of how close he had come
to such a death sent her stomach into an agonising knot,
and froze her heart and mind in a way that she had not
experienced since Yashi had died.

'I have distressed you,' he said, his tone softening
suddenly as he studied her face. 'I should not have
spoken of such things.'

'No. . . I'm sorry,' she said, stricken by the anguish
that lingered in his grey eyes, and cursing herself for the
thoughtlessness of her question. 'I should not have
asked; you must want to forget.'

'Forget?' He laughed bitterly, his voice harsh again.
'No. The day I can forget such atrocities is the day I
cease to be human. War is terrible, savage and wasteful,
and if more people remembered that perhaps they would
be less eager to begin another.'

'I suppose you are right,' she agreed a little ashamedly,
staring down at the table. She knew she had been
clinging to her initial impression of him out of an instinct
for self-preservation. Whatever Tristan Beaumaris was,
he was not the arrogant, brash soldier she had first
judged him. In spite of what had been done to his men,
he had given her the opportunity to arm herself, even
though he believed her to be his deadly enemy, whom
he had every reason to hate and to fear. She knew
suddenly, with an unquestionable female instinct, that it
was not simply his physical stature that would always
place him head and shoulders above most other men,
but his courage and generosity of spirit. There was
something about him that was indomitable. She had
never met a man to match him before, and doubted she
ever would again. But to let her thoughts go in such a
direction was like taking a step into quicksand. She
forced herself to regard him as coolly as he was looking
at her. 'So how did you come here, Captain?'

'Luck,' came the laconic reply. 'My wound looked

worse than it was. They assumed I would not have the strength to escape, so they were careless. They left me in a barn with only one guard, who drank himself senseless on vodka. And then I found Montespan and my weapons in the next stall. . .so I mounted, waited for them to open the door and then rode for my life. If it hadn't been for the blizzard, I doubt I would have got away with it. . .but the snow was so thick that it was impossible for anyone to see where anyone else was. Eventually we came to this place. And then. . .' he paused and surprised her with a sudden vivid smile '. . .you arrived. . .my very own guardian angel.'

The all too familiar teasing note was back in his voice, and she looked at him sharply, but there was a genuine warmth in his eyes that made it impossible for her to be really annoyed.

'And what of you?' He added, 'How did you come to be travelling alone? I should have thought there would have been a dozen men willing to have assisted your flight from the odious André. Was there no one who met with your approval?'

His compliment caught her off guard, touching old wounds that she had thought long-healed.

'You do not know the Russian nobility,' she countered with a brave effort to match his bantering tone. 'I am beyond the pale on three counts: first I am illegitimate, second I am the daughter of a foreigner, and last and worst of all I am penniless.'

'Grave crimes indeed, *mademoiselle*,' he said softly with the faintest lift of his black brows. 'But none of which would matter to a man of any sense.' He could not have told her more clearly that he had seen through her paltry defence.

'Perhaps men and women of sense prefer not to marry,' she snapped, angry suddenly, because she knew the last thing she wanted from him was pity.

'That's an opinion I should take care not to voice in

front of society.' He grinned provocatively. 'You could find it misinterpreted.'

'I did not mean. . .' she said hastily, seeing the devilish gleam in his eyes. 'I meant only that sometimes all that binds a married couple is hatred.'

'You do not need to tell me that,' he said drily. 'But what of you? Do you regard marriage as such an awful fate?'

'I do not where there is love,' she answered, feeling suddenly very uncomfortable about the direction of the conversation. 'But that is rarely a consideration between people of our class.'

'I am flattered you consider me your equal, *mademoiselle*.' He lifted his goblet to her in a mocking gesture. 'I am simply a citizen of France, no better, no worse than any other.'

'I had forgotten you are a Bonapartist and upholder of the revolution,' she replied defensively, resenting his implied criticism of her values. 'To think I had almost begun to mistake you for a gentleman.'

He laughed good-humouredly. 'I make no apologies for it. I am proud to serve the Emperor.'

'And what of the revolution? Are you proud of the murder that went on in its name? Proud of the way that people were driven from their own land by fear?' Deliberately she goaded him; for some reason she felt safer when they were arguing.

'No one is proud of the Terror,' he said, his smile fading. 'But as for the *émigrés*. . . I reserve my sympathy for those who were too poor to leave. Do you know that the largest number of those who went to the guillotine were not aristocrats, but poor, ignorant people who broke trivial rules over pricing as they tried to get a living?'

'No,' Angèle confessed grudgingly. The letters that her mother had received from her aristocratic friends had been entirely concerned with their own misfortunes.

She could not ever remember any of them commenting on the fate of ordinary people.

'No,' he shook his head, 'I did not think so. The Bourbons and their supporters were ever more concerned with their own interests than those of France or the French people.'

'That is unfair. Many of them are honourable men!' she countered hotly.

'Name one,' he scoffed.

'The Duc de Lucqueville,' she answered instantly, naming her real father.

'Lucqueville!' He threw back his head and laughed scornfully. 'Let me tell you about Lucqueville; he has quite a reputation, *mademoiselle*. First, in 1789 he couldn't leave the country fast enough. He didn't stay to see what became of his king and liege lord, nor did he go to assist his widowed mother as she tried to quell the rising on his family estate.'

'You are mistaken! He is a brave man. I know he has often fought for the Bourbons!' she protested vehemently as his words destroyed the fragile rapport that had grown between them in the last hour. He was denigrating the man whose picture had hung about her neck in a gold locket since she was three years old. The handsome young Duc in the miniature had always been her image of a perfect knight. Something to cling to and dream of as compensation for the lack of love from the Count and her mother's uninterest.

He snorted derisively. 'The nearest Lucqueville gets to a fight is a dispute with his valet over which neckcloth to wear. He does not join his allies in the field, *mademoiselle*. He and rest of the Comte d'Artois's cronies have other methods, such as assassination and murder!'

'He would not sully his hands with such work,' she began furiously, getting to her feet and leaving the table. 'I will not listen to such ridiculous slanders!'

'You shall!' He followed and caught her arm. 'It's a

pretty tale. The Comte d'Artois and Lucqueville thought
to assassinate Napoleon by planting a bomb in a wagon
outside the Tuileries. Lucqueville and two other men
came to Paris. Lucqueville didn't have the nerve to
position it himself, of course,' he scathed. 'Do you know
who these Bourbon heroes got to hold the horse and
wagon in place?' His hand came to her chin, forcing her
head up so that she had to look at him. 'No, I can see
you don't. It's not the sort of thing your mother's
Bourbon friends would have boasted of. A twelve-year-
old girl, *mademoiselle*! A child, blown to a thousand
pieces.'

'Stop it! Stop it!' Angèle begged him. She felt as if she
were being torn apart. It could not be true; she would
not believe it. 'You are lying!' In her agony she lashed
out heedlessly, wanting only to hurt him as he had so
unwittingly hurt her. 'The Duc de Lucqueville is a
gentleman, a man of honour. Something that you and
your rabble would know nothing of! How could you,
when even your Marshals are drawn from the gutter?
What can the sons of coopers be expected to know of
honour and loyalty? Do you think I would believe such
Bonapartist propaganda?'

'Propaganda?' he roared back at her. 'I do not need
it—Lucqueville condemns himself. Let me tell you,
mademoiselle, that I should rather spend a thousand years
in the company of a man like Marshal Ney than a second
with Lucqueville!' His eyes were blazing as they met her
brilliant gaze. 'He has more honour and courage in his
little finger than Lucqueville has in the whole of his
cowardly frame!'

'How dare you?' Her free hand collided with his face.
The impact stung her palm, and left a livid white imprint
on his bronzed cheek.

For a moment he did not move. But the expression in
his eyes held her motionless. Never in her life had she
seen such rage. She saw his chest rise and fall as he took

a deep breath. The hand on her jaw shifted to her throat and closed, half choking her.

'No one strikes me with impunity,' he said with a control that frightened her far more than if he had shouted. 'Man or woman. Apologise.'

'To one of Bonaparte's lackeys!' She masked her fear with contempt. 'Never!'

'Then I will make you!' His restraint snapped. White with fury, he caught her shoulders and half lifted her off her feet as if about to hurl her across the room.

'I thought you did not make war on women!' she sneered, too angry now to be afraid.

'I don't, and this isn't war!'

Expecting him to strike her, she was more than ready to defend herself. But she had not anticipated this, the punishing, numbing impact of his hard, lean mouth on hers. Outrage held her immobile for a second, then her hands lifted to push, to hit, to do anything to escape his embrace. But it was too late. As she had stopped moving the anger had gone from his mouth and hands. His lips were gentle now, exploratory, a thousand times more dangerous because she no longer wanted to resist. . .or could. Her hands stilled helplessly on his chest, her body swaying towards his, demanding a closeness she had never known before. Then, as if he sensed victory, his kiss became more insistent, shockingly invasive. No one had ever kissed her like this before. The sensation made her weak, dizzy, and her knees buckled. She felt laughter ripple through his chest as he caught her, crushing her against him. And then she was aware of nothing except his mouth, his touch, the fire that he was spreading through her body. She felt cherished, protected, intoxicated all in an instant, and then unbearably alone and vulnerable as he abruptly lifted his mouth from hers.

She opened her eyes to his and for a second that shock of recognition sparked between them again. As if for all of their lives both of them had been waiting for this

moment, this devastating contact. But then his face
hardened, making her think she had imagined the softness in his eyes a moment before.

'You see, it is possible to learn something useful in the
gutter, *mademoiselle*. There is little difference between a
coquette on the rue St-Jacques and a Bourbon *lady*.' He
paused, his mouth curving cruelly. 'They are both
equally easy to please.'

'What makes you so sure you pleased me?' Pride came
to her defence as she lifted her chin to look him in the
eyes. His mouth tightened, and she felt a flicker of
triumph that she had dented his masculine ego. Her
small victory made her reckless, and she smiled at him
tauntingly. 'You see, Captain, there is a difference: your
friends on the rue St-Jacques are paid to pretend; I am
not.'

'I have never had to pay for my pleasure, *mademoiselle*,' he rasped, his eyes slicing into hers like sabre
points. 'Would you like me to show you why?'

'No!' Her brave façade crumbled into panic; she would
not allow him to humiliate her again in such a fashion.
'Let go of me! I hate you!' She meant it as she struggled
against the restraining band of his arm.

'Do you, now?' he said unconcernedly, his hand
coming to her chin, forcing her to meet his gaze. Then
he laughed, reading his victory in her blazing eyes.
'Don't you know that hate is only a hair's breadth
from——?' He stopped, the fire in his charcoal eyes
dying instantaneously. 'Did you hear that? Outside?' he
whispered harshly.

'Yes,' Angèle answered raggedly as she fought to
master her see-sawing emotions. She had registered the
hissing sound and clink of harness at the same moment.
'It is a sleigh.'

She had not thought it possible that anyone could
move so quickly and silently. In seconds Beaumaris had

released her, caught up his sword and positioned himself by the door.

But who would come here on such a day? André. The thought filled her with a cold dread. Not for herself, but for the man whom she had thought she hated a moment ago. André would kill him. And in spite of everything she could not let that happen. Inspiration sent her flying across the room towards him.

'Put your arms around me!'

'What?' He stared at her as if she were mad.

'Do as I say and tell them I am your hostage, and if they move against you you will kill me.'

'Angèle.' He sighed bitterly as he put her aside. 'Chivalry is one of the first casualties in any war. Do you think such a threat would prevent them from shooting me, and perhaps you in the process? I would not go to my maker with that on my conscience.' Then he smiled at her. A smile that tore her heart in two. 'Not even if you were Lucqueville's daughter. Now stand by the stove and don't move!'

CHAPTER THREE

THE door of the lodge opened an inch. Angèle watched
helplessly as she saw Beaumaris tense, every muscle
bunched and ready to strike.

'Angèle? Are you there?' The voice was low, feminine,
unmistakably that of her closest friend.

Weak with relief, Angèle signalled frantically to
Beaumaris to move away from the partially open door.
For a moment he hesitated, a flicker of suspicion in his
eyes as he regarded her eager face. 'Please,' she mouthed
at him as she ran to the door. He shrugged and moved
back to the other side of the room.

'Irina, what are you doing here? Are you alone?' she
asked hastily in French so that Beaumaris could follow
the conversation.

'Looking for you,' came the tart reply. 'Katja told me
you might be here. My driver, a guard and my maid are
with me, but I have told them to stay outside. Now open
the door and let me in.'

Angèle opened the door just sufficiently for the petite
mink-swathed figure to enter, and then shut it again.

'How could you, Angèle?' Irina began accusingly as
soon as she was through the door. 'To leave without a
word to me. You know I love you like a sister. I have
been mad with worry about you.'

'I did not want to involve you. I knew there would be
talk,' Angèle apologised hastily. 'And I am quite safe.'

'For the time being,' Irina scoffed. 'I could not believe
it when Katja told me what you had done, to go off
alone. . .' She stopped in mid-sentence and took a step
back, her hazel eyes widening in surprise.

'Irina, please don't be alarmed; this is. . .a friend,'

Angèle said quickly as she followed the direction of Irina's gaze to Beaumaris's tall figure.

'A friend!' Irina laughed. 'Really, Angèle, must you always be so understated? I have only to see the way you look at him to see that you are besotted. You are eloping! It is simply too exciting!'

Angèle flushed scarlet and stared at Irina in bemusement, unable to say anything coherent. She was all too aware of how Beaumaris's eyes had shifted suddenly from Irina back to herself.

'You need not look so amazed,' Irina continued cheerfully, 'I knew you would not really have countenanced running away alone. Now how long has this romance been going on? And how could you keep it from me? She is too cruel, is she not. . .?' She smiled at Beaumaris and waited for the introduction.

It was only then that Angèle realised that Irina had taken Beaumaris for a Russian, dressed as he was in the black wool tunic, soft trousers and boots.

Before she could say anything he sheathed his sword and made a low bow. 'Captain Beaumaris, Chasseurs of the Garde Impériale, *mademoiselle*.'

Irina was momentarily transfixed, and then she turned for the door. But Angèle was there before her.

'Irina, please,' she begged. 'Don't call your men; Captain Beaumaris has not harmed me. He came here only to shelter from the storm, like myself.'

'But he is a Frenchman, our enemy. . .my enemy,' she corrected slowly as she read the expression in Angèle's eyes. 'Tell me the truth, Angèle,' Irina said quickly in Russian. 'Are you attracted to him?'

'I do not even like him!' Angèle said shortly, looking everywhere except at her friend's face.

'Then I shall call my men,' Irina said dispassionately.

'No!' The protest tore itself from Angèle's lips.

Irina laughed and shook her head. 'Oh, Angèle, you are a terrible liar!' Then her expression became more sombre as her eyes went back to Beaumaris. 'You must understand, this is not an easy decision for me. I am Russian, this is my country and you are an invader.' Irina reverted to French as she addressed him. 'I need a moment to think.'

'My fate is in your hands, *mademoiselle*,' he replied calmly. 'And I could not ask for a fairer judge.'

How could he flirt in such circumstances? Angèle thought angrily as Irina gave him a surprised but radiant smile before turning away and walking to the other side of the room.

She had not meant to look at him as Irina stood with her back to them, but her eyes were drawn to his face as surely as if she were a marionette and he a puppeteer, tugging on invisible strings. His eyes were speculative as he surveyed her face. The faint lift of his black brows brought her eyes to his. Grey collided and merged with glittering turquoise, making her heart pound as if he had caught her in his arms again. Then his mouth curved, and the uncomfortable suspicion that he had understood the general drift of her Russian conversation with Irina turned to a certainty.

She dropped her gaze in utter confusion. How could her heart betray her reason in such a way? He was a Bonapartist, he despised her father, and there was Blanche, whoever she was. . .

'Angèle.'

With a start she realised that Irina had spoken her name a second time. 'I am sorry, Irina; what is your decision?'

'I am not sure,' Irina said in Russian. 'Please will you not consider giving up this ridiculous idea and return to the dacha? At least wait until the spring.'

'Do you think André will wait until the spring?' Angèle returned bitterly.

Irina pursed her pretty rosebud of a mouth in distaste. 'He has been paying you unwelcome attentions again.'

'A little more than that,' Angèle muttered, uncomfortably aware of the sudden interest in Beaumaris's eyes at the mention of André's name. 'The night before last he was drunk on vodka again; he came to my room and tried to force me. . .if it had not been for the arrival of the messenger with the news that the French were so close. . .' Her voice tailed off and she shuddered with unmistakable revulsion as she recalled André's bleary, red-eyed face and the smell of the alcohol on his breath.

Irina was shocked. 'You do not think he would have——?'

'Would I be here otherwise?' Angèle said. 'He frightens me, especially since my mother died. She had a little influence with the Count, and that kept André in check. But now. . .' She left the sentence unfinished; with Irina there was no need to say more. . .nor with Beaumaris, she thought as his eyes lanced across her face and his mouth tightened.

'You cannot go back to the dacha,' Irina said, turning her fur muff over and over in her hands. 'Perhaps. . .' she went on more eagerly '. . .if I spoke to Papa you could come to St Petersburg with us next week. Count Kerenski might listen to him.'

'No.' Angèle shook her head. 'He will not agree now, when it seems as if. . .' she hesitated, wondering why on earth she should feel as if she was being disloyal to the man who was regarding her so steadily '. . .as if Bonaparte is about to be defeated,' she continued with a mixture of defiance and regret as she risked meeting Beaumaris's eyes over Irina's shoulder. 'You know he has always had high hopes that the estates my mother lost in the revolution will be returned to me. He believes the income from those estates to be his reward for marrying my mother when she was carrying another man's child.'

'You are probably right.' Irina sighed, anxiety written

across her heart-shaped face. 'But where do you plan to go?'

'England,' Angèle answered a little shortly, all too aware of the cool grey eyes on her face. Just how much of this conversation was he following? she wondered, and was answered by the faint, but unmistakably censorious lift of his black brows. She felt an inexplicable pang of guilt, and then, suddenly angry, tore her eyes away from his. She was doing nothing to be ashamed of; England was not France's enemy, merely Bonaparte's.

'England! Whatever for?' Irina was startled. 'From what I have heard, the men there reserve their affections for their horses, and they put milk in their tea!'

Judging by Irina's expression, the latter was an even worse crime than the first, and in other circumstances Angèle would have laughed.

'To find my natural father. My mother made me promise when she was dying that I would go to him if it was at all possible.'

'You are going to the Duc de——?'

'Yes,' Angèle interrupted abruptly, hating herself for her own weakness. For some reason she could not bear the contempt she knew would be in Beaumaris's eyes if he discovered she was the Duc de Lucqueville's daughter.

'But Angèle. . .' Irina was horrified '. . .so much has changed. . .the revolution . . .he may not wish to be reminded. . .supposing he does not acknowledge you— what will you do in a foreign country without friends or family?'

'I am sure he will help me. Maman said he was a man of honour. . .'

'So much so that he did not marry your mother!' Irina muttered, only half beneath her breath.

'If he won't I shall manage,' Angèle went on determinedly, with a confidence that she was far from feeling.

'But I am sure he will help me find some useful employment as a companion or governess.'

'Employment! A governess!' Irina could not have looked more horrified if Angèle had announced she intended to sell her favours. 'Angèle, this is madness! Your mother was utterly irresponsible to suggest this to you. It makes me so angry! If she had been more discreet and hidden her passion for her precious Duc, the Count would have accepted you as his daughter and protected you from André! Instead of which she made a fool of him in society. . .and ruined any prospect you might have had of a normal life here!'

Angèle was silent, having no adequate defence against the truth. She knew her mother's weaknesses too well. She averted her face from Irina, and then turned back, realising that to look at the tall silent figure who lounged against the wall beside the stove was infinitely worse. While she and Irina argued, his life was hanging in the balance, and he seemed utterly unconcerned. If it had not been for their earlier conversation she would have thought him inhuman.

'Angèle.' Irina touched her arm, regaining her attention. 'I am sorry, Angèle, I did not mean to insult your mother or your father. It is just that I am so afraid for you.'

'I know that. . .goose.' Angèle managed a watery smile. 'But my mind is made up.'

Irina shrugged, accepting defeat. 'Very well. But will you not at least take my maid with you to give some protection to your reputation?'

'No.' Angèle shook her head. 'It is not fair. The journey will be hazardous enough, but if I am caught my stepfather and André will certainly kill any serf who accompanies me. I shall hire a companion once I am safely out of Russia.'

'If you get that far,' Irina said gloomily. 'It is the middle of winter! And the country is at war. . .' Then she stopped as her eyes alighted on Beaumaris and she saw the way he was watching Angèle. Some of the anxiety faded from her pretty face and a half-smile came to her lips.

Angèle looked at her curiously, wondering what was responsible for her mercurial friend's sudden change of mood.

'I am a fool not to have thought of it before,' Irina said cheerfully in French.

'Thought of what?' asked Angèle.

'Captain Beaumaris.' Irina paused significantly.

'What of him?' Angèle forced herself to ask calmly, not daring to look at him. Why did it matter so much to her what became of him? It made no sense. . .

'I shall not reveal his presence,' Irina went on in French, smiling at Beaumaris. 'On one condition.'

'What is it?' Angèle asked instantly, forgetting her resolution to appear unconcerned as to his fate.

'That you give me your word, Captain, that you will do your best to ensure my friend's safety until she is on a boat for England.'

Beaumaris looked thunderstruck. 'I cannot, *mademoiselle*! My route out of Russia is with the French army; I have a duty to my men. . .the Emperor. . .it is too dangerous.'

'Irina!' Angèle broke in, humiliated by his transparent opposition to the suggestion. It was obvious that he could not wait to be rid of her. 'I do not wish to make the journey in Captain Beaumaris's company, and you cannot impose such a condition.'

Irina appeared not in the least put out as she glanced from Angèle's stricken face to Beaumaris's. 'It is my only offer,' she said as calmly as if she were serving tea. 'You may take it, Captain Beaumaris, or accompany me outside to my men. Angèle is my dearest friend, but she has little experience of the world. Her happiness and safety mean much to me. Since she is determined to travel, I am determined she should have an escort, however *unsuitable*. It is for this reason alone that I will not tell anyone that you are here. I am sure you understand me, Captain.'

'I understand,' Beaumaris answered with an odd, grim smile. 'Do you always get your own way, *mademoiselle*?'

'Mostly,' Irina confessed with an impish grin. 'I may take it my offer is accepted?'

'You have my word. I will do my utmost to ensure her safety,' Beaumaris said gravely. 'Her happiness I cannot answer for.'

'You think not, Captain?' Irina said with a raise of her finely arched brows. 'And to think I had judged you an astute man.'

To Angèle's utter astonishment, Beaumaris laughed aloud and there was an expression on his face as his eyes met Irina's sparkling gaze that sent a surge of unmistakable jealousy through her veins. She felt excluded and ridiculously envious of the unspoken and instant rapport that seemed to exist between them.

'Irina!' She spoke more sharply than she had intended, using Russian again, in the hope that his grasp of the language was not as good as she suspected. 'I have had enough of this nonsense; I will not be handed over like an unwanted parcel to Captain Beaumaris.'

'As you like.' Irina smiled. 'Then I must hand Captain Beaumaris over to the authorities.'

Angèle gasped. 'That is blackmail!'

'Yes,' Irina agreed, unperturbed. 'And I'll wager you'll thank me for it in due time. And, speaking of time, I must leave—my family think I am in bed with a headache. Oh! I nearly forgot the very reason I came to find you. Your captain is quite a distraction.'

'He is not *my* captain!' Angèle said, squirming inwardly as Beaumaris glanced at her with amused eyes.

'No?' Irina purred. 'I shall not argue with you now. Listen to me. André knows you are missing. He arrived at the dacha while I was there with Katja. I told him that I thought you had eloped to St Petersburg with Boris Lushenkov.'

'Did he believe you?'

'Yes. But it will not be long before he catches up with the Lushenkov party and guesses that I have deliberately sent him in the wrong direction. André is not a fool. I think he will guess you are heading for the border, and he will be determined to bring you back before the Count returns and discovers he has failed to guard you properly.'

'I am sorry you have become involved in this,' Angèle apologised, forgetting her momentary irritation with Irina as she assessed the implications of the news.

'Worry about yourself, not me,' Irina scolded affectionately. 'I can handle André.'

'It is not as much of a start as I had hoped,' Angèle admitted, trying to quell her rising fear.

'Yes. I know. That is why I came to find you as soon as there was a lull in the storm,' Irina said worriedly. 'It is not too late. Come back with me. . .you could say you were out tending a patient——'

'No.' Angèle shook her head, aware that Beaumaris was regarding her intently. 'I cannot face him again. . .'

'Then it seems I must leave you in the hands of the Captain. Write to me when you get to. . .' she paused as her eyes flicked to Beaumaris and then she smiled '. . . England.'

'She is a good friend.' Beaumaris broke the silence that fell after Irina had taken leave of them.

'Yes,' Angèle replied shortly. Now that the immediate danger was past, she found her resentment returning. 'But you need not worry, Captain, I have no intention of holding you to this ridiculous arrangement.'

'I see nothing ridiculous about it.' His voice was cold. 'You have a sleigh and provisions, and you know the country. I can offer you some protection against wolves of both the four-footed and two-footed kind. It seems a fair arrangement to me, *mademoiselle*. We both gain.'

'You talk like a tradesman! I am so glad you think me of some use, Captain,' she scathed. For some unfathomable reason his cold logic angered her further. 'Not that I wish to keep you to your word. I have no desire for the company of a man who. . .' Insults my father. She bit back the last three words. She would not give him the opportunity to gloat over how easily the Duc de Lucqueville's daughter had succumbed to his kiss.

'A man who?' Beaumaris raised a taunting black brow.

'A man who serves a Corsican mountebank,' she snapped, and saw his face darken.

'For one who could be called far worse than mountebank, you are very free with your insults, *mademoiselle*,' he sneered. 'Have you considered that I have no desire for the company of a spoilt little Bourbon lily? Your snobbery bores me, *mademoiselle*. Are you so unsure of your own position that you must attack everyone else's?'

She flinched as if he had struck her. Not simply because of his derisory reference to her illegitimacy, but because there was a thread of truth in his words. She had often thought the same about her mother's excessive concern with gentility, breeding and titles.

Beaumaris saw that he had hurt her and sighed.

'I meant to apologise to you, *mademoiselle*, not argue. I am sorry for——'

'Sorry for what, Captain? Insulting me, disbelieving my story or kissing me?' she cut in tersely, confused by the softening of his expression as he stared at her.

'All of those things. I mistook you for a woman of. . . experience. I did not mean to insult you and I regret that your first kiss should be one taken in anger.'

'I have been kissed before,' she replied defensively.

'I don't doubt it. But I was not talking about a childish peck on the cheek in some alcove between dances at a ball.'

'It was nothing like that,' she retorted, angered by his patronising tone. But he was right in spirit if not in substance. There had been nothing passionate about that one brief embrace with Yashi, her first and last kiss. . . until now. One innocent kiss and Yashi had paid for it with his life.

Seeing the bleakness in her face, he took a half-step forward. 'Angèle, I did not mean to hurt you.'

'Hurt me!' She forced a harsh laugh. 'Do not concern yourself. Do you seriously believe anything you say could affect me?' Why did he make her wish to provoke him? she wondered as she saw the contempt in his eyes. Why was she saying things that she had never thought for a moment to be true?

'Then I will not waste my breath, *mademoiselle*,' he said resignedly. 'From what your friend said, it seems that we had best leave at once.'

'You speak Russian well?' she asked after a moment of silence in which she could not meet his critical eyes.

'A word or two. Enough to understand your friend,' he said laconically. 'There was a ballet dancer at the Comédie Française. It is surprising what you can learn of a language while in bed.'

A flood of colour rose to her face. Partly caused by the recollection of what Irina had said, partly by a memory of that morning. She had been right; sharing a bed was nothing new to him. And for some reason the thought was deeply disturbing to her.

'It is not polite to eavesdrop.'

'Neither is it mannerly to converse in a language that all persons present do not understand,' he countered icily.

'I did not think a Bonapartist knew the meaning of the word manners,' she said unfairly.

'Angèle,' he exhaled wearily, 'it is time to call a truce. If we do not co-operate we will not survive.'

'You take back what you said about the Duc de Lucqueville?' she demanded.

'I cannot do that, but I will not mention his name again if you will desist from referring to the Emperor as a Corsican mountebank.'

Reluctantly she nodded her assent. He was right; all their attention had to be given to the journey ahead of them—they could not afford to quarrel over politics.

'Thank you.' There was unmistakable relief in his face. 'I'll harness the sleigh and Montespan. It is snowing again, so our tracks and the disturbed snow around the lodge will soon be covered. Can you remove all traces of our presence and pack our things?'

'Of course.'

'Good,' he said, and turned towards the door that led into the barn.

'Wait! Captain.' She went to the bed and pulled the largest fur from it. 'Use this as a rug for your mare—she is too thin-skinned for this climate. It will help keep her warm.'

'*Merci*.' He smiled with genuine gratitude. 'I wish it was as easy to solve all our problems.'

'Something is worrying you?'

'Yes; I should give anything to have a shot or two for my pistols, but it can't be helped.'

'Perhaps it can,' she said, bending and pulling out a wooden box from beneath the bed. Inside was a leather satchel, the contents of which she tipped out on to the bed. 'Count Perenskov's hunting pistols,' she explained.

'Pistols, powder and shot! You angel!' Taking her entirely by surprise, he picked her up and spun her exuberantly through the air.

'We called a truce, Captain,' she said breathlessly as her feet touched the ground again and he gave no sign of letting go of her. 'We did not form an alliance.'

'Perhaps we ought to?' He was half teasing, half serious.

She had not the slightest doubt what sort of alliance he meant. She stared at him, speechless with shock, uncertain whether to slap his face or to laugh at his outrageous impertinence.

For a moment he held her gaze in silence, and then with a half-smile he shook his head and released her. 'On second thoughts. . . I'm beginning to think it is safer to be at war with you, Angèle Kerenski. I have a feeling you wouldn't stick to the terms of the treaty. . .'

'Live for today, the devil take tomorrow?'

'You know me too well,' he complained with a rueful grin.

She managed a laugh, wondering why she felt such a nagging sense of disappointment. 'I might surprise you, Captain.'

'That, *mademoiselle*, is what worries me,' he said softly, and then turned away to pick up the pistols.

CHAPTER FOUR

'WE OUGHT to take more fodder for the horses,' Beaumaris said as he looked at the sleigh. 'But there is not room.'

'Take out my trunk—there is nothing in it but gowns, and I have all the necessities I need in my valise,' she offered at once.

He looked at her in astonishment, and then laughed suddenly.

'What is so funny?' she asked suspiciously.

'Nothing. It is just that I have never known a French-woman to part willingly with her wardrobe before.'

'There is a first time for everything,' she replied with more than a little satisfaction at having taken him off guard for once.

'Very true.' He grinned at her as their eyes collided.

She went scarlet and turned away to rummage in the sleigh, knowing he was thinking of that brief, angry kiss.

'It's hardly the time or place for beautifying yourself,' he observed drily as he watched her take out a jar of salve and smear it on her face.

'It is not a beauty aid, Captain,' she snapped, irritated that he should still think her so frivolous. She went over to him and held the jar out. 'It will save your skin from the worst effects of the cold. I suggest you use some as well.'

'My apologies,' he said as he took it. 'You are right, you do surprise me, *mademoiselle*.'

'I don't like being driven by a woman,' Beaumaris said when they were ready to leave. 'Give me the reins.'

'Not unless you have driven a sleigh before.'

'I haven't,' he admitted reluctantly.

'Then you had best let me drive this morning,' she told him briskly, 'otherwise we will be overturned before we've done a mile. You may take a turn later when you have seen how it is done.'

'Very well.' He conceded defeat with a slightly bemused smile and made her a mocking salute. 'On one condition.'

'What is it?' she asked suspiciously.

'That you call me Tristan.'

'If you like. . .Tristan.' His name came more easily to her tongue than she had expected.

'You see, it is not so difficult,' he said as he tucked the fur rug on the seat more firmly about her knees.

No, she thought. It was not difficult. It was all too easy. As easy as it was to allow her thoughts to dwell on the colour of his eyes, the shape of his mouth and the way he had kissed her. She shifted away from his disconcerting nearness and cracked her whip over the head of the lead pony. The sleigh leapt forward as the ponies surged into a smooth canter, there was a slight jerk as Montespan baulked, but a moment later she was following willingly enough.

'We will head for Borisov,' he told her. 'I am sure that is where the Emperor will attempt to cross the Berezina, and we can rejoin the army there.'

'It is about three days' journey from here,' she replied, 'and I heard André say that Admiral Chitchagov intends to retake Borisov before Bonaparte arrives.'

'The *Emperor* has sent Marshal Oudinot to hold him off,' he answered shortly, his eyes dark with anxiety. 'Please God he succeeds.'

'If he does not?'

'Then thousands more Frenchmen will die.'

Sensing that he did not wish to discuss the matter further, she was silent and gave all her attention to directing the ponies. Soon there was nothing to see but whiteness that seemed to stretch for eternity, and it was impossible to tell where the land ended and the sky began. Familiar as the landscape was, she still found herself overwhelmed by the sheer vastness of Russia.

'Someone told me once that a mile in Russia is ten times as far as anywhere else in the world.' He startled her by echoing her thoughts aloud. 'I didn't understand until we came here.'

'No,' she agreed. 'It is impossible to imagine such space and distance without seeing it. Sometimes I think that it would be possible to travel the length and breadth of the country without meeting another living soul.'

'Does anyone in this benighted country have a soul?' he asked cynically. 'I have not seen much evidence of it. We thought the serfs would welcome us as liberators; instead they lie and murder to protect masters who treat them worse than animals.'

'They do not know any different. To disobey your master means death—by hanging if you are lucky, the knout or worse if you are not. There are no judges or juries here; to a serf, his master is next to God,' she tried to explain. 'They are not bad people; to their own kind they are generous and I do not think their love of their country can be equalled. The serfs have a saying: "I belong to my masters, but the land is mine." A man might die but the land lives on.'

'They must have little joy in life if they find any consolation in that.' He grimaced as he stared out across the icy waste. 'Did it not disturb you to live in a country where human life is held so cheap?'

'Yes. Often, since I was old enough to form my own opinions. It did not make me very popular. My stepfather was forever telling me to learn to hold my tongue.'

'Did you?'

'Oh, yes,' she paused, her eyes going dark with memories, 'when I was seventeen.'

'It was a painful lesson?' he asked, glancing at her face.

'You could say that,' she answered bitterly.

'Tell me about it.'

'It is not a pretty story.'

'But I wish to hear it.'

'There was a boy called Yashi,' she began reluctantly. 'The youngest son of my stepfather's house-steward. He had been very ill as a child, and was not very strong physically, but everyone liked him; he was bright, intelligent, always laughing. Even my stepfather had a soft spot for him. He allowed him to learn to read and to use his library. He was the only child of my age on the dacha, and we grew up together.'

'You were very fond of him,' Tristan prompted when she paused.

'Yes. He made me laugh, and there was so little laughter in our house. And when I was with Yashi it did not matter that my mother and stepfather detested each other, or that I was illegitimate. Of course, as we grew older the difference in our ranks made our friendship more difficult. But Yashi looked after my horses, so we still saw each other every day. On the morning of my seventeenth birthday I went riding, with Yashi as my escort. We stopped by a stream to let our horses rest. He picked me a bunch of wild flowers as a gift, and somehow. . .' her voice caught in her throat as she remembered '. . .we kissed. . .'

'Were you in love with him?' he asked, wondering why he should care either way.

'No. Nothing like that. It was gentle, innocent. A kiss between friends—nothing more. It did not last more than a second or two, and neither Yashi nor I would have been foolish enough to let it happen again. He was more shocked than I was. I reassured him that it didn't matter, it was unimportant. It would have been if my cousin André hadn't seen us.'

'He told on you?'

'No.' She shook her head, her lip curling in distaste at the memory. 'He tried to blackmail me into granting him the favours he thought I was giving to Yashi. I refused, of course; I detested him even then. If he had told we would both have been punished, but I knew the Count liked Yashi, so I did not think there was much to fear. I was a fool to underestimate André. The next week, when the Count had left for Moscow, André accused Yashi of stealing oats from the stables. In my stepfather's absence André presided over the district court. Yashi was sentenced to exile in Siberia. I was there and I begged André to change his mind, since I was sure Yashi would not be strong enough to withstand the journey on foot. André said that since I asked it, he would be merciful.' Her hands clenched on the reins as she felt a wave of anger as if it had been only yesterday, not seven years ago, and her voice was brittle as she continued. 'He said Yashi would be spared a slow and lingering death and gave the order for him to be hanged. There was nothing I could do to prevent it.'

Angèle took a long, juddering breath as she finished, and turned to look at his shocked face. 'So you see, Captain, after that I learned to think before I spoke.'

'And you still blame yourself?' he asked, leaning over and taking the reins out of her slack fingers.

'Yes.' His perspicacity jolted the admission out of her.

'You shouldn't,' he said brusquely. 'If you had not intervened Yashi would probably have died anyway. And then you would never have forgiven yourself for not trying to save him. You were in an impossible situation, Angèle; you did what you could.'

She made no reply. She had never told anyone about Yashi before and she felt awkward, as if she had revealed too much of herself to Tristan. And then as she remembered that morning a half-smile came to her mouth. It was a little late to worry about that in every sense.

'How did you know that I blamed myself for Yashi?' she asked later.

'Something in your eyes. . .' he replied after a moment's hesitation. 'I've seen it often enough in my mirror the morning after a battle. I stand there asking myself, if I had given a different order would this man still be alive, or this one not be maimed. . .? During a battle there is no time for doubts, but afterwards when you're still alive and your friends are dead. . .'

'You've lost many friends,' she stated rather than asked as their eyes touched accidentally and held, and she glimpsed the man beneath the cynical, humorous veneer. 'It must be hard. . .'

'It gets easier,' he said slowly. 'After a while you learn never to let anyone become too important to you, never to let anyone too close, then. . .it becomes bearable. . . and that frightens me more than any enemy. . .'

Then with a suddenness that took her unawares his mood changed and she felt the barriers go up again. 'But an army life has its moments—all that looting, pillaging and women. . .'

'Are you trying to shock me?' she asked, mortified by how clearly her thoughts must have shown on her face when she had first set eyes on him. 'I do not think you have ever looted or pillaged in your life.'

'But you have your doubts about the women?' he said with a gravity that should have warned her.

'I do not doubt there have been plenty who were willing. There are always women who will be more influenced by a handsome face than good sense—— Oh. . .' bright colour flooded her cheeks as she caught the flash of silver in his eyes '. . .you are teasing me again.'

'Guilty.' His mouth curved into the grin she was beginning to find irresistible. 'But thank you for the compliment.'

'You are the most provoking. . .' she began, and then

had to bite her lip and turn away so that he would not see how close she was to laughter. Some instinct told her that to laugh with him would be as dangerous as to touch him. She was deeply grateful that the track they were travelling on became deeply rutted at that point and he had to give all his attention to the ponies. As she watched him deftly manoeuvre the ponies so that the sleigh did not overturn she found herself wondering if there was any physical skill that this man could not master. He seemed to have learnt in hours what took most people several days.

'Why didn't you leave before?' He broke into her thoughts. 'Didn't your mother want to leave? Couldn't she have appealed to your father for help to get away?'

'She did write once, but the letter did not reach him. Then she became ill and she was too frail and too frightened to take the risk.'

'Aren't you frightened?'

'I am terrified,' she admitted honestly. 'But I was more frightened of giving in to André, of the sort of person I should become if I did. . .'

'I cannot imagine you any different.' His eyes were warm blue-grey as they found hers.

'Dressed like a Cossack and covered in grease, you mean?' Her arched brows tilted up in self-mockery.

'No.' He laughed and shook his head. 'That was not what I meant. Though I have to confess to wondering what you would look like in a gown.'

'Your curiosity is unlikely to be satisfied, since we left my trunk at the lodge.'

'It does not matter. When we get to Paris I'll take you to Madame Chantelle's and order you the prettiest gown in France.'

'I am not one of the *demi-monde*!' she gasped, half annoyed, half flattered.

'No, I'm sorry. . .' he apologised swiftly. 'I have

become too used to the company of actresses and ballet dancers of late. I meant only to raise your spirits. . .'

'Thank you.' She accepted his apology with a smile. *Actresses and ballet dancers.* For no reason her heart soared. Perhaps Blanche was not so important to him after all. 'But I do not mean to set foot in France,' she added, her elation dying as she remembered how little time they were likely to spend together. 'I thought to take a boat from Germany.'

'Of course. I had forgotten you are set on going to England. Do you have no desire to see your native land?' There was the faintest hint of criticism in the question.

'Of course. But I promised my mother I should find my father first.'

'I gathered from your conversation with Irina that he is an *émigré.*'

'Yes,' she answered tersely, aware that the conversation had veered on to dangerous ground again. 'He has vowed not to set foot in France until King Louis is restored.'

He shrugged. 'You need not sound so defensive. A man has a right to his own opinions. Loyalty is a quality I admire, even if I think it misplaced.'

'Misplaced?' She bridled.

'Yes.' He was vehement. 'A man's loyalty should be to his country, his nation, not to an individual, however blue his blood.'

'And what of your precious General. . .Emperor?' she corrected herself hastily. 'I do not doubt you would give your life for his.'

'You are right. Because Napoleon *is* France. He saved what was good from the revolution and he is making France a nation to be reckoned with. Why do you think the English refuse to make peace with us? It is not for your beloved Louis, but to prevent Napoleon making France an industrial power to rival England.'

'You think it is the Allies who are the warmongers!'

Angèle began angrily, and then, seeing his expression, she smiled wrily. 'I think it is best we agree to differ. I do not wish to quarrel with you again.'

'Nor I with you.' The line of his mouth softened as he looked at her anxious face, but he remained silent as they drove onwards.

The short winter day was fading into dusk when Angèle brought the sleigh to an abrupt halt.

A moment later Tristan stuck his head out of the back, where she had insisted he take some rest a few hours before, having observed that his wound was causing him some discomfort.

'You should not have let me sleep so long,' he told her as he got out and then stopped, instantly alert as she held her finger to her lips. 'What is it?' he asked, low-voiced.

'There are fires ahead. Several. To the right.'

'Soldiers?'

'I think so. I saw riders.'

'They are almost certainly Russian. The French do not have that much firewood left,' he said after one glance, taking the pistols from his pockets and beginning to load them. 'We will try and skirt them, but we'd best agree what action we are going to take if we are challenged.'

'Yes.' She strove to match his coolness. 'With the clothes you are wearing and your bearing, no one would ever believe you to be a servant. You are too much the soldier. So if we are stopped I will say my father's dacha has been overrun by the French, and that you are one of my father's Cossacks, accompanying me to my aunt's house near the Berezina.'

He nodded, a new respect in his eyes as he scanned her face. 'I had more or less the same idea in mind. I have enough Russian to get by.'

'No.' She shook her head. 'Your accent would give

you away immediately. I will let it be known that you have been a mute since you saw a shaman change his shape when you were a child.'

'They'll never believe that,' he scoffed.

'Trust me. They will. The Russians are the most superstitious people on earth.'

'I hope you are right.' He sighed. 'And what of Montespan? Not even the most dimwitted serf could believe she was bred in a northern climate.'

'I will say that a wounded French officer asked us for help, and you murdered him and we kept his horse,' she said, deciding that the closer they kept to the truth, the easier it would be to carry out the charade.

'That I do not doubt they will believe,' he said with feeling. 'After seventeen years of soldiering I did not think there was anything left to shock me. But on this campaign I have seen. . .' he stopped as he saw the apprehension in her face that she was trying so hard to hide '. . .things that are best not spoken of,' he finished abruptly. 'You had better get in the back.'

'Yes.' She let him lift her down. There were layers of leather and wool between their flesh, but it made no difference as his hands gripped her waist. She could not prevent the leap of her heart, or the flare of colour to her cheeks as their eyes met.

Beaumaris swore inwardly. He too felt the spark that seemed to leap between them whenever they touched, but he had been too long a soldier not to know that there was no place for such emotions in the midst of war. They blurred a man's judgement, slowed his reactions.

'Angèle.' He was deliberately cold as he handed her into the sleigh. 'If things go wrong and there is the slightest hint we are suspected, you must denounce me, say that I have taken you hostage and forced you to travel with me.'

'I could not,' she protested instantly, outraged that he

could even think for a moment that she would obey such an instruction.

He saw the angry emerald flecks in her eyes and a flicker of a smile transformed his stern face. 'What am I to do with you, Angèle Kerenski?' he muttered, shaking his head. Then he was harsh again. 'You must do as I say. They could shoot you as a traitor. Do you understand?'

'No.' She shook her head emphatically, wondering why she should feel so ridiculously happy because he seemed to care a little about what became of her.

'Then I will do it myself,' he said brutally.

'But why?' The question came unbidden from her lips. 'I have not asked you to take my share of the risk. I have no claim on you.'

'Don't you?' What the devil had made him say that? he wondered angrily as he turned away. He had intended to kill whatever it was between them, not feed it.

Angèle stared at his back. No doubt he had been referring to the bargain that Irina had forced on him. Meaning to tell him that she would never seek to hold him to it against his will, she reached out and touched his shoulder.

He jerked around, his face cold and masklike.

'Tristan. . .' she began, but the words died in her throat as she saw the flinty chips in his eyes. She did not need to ask whether or not he was already resenting the promise Irina had forced from him; it was obvious.

'What is it?' He was curt.

'Nothing. . . Just that I am scared.'

'I know.' His voice softened a little as he held her eyes with his cool silver stare. 'So am I.'

Then, taking her entirely by surprise, he caught up her gloved hand and raised it to his lips in a fleeting gesture.

A moment later she was alone as he closed the leather doorflap and made it fast. She fought off a wave of panic as she sat in the darkness; she had to be calm for his sake. Taking a kerchief from her pocket, she began to wipe the remnants of the grease from her face.

As the minutes went by with no other sound than the hiss of the sleigh's runners on the snow she began to hope that they might manage to pass the encampment unchallenged. But then her stomach contracted as she heard the dull thud of horses' hoofs and the chink of bits and stirrups.

'Halt.' A shout rang out in Russian. Her heart stopped beating as she prayed that Tristan had understood it. A moment later the sleigh slowed and came to a stop.

She put aside the window flap and looked out. Cossacks. But not from the same area as her stepfather's men, she thought with relief as she looked at their distinctive ankle-length tunics and coats, with cartridge cases sewn like decorations on either side of the breast. These were Kuban Cossacks, not Dons.

'What do you want?' she snapped at a man on a bay horse that was of markedly better quality than those of his companions. She stared at him with every ounce of imperiousness that she could muster, knowing that in Russia nothing was respected so much as authority. 'I am in a hurry.'

'A thousand pardons, *sudarinia*.' The man bowed in her direction and brought his horse up to the sleigh. 'We have orders to stop all traffic going in the Borisov direction. I must ask you your destination and your identity.'

'If you must, *starshina*.' Deliberately she flattered him, according him the rank of lieutenant-colonel, though she guessed he was unlikely to be more than a major. 'I am the daughter of Count Stefan Kerenski, and he is my escort.' She gestured dismissively towards the front of the sleigh.

To her relief, the Kuban glanced at Tristan without interest and returned his attention to her.

'Major Platov at your service, Sudarinia Kerenski.' He bowed again and smiled, revealing white teeth beneath his flowing black moustache. 'It is an honour to meet the daughter of such a great warrior.'

'You know my father?' She forced herself to smile back, disguising her panic.

'Not personally. But we have often ridden into battle beside our brothers from the Don, and your father's reputation is well known.'

'He will be pleased to hear it.' She laughed with genuine relief.

'But you should not be here, Sudarinia Kerenski.' The major was sombre again. 'The French are very close; you could be in danger.'

'I do not need reminding of that, Major!' She shuddered in what she hoped was a convincing manner. 'My father's dacha was overrun by them yesterday. I was forced to flee—hence my appearance.' She made a depreciatory feminine gesture towards her masculine clothes. 'I am now on my way to my aunt's to seek shelter.'

'By the hosts! You can be sure such an insult will be avenged, Sudarinia Kerenski.' The major was indignant.

'Thank you, Major. But I have already taken my own revenge.' She leant out of the window and pointed to Montespan. 'We came across a wounded officer. He appealed to me for help—so we gave him some.' Drawing her finger across her throat in a graphic gesture, she laughed.

The major guffawed his approval, as did several of his men. 'You are truly a Cossack's daughter, *sudarinia*. Your father will be proud of you.'

'I hope so. Perhaps it will provide some consolation for the destruction of our dacha; and now, if you are satisfied, Major, may we continue our journey?'

'If you wish. I would not detain you further, but I must warn you that you are not far from the French

army, and there are known to be wolves between here
and the next village.'

'Wolves.' Paling, she bit her lip. She did not share
Tristan's confidence that he would be able to defend
them from the four-footed variety single-handed. To
small groups of travellers, wolves were a serious threat.
Tales of men and horses being eaten alive were not
unusual, and even gunshots were not always an effective
deterrent if the animals were starving. It was not easy to
hit a flitting grey shadow in the dusk from a moving
sleigh.

'You are welcome to stay at our camp this evening,'
Major Platov offered. 'We leave for Borisov at dawn, so
we can give you an escort for part of the way.'

'Thank you. That is most kind.' She accepted the
offer after a moment's hesitation. To have refused it
would have been madness and might have aroused his
suspicions. 'We will stay here the night,' she told Tristan
brusquely, hoping that he had followed enough of the
conversation to realise that they were in no immediate
danger.

Surely it had been the longest evening of her life, Angèle
thought several hours later as she sat with the major
beside the largest of the flickering fires.

'No, thank you.' She declined the piece of roast
chicken he waved at her on the end of his knife and took
a sip of vodka from the flask beside her. It was rough
and fiery, making her eyes water. But at least it took
away the nausea she was feeling. The major seemed to
have assumed that she was indeed her father's daughter
and had regaled her with sickening tales of attacks on
the frozen and helpless French. Somehow she had forced
herself to smile and laugh, to make approving and
encouraging comments. But she could only guess at how
Tristan, sitting in the shadows slightly behind her, must
be feeling.

'It is good?' The major grinned through a mouthful of chicken.

'Yes,' she lied and took another more cautious sip of the vodka.

'But not as good as this.' He drew a silver and leather flask from his tunic. 'I am saving it for when Napoleon is dragged in chains to Moscow.'

'You think he will be captured?' she asked.

'He cannot escape. The temperature has raised just enough to thaw the Berezina. Now it is in full flood. And we heard this afternoon that Chitchagov has destroyed the bridge at Borisov and has artillery on the far bank. The French will not be able to repair the bridge and there is no other way across, unless they know of the ford at Studenka, which I doubt! They are trapped!'

He laughed uproariously and took a swallow of vodka from the open flask and then held it out to Tristan. 'Is that not worth drinking to, fellow?'

Tristan turned his head towards them and she saw from the savage line of his mouth what it was costing him to suppress his anger. Her heart stopped as she saw his hand come up abruptly as if to knock the flask aside. Then, to her infinite relief, he accepted it and put it to his lips.

'Well?' the major demanded as Tristan handed back the flask, stony-faced.

'He cannot answer you. He is a mute.' She spoke hastily. 'He saw the shaman change his shape when a child and has never spoken since.'

The major crossed himself in an automatic gesture as he stared at Tristan. 'So that's why he's such a surly brute. From his expression, you'd think he trusts no one to be near you.'

'He does not. My father charged him with my safety.'

'He need not fear for you here.' The major was affronted. He scowled as he rested his elbow on his horse, which like all Cossack mounts was trained to lie on the ground beside him. 'You are under the protection of Major Platov. Anyone who dares to touch a hair of your head will answer to me. Do you hear that, fellow? Or should I call you nursemaid?' He cackled, delighted with his own joke.

For St Peter's sake, smile, she willed Tristan as the antagonism between the two men seemed to crackle in the air.

Grey eyes held black for a long moment, then Tristan managed a grimace and inclined his head to the major. When she risked a glance at him a few minutes later he was staring, tight-lipped, into the flames of the fire, turning a twig over and over in his hands.

Wearily she slumped back against the quarters of the major's chestnut horse, allowing her heart to return to a more normal beat.

The major too settled himself more comfortably, and threw his arm out along the horse's back, brushing her shoulder and making her start.

'Your pardon. . .' the major began to apologise.

The twig Tristan had been holding snapped like a pistol shot as he came to his feet, unmistakable murder in his eyes. Every head around the fire turned towards him, and hands went for sabres.

'Be seated!' Sheer panic made Angèle's voice harsh as she gestured to Tristan sharply. He ignored her and continued to glower at the major.

'What in the name of the brotherhood is wrong with the man?' the major growled. 'If it's a fight he wants——'

'No!' She smiled at him desperately, fanning her eyelashes as she had seen Irina do so often. 'This is no time for brother to fight brother when we have a common enemy.'

'You're right,' the major agreed grudgingly. 'But he obviously seeks one.' Then he laughed. 'There is another way to cure his pride. The Dons are proud of their skill as dancers, are they not? Well, let him see how well he does against my men. I'll wager he'll run out of breath before they do.'

There was a murmur of approval, and several of the younger men got to their feet. And from somewhere a young trooper produced a balalaika.

For a moment she froze, incapable of thought or action. No one had questioned her explanation of Tristan's muteness. But a Don Cossack who did not know how to dance? It was unthinkable. She looked at Tristan and saw that he was coolly assessing the men who were on their feet, deciding which to take first.

Inspiration came from nowhere.

'No,' she protested. 'I could not possibly allow him to defend the honour of my father's people. His dancing is on a par with his conversation.'

As she had hoped, there was a roar of laughter, and some of the tension in the circle vanished.

'But I should be happy to do so myself.'

'Do the Dons let their women dance for them now? They'll be doing the fighting for them next!' someone taunted, and there was another ripple of laughter.

'No,' she retorted, 'but they leave the singing to us.'

As she had hoped, the major intervened. 'Enough.' He gestured to the heckler to sit down. 'We should be honoured to hear you sing, Sudarinia Kerenski.' He nodded to the balalaika player to come and sit beside them.

Her heart was still pounding with fright as she took off her hat and shook out her hair, deliberately drawing the eyes of every man in the circle as Tristan eased himself back into the shadows.

There was a low hum of approval as she began to sing. She had picked an old ballad about a woman reassuring her sweetheart that he would not be forgotten when he went off to war.

'My heart was yours before we first touched,
When the south wind whispers in your ear,
Remember it has run its fingers
Through my hair. . .'

Her voice faltered momentarily as she glimpsed
Tristan's oddly intent face watching her from the
shadows. As she saw the all too obvious message in his
eyes her cheeks grew hot in a way that had nothing to do
with the fire. Why was it only now, when she had sung
the song a hundred times without thinking, that she
should become aware of the sensual implications behind
the simple words? But it was too late to stop now. And
as she came to the last line she could not help but look
at him again.

For a long unguarded moment her gaze merged with
his in a mutual unspoken acknowledgement. And then
he moved back abruptly into the shadows and she was
left staring into the empty darkness, wondering if she
had imagined what had been in his eyes and face.
Perhaps she had, she told herself sternly. A love-song
was one thing, real life another. Common sense told her
they could never be more than travelling companions.
He was a Bonapartist, he despised her father, and he
loved a woman called Blanche. But inside her head a
stubborn little voice kept repeating the last line of the
song, over and over: 'We were never strangers, nor ever
will be.'

The song had changed the mood of the Kubans around
the fires. Tristan was forgotten; they were quiet now,
thinking of the women they had left behind, and the
protests when Angèle bid them goodnight a few minutes
later were polite rather than pressing.

The major insisted on escorting her to her sleigh, and
holding her arm as they threaded their way through the
prone horses and men. Some of the Kubans were already
snoring, their heads pillowed on their saddles between

their horses' forelegs and their backs to their horses' bellies for warmth. To her infinite relief, the major did not linger as he wished her goodnight. As soon as he had left, Tristan stepped out from the shadows beside Montespan.

She dared not say anything to him for fear of being overheard. The glow from one of the nearby fires illuminated his face and she found herself staring at him helplessly, unable to look away. But he seemed to be barely aware of her presence as he helped her into the sleigh. The expression on his face disturbed her. He looked not simply tired, but racked, as if he were being torn in two. It was the news about the bridge, she guessed. Out of blind instinct she took off her glove and touched her hand to his cheek, wanting to offer the sympathy she could not put into words.

He froze, and she heard his breath catch in his throat. Then slowly, like a man drugged, he raised his hand to hers and cupped it against his lips. The warmth of his breath against her palm sent a searing, unfamiliar heat through her veins that made her dizzy. A moment later he released it abruptly and took a step back, leaving her shaken to the core by the intensity of her reaction to his caress.

Why had he looked at her like that? she wondered as he let the hood of the sleigh fall back into place. For a second his shadowed eyes had seemed almost accusatory, as if instead of giving comfort she had made things more difficult for him. Miserably she leant back against the velvet cushions and pulled a fur rug around her. She was behaving like a fool of the first rank. Had he not told her at the lodge that he thought her a boring little snob? They had nothing in common except their danger, nor were they ever likely to. She shut her eyes against the sudden hot tears that trickled from beneath her lashes.

At dawn the next morning Angèle was awoken by the shouts of command as the Cossacks struck camp. As she got out of the sleigh her first glance was to the driver's seat. Tristan wasn't there. With a sick feeling in the pit of her stomach she turned to the back of the sleigh, instinct already telling her what she would see. Montespan had gone. She should have guessed last night that he would try to reach the army with the news about the bridge at Borisov. . .and the ford at Studenka. She could not even blame him; there were thousands of lives at stake, and little wonder he gave such scarce importance to hers. Leaning against one of the cream ponies, she half laughed, half sobbed at her own stupidity. If she had any place at all in his affections her rival was not just Blanche, it was Napoleon Bonaparte and his army.

CHAPTER FIVE

HALF an hour later the major and his men were nothing more than black dots on the pale orange horizon. With a sigh of relief Angèle slumped against the wooden back rest of the driver's seat. Major Platov was a simple man, with simple patriotic beliefs, but he was not an utter fool; if he had begun to doubt her story about Montespan's straying and Tristan's going in search of her. . .if she had not convinced him that her aunt's house was close enough for her not to need an escort in daylight. . . It did not bear thinking about.

Picking up the reins, she turned the sleigh to the west. If the French could cross the ford at Studenka, so could she. It was the quickest way, she told herself; her decision had nothing to do with the insane, ridiculous hope that if she found the French army she might find Tristan Beaumaris again.

By late afternoon both she and the ponies were urgently in need of rest and shelter. She stopped in the lee of a small wood, fed the ponies and then herself. Climbing into the sleigh with the hot coffee she had made over a small fire, she stretched out on the cushioned seat. She would doze for an hour or two, no more, then she would move on.

It was dark when she was jolted awake by the ponies buffeting the sleigh. She could hear them blowing, stamping their feet: something was wrong. Still half asleep, she scrambled out of the sleigh, forgetting to put her hat on. How long had she been asleep? Too long. The fire she had lit earlier was nearly out and the only illumination was from the silver light of the full moon that filtered through the trees on to the snow-covered ground. The ponies were tossing their heads, jerking at their tethers, rolling their eyes. In the moonlight they looked almost like ghost horses, but their fear was all too real.

An icy trickle of unease went down her spine as she peered into the darkness of the woods. She could see nothing, but an instinct as old as time made her scalp prickle. The ponies were stock-still now, stiff-legged, their ears pricked and nostrils flaring as they stared into the darkness.

The slightest of noises to her right sent her spinning around, her heart in her mouth as she scanned the expanse of moonlit snow about the sleigh. Nothing. Just the trunks of the silver birches shimmering like satin in the moonlight, but the shadows behind them were black as soot; anything could be hidden there.

Her eyes went to the glowing orange embers of her fire. A cheerful blaze would do much for her fast-dwindling courage, she decided, taking a step towards it.

Her shoulder-blades knitted together as she moved away from the sleigh and instantly felt twice as vulnerable with nothing to protect her back. The few yards to the fire seemed endless. The night was clear, still, silent, except for the crunch of the frosted snow beneath her feet. Halfway to the fire, she halted and spun round. She had heard something, a tiny rustling sound. Her stomach lurched as she saw the ponies' heads turn as one in the same direction. She had not imagined the noise. Another rustle, this time from the other side. She wheeled, to see snow cascading from a branch. What had caused it? There was no wind, only a terrible stillness. Just the weight of the snow—you have seen it a thousand times, she told herself—but her skin had gone cold and clammy with fear, and her heart was hammering against her ribs, so loud that it seemed to echo about the clearing. There

was something out there in the darkness, she could feel
it. . . There was nothing she would not have given at
that moment to have Tristan beside her, but it was futile
to think like that. With trembling fingers she reached for
the knife in her sleeve. It wasn't there. She had used it
in the sleigh to cut a piece from the smoked cheese and
forgotten to replace it.

She turned back and then froze as she saw what had
seemed a grey shadow move, low-bellied, across the
snow towards the ponies. How could she have been so
stupid as not to realise it at once? Wolves! For a moment
she was too horrified to do anything as the ponies erupted
into a stamping, snorting mass of equine panic.

'No!' Her voice came out as little more than a gasp as
she began to run for the sleigh and her knife. It was too
late. A pony reared, snapping its tether as a wolf sprang
out of the darkness and landed on its back, sinking its
teeth into its woolly mane. The animal screamed in
terror, lost its footing on the icy snow and went down,
its legs kicking and flailing, but the wolf had kept its
grip.

She had to do something. The whip! She snatched it
from the driver's seat and sent the lash snapping out. It
caught the wolf across the muzzle. Dog-like, it yelped in
pain and retreated momentarily. But there were others
now. She was encircled by what seemed like a hundred
baleful yellow eyes.

Her scream was cut off as the pack leader leapt. Its
weight took her down. Its forefeet were on her chest, its
jaws open, ready to seize her throat. In an unthinking
reflex she thrust the heavy stock of the whip into its
mouth, jamming it open. It stopped it only for a moment
as it shook its head to clear the obstruction. But it was
enough for her to do as an old Don Cossack had once
told her and curl herself into a tight ball, using her arms
to protect her head and throat.

But it would not help her for more than seconds. The

beast was strong, catching at her coat, shaking her, scrabbling with its forefeet. Terror blotted out everything except the horrid, fetid stench of its breath as it worried at her. Now there were others, a maelstrom of snapping, snarling yellow teeth and razor claws. Growling, tearing, snapping at her coat, boots, hair. Another moment and they would find her flesh. One caught her sleeve, tugging her arm so that her throat was left exposed as another moved in for the kill. Her mouth opened in a scream that had no end, merging and reverberating with the shrill whinnying of the ponies. And then came a noise like thunder, a flash of searing pain, and instant merciful blackness.

The wolves scattered, melting into the shadows as the pistol shot echoed around the clearing, all except the one that had been poised at Angèle's throat. It yelped, rolled, ran a few paces and then crumpled, a ragged black shadow on the snow.

Tristan swore as he swung down from Montespan's back and ran forward. She was so still, sweet heaven; let him not have arrived too late or have misjudged the shot. . . If the ball had passed through the wolf. . . Ashen-faced, he bent over her, the smoking pistol in his hand.

'Angèle. . .' His voice broke on her name as he rolled her on to her back. A numbing black horror squeezed the breath from his lungs as he saw where her hair clung to her temple, sticky, matted, and the trickle of blood, black in the moonlight, that ran down the side of her face and on to the collar of her coat. She was white as the snow, cold, lifeless.

He had killed her.

A sharp stinging pain that made an unwelcome counterpoint to the dull pounding in her skull brought Angèle back to consciousness. She opened her eyes and saw Tristan's face. Exhausted, gaunt, a thousand years older,

but his face nevertheless. It couldn't be. Tristan had
gone. She shut her eyes and opened them again. He was
still there. An overwhelming sense of relief and joy swept
through her. He had come back for her!

She tried to form his name but her tongue seemed
glued to the dry roof of her mouth.

'Angèle?' Some of the anxiety left his face as his eyes
came to hers and saw the recognition in them. Very
gently he pressed to her temple a cloth that was, from
the smell of it, saturated in vodka. 'Does this hurt
much?'

'No. . . I don't think so,' she answered slowly, aware
for the first time of the source of the throbbing pain in
her skull. 'Was it. . .?' What was it? She frowned; there
was a blankness in her mind, some horror that nagged at
her but refused to take shape.

'No,' he said, some of the grimness coming back to
his face. 'This was my fault. . .'

'Your fault. . .?' She was bewildered.

'Yes. Mine.' He was terse. 'A wolf was at your throat.
I had to shoot at once. . .the ball passed right through it
and grazed you——'

'Wolves!' She only took in one word of what he said.
Jerking upright, oblivious to the pain in her head, she
looked about her wildly as her terror returned all too
vividly.

'It's all right.' He put his hands on her shoulders,
steadying her. 'They've gone. They were mostly young
ones. I managed to hit several, and the rest seem to have
been frightened off by the shots.'

'You don't understand!' she blurted, still rigid with
fear. 'They'll come back for me—they always do for a
kill. . .'

'Not through the fires.'

'Fires. . .' This time as she looked around she realised
he had made a circle of fires around them and the ponies,
which were huddled together but apparently unharmed.

'The leader lost a mouthful or two of mane but that's all,' Tristan said, following the direction of her gaze.

With a sob of relief she brought her eyes back to his face. He was here; she was safe. That much her mind could grasp, but her body was trembling from head to foot and she could not stop.

Without a word he let go of her, picked up the flask of vodka and poured a large measure into a metal beaker and held it to her lips.

'Drink; you'll feel better.'

Grim-faced, he watched her drain the beaker and then took it from her shaking fingers.

'I knew I should not have left you. . .' he said, more to himself than her.

'You had. . .to. I understood. . .'

'Then what possessed you to leave the Cossacks? Surely you knew I would come back for you as soon as I could?' His eyes were flinty with anger as he scanned her face. 'Do you realise if it had snowed or if there hadn't been a full moon I'd never have found your tracks and realised you'd gone off on your own?'

'I didn't expect. . .you to come back.' She forced the words out between her chattering teeth.

'Sweet liberty! Is that what you think of me? Can't you discard your damned Bourbon prejudices for once? Do you think I have so little regard for my obligations, for my honour?'

Honour and obligation. Was that all that had brought him back? How could he be so cold, so angry. . .? She wanted to hit him, or to weep. But she could do neither. She turned her face away so that he would not see her hurt, her disappointment, not realising that it was written in every quivering line of her body.

'Damnation!' Tristan groaned, and then against his better judgement he reached out to her. 'Come here, you fool.'

A second later Angèle was cradled in his arms, her

face against his chest. The silken frogging that fastened his coat dug into her cheek, but she did not care. He was holding her, his arms were around her, his hands were stroking her hair, taking away her terror and the throbbing pain in her head.

He held her close in silence until her trembling had ceased.

'I'm sorry,' he murmured against her hair. 'I am angry with myself, not you. When I picked you up I thought you were dead. . .' His voice cracked suddenly and his arms tightened around her. 'I thought I'd killed you. . .'

She lifted her head; his eyes were dark, haunted. 'It wasn't your fault,' she hastened to reassure him. 'If it had not been for you I should have died. You saved my life——'

'I nearly took it!' he rasped, his face stiff with self-contempt. 'A fine protector I am proving to be!'

'I do not think I could ask for a better one.' Her response was unthinking, instinctive.

'Don't you?' His voice was jagged with a mixture of self-contempt and amusement. For an instant, as he met her shining, clear eyes, he forgot everything except that he wanted to go on holding her close, wanted to explore her sweet, soft mouth again, wanted her so much that it hurt. But his conscience overrode his desire. 'I'm the last person who ought to be entrusted with your protection. . .' Tristan sighed, and, lifting a hand, he touched her cheek where the frogging on his coat had left a livid red mark. 'I could hurt you so easily, Angèle. . .'

'Hurt me?'

'Yes. By accepting the invitation in your eyes and kissing you.'

'Could there be so much harm in a kiss?' A stranger seemed to have taken control of her mouth, saying what she was not even aware that she thought.

'A kiss?' His brows rose as he looked at her. Then he shook his head at her innocence. 'You must know how it is between us. Do you really think it would stop at a single kiss?'

'Would it matter if it did not?' Shock, vodka and the wound to her head must have affected her reason. She could not believe she was saying these things, but she could not stop herself. Nor could she smother the joy that lit her face. He felt it too! Her instinct at the Cossack camp had not been wrong.

'Yes, dammit! It would!' he grated, releasing her abruptly and getting to his feet, his face chalk-white in the moonlight as he glared down at her incandescent face.

'Why?' The stranger who was speaking through her mouth breathed the question.

'Why?' He inhaled sharply. There was going to be no easy way to say this. He might as well get it over with. 'Because tomorrow I am taking you back to the lodge, and you can travel back to the dacha in daylight the following day.'

'What are you talking about?' Angèle was bewildered. This was the last thing she had expected him to say.

'Saving your life,' he answered flatly. 'You must realise what it means now the bridge is destroyed. . .'

'I know it will be dangerous,' she broke in, 'but you cannot really mean to make me go back. . .' She stared at his set face, and for the first time real doubt crept into her mind, freezing her heart. 'Can you?' The question came out as a whisper.

Tristan dragged his eyes from hers, swearing beneath his breath. He had been prepared for her to be angry, outraged, hysterical even, but not for her to look at him with such disbelief, such trust.

'Listen to me!' Self-contempt made his voice as vicious as a whiplash. 'Khutuzov's army is two or three days behind us, Wittgenstein's Cossacks are coming in from the north, Chitchagov is waiting for us on the west bank of the Berezina and we have to cross a river in full flood. . .' He paused, searching for the words to make her understand. 'We don't even have pontoons; they were burnt at Orsha to save the horses.'

'But the ford at Studenka——' she began to argue.

'An officer crossed it a few days ago,' he interrupted sharply. 'It's deeper than a man's height in midstream—infantry will be swept away like driftwood. . .unless General Eble can cobble together a bridge before Chitchagov realises where we mean to cross. . .we'll be caught like rats in a trap. . .'

'It might not be as bad as you think,' she protested, forgetting her own situation in the desire to offer him some comfort.

'It'll be worse!' he said savagely. 'I saw the army at dawn this morning! The men are frozen and hungry, and half of them are too exhausted to carry their weapons! Not even the Emperor can fight off three armies with a rabble! If the diversions fail and Chitchagov attacks before we can regroup, it will be a massacre! And don't think waving a white cockade will save you—a Russian soldier isn't going to differentiate between a Bourbonist and a Bonapartist. . .' He stopped and then went on more gently, 'So you understand why you must go back?'

'I cannot,' she answered slowly. 'Dying in battle does not frighten me as much as my cousin André. . .'

'It damn well ought to!' His voice rose again, edged with desperation. He had to make her see sense. 'For every man who dies cleanly, there is another who lies in agony with smashed limbs, bleeding to death without as much as water or a word of comfort to lessen his pain! This cousin of yours, surely you can bring him to heel? It didn't take you long to wind your way around my——'

'Your what? Heart? I doubt you have one! And you're wasting your breath. I am not going back!' she interrupted, her own temper snapping. How could he speak so dispassionately about sending her back to another man? Because he loves someone else. An unwelcome voice in her mind supplied the answer and fuelled her anger with him and herself. His heart, and most likely his future, lay with Blanche, something she had forgotten in her fear and shock. She had always thought women who set their caps at men who were committed to others were both selfish and foolish. And now she was behaving like the worst of them.

'For God's sake,' he was too angry to see her sudden despair, and went on relentlessly in his attack, 'don't you see? Even if by some miracle we get across the bloody river, have you any idea what a forced march in this weather is going to be like, with no supplies, no shelter? You must go back!'

'I can't.'

Their eyes clashed and locked in a duel of wills.

'Here!' He broke first, catching her hands and pulling her on to her feet and thrusting a pistol into her hand. 'If you're bent on killing yourself, why didn't you just say so! It'll be simpler and quicker! You just put the barrel in your mouth, and pull the trigger. Not very pretty, but a much easier death than having a limb torn off by cannonshot, or being so desperate for food that you begin to gnaw your own flesh!'

Nauseated, she flung the pistol back at him.

'There is no need for you to try and frighten me! I should have guessed you'd want to be rid of a royalist embarrassment before returning to your precious regiment!'

'Politics don't enter into this and you know it!' he bellowed as he pushed the pistol back into his belt. 'Can't you see beyond the end of your blue-blooded nose? I'm simply trying to keep my word, to ensure your safety. Surely even you can understand that?'

'I understand that you despise me for my convictions and my breeding!'

'It's not you I despise! Damn it! I wish I could!'
Tearing his eyes away from her hurt white face, he bent,
picked up a stick and hurled it into the fire with such
violence that a spiral of orange sparks shot upwards. It
was only after he had watched them vanish into the clear
star-studded sky that he trusted himself to go on. 'It is
myself I despise for ever agreeing to this bargain in the
first place.'

'You can consider yourself released from it.' She
jerked the words out, staring up into the darkness; she
would not cry, she would not.

'Can you release me from my conscience so easily?' he
asked brutally. 'You know I can't just leave you here. . .'

'I can take care of myself.'

'The way you did tonight?' He laughed mirthlessly.
'For the last time, will you go back?'

She shook her head, letting her hair fall forward over
her shoulders in a golden-bronze curtain that shielded
her face from his gaze.

'Please. . .'

'No!' She shrank from his touch as he put out a hand
to her cheek. 'I will travel on alone.'

'I can't let you. . .' His voice faltered and softened as
he saw a tear, golden in the firelight, that rolled down
her pale face and touched the corner of her mouth. 'I
didn't mean to make you weep. . .'

'You haven't. It is the smoke that makes my eyes
water!' she replied, rubbing her eyes with the back of
her wrist.

'I wish I could believe that.' Suddenly he sounded
utterly weary, defeated.

'I'm sorry. . .' She found herself apologising without
even knowing why.

'So am I,' he said grimly, turning away from her. 'So
am I.'

'Where are you going?' she asked in sudden panic that
he might leave her after all.

'To get some more firewood,' he answered roughly. 'You'd best see to those scratches, and then perhaps if you're feeling well enough you can find me something to eat.'

'Yes. Of course,' she answered thickly. The distance between them now was as great as when they had first met, and she did not know if she could bear it. Then as she watched him walk away into the darkness she called after him; there was something she had to know, something she simply did not understand. . .

'Tristan!'

He halted and turned, his face a harsh mask of firelight and shadow. And for the first time since he had held his sword to her neck at the lodge she felt truly frightened of him. Then she had been in fear of her life, now for her heart, and there seemed to be little difference.

'What is it?' There was no encouragement in his voice.

'Why. . .?' Her nerve failed her beneath his cold scrutiny of her face.

'Why did I come back for you?' He guessed her question accurately. 'I told you, it was a matter of honour.'

'That was the only reason?' She forced the words past the lump in her throat.

'Should there be another?' he said with the coldness she was beginning to dread above all other things.

She flinched as his eyes drifted disparagingly from her unkempt hair to her ripped and tattered sheepskin coat.

'No.'

'Then you won't be disappointed, will you?'

'Disappointed?' Somehow she salvaged enough pride to produce a bitter smile. 'You flatter yourself, Captain; relieved would be nearer the mark.'

Tristan said nothing. His mouth twisted as he saw the tautness of her slender body, how she held herself poised like a fencer, ready to repel his next thrust. She lied so bravely. . .and so very badly. He was exhausted, men-

tally and physically. But it didn't stop him wanting her.
It would be the easiest thing in the world to catch her up
in his arms and lay with her among the furs in the sleigh,
to wipe out the hurt he had done her with kisses and
caresses. . .and with promises he could not keep. No.
He had no choice. Cursing the fates that had thrown
them together at such a time and place, he turned on his
heel and walked away.

When he had gone she slumped down beside the fire.
Part of her hated him, and part of her had an all-
consuming longing to be in his arms again, to be held,
protected by him, even if he did love another woman.
Bringing her knees up to her chin, she wrapped her arms
around them and stared into the fire. England; she
should think about her future there, not Tristan. . .but
there was little comfort in that. What Tristan had said
about the Duc de Lucqueville had set a seed of doubt in
her mind. Supposing her mother's confidence that he
would receive her as his daughter was misplaced? Supposing he would not acknowledge her or help her to find
respectable employment? Supposing she could not find a
position before the gold and jewellery she had stitched
into the hem of her tunic ran out? It was best not to
think about it. Best not to think of anything, but just to
watch the flames consuming the wood, until it collapsed
into ashes like the ridiculous, childish hope that Tristan
had come back because he was beginning to care for her.

CHAPTER SIX

'DAMNATION!' Tristan swore as he looked at what was left of the army. It was worse even than he had feared. There had been warning signs, of course. For the last day and a half they had been travelling through a nightmare. Mile after mile of brown slush, studded with broken guns, abandoned wagons, dead horses, dead men. And, worst, dying men. Dying men he'd refused to allow Angèle to help because there were too many of them. She had accepted his decision without a word. But the silent reproach in her eyes every time they passed one of the pathetic bundles of rags on the snow tore at his conscience, making him blindingly angry. Couldn't she see there was nothing they could do? Not a single damned thing? Cossacks he could fight, but not the bloody Russian winter!

He lowered his field-glass and glanced at her. She was pale, her eyes dark and enormous in her strained face. His anger with himself for giving in and bringing her with him increased.

'Here, take a good look!' he said roughly, thrusting the field-glass into her hands. 'Behold the *grande Armée*! It should make a tale to amuse your mother's *émigré* friends over the dinner table!'

Angèle bit her lip. Her nerves were jangled enough without his insults. She had felt for him, knowing it was tearing him apart to see the army that had been his life for years being destroyed, hour by hour. But it was almost as if he blamed her personally, as if he sought an argument. And if he made one more gibe about her royalist sentiments he could have one, she decided furiously.

Without a word she took the field-glass and raised it. There was nothing to see but thousand upon thousand of ragged, skeletal men, stumbling through the icy slush, half with nothing more than rags to protect their feet. After a minute or so she lowered the glass slowly, sick to the stomach with pity and anger at the sheer scale of the suffering.

'Well?' Tristan demanded impatiently.

'I never imagined it would be like this. . .'

'Didn't you?' His eyes skimmed derisively across her anguished face. 'You must be pleasantly surprised. Don't you find it a sight to warm your loyal Bourbon heart?'

'How dare you?' she seared, swivelling sideways on the driver's bench to face him. 'Do you think you are the only one with compassion? The only one to feel guilt every time we pass a man lying in the snow? The only one to feel anger at your own helplessness?'

Her hand closed involuntarily on the sleigh whip as she held his contemptuous gaze without flinching, meeting frosted silver with splinters of emerald fire. Just one more insult! Just one and she would not be responsible for her actions!

His hand shot out with the quickness she had almost forgotten and caught her wrist. Even through the thickness of her clothes she could feel the steely strength of his fingers. They had both been scrupulously careful not to touch each other since the evening of the wolf attack, not even letting their sleeves brush as they sat beside each other on the driver's bench. Now the suddenness of the contact made her tremble. The whip fell from her suddenly slack fingers and clattered into the footwell.

Grey eyes met turquoise. His intake of breath was audible as Tristan felt the tremor that shook her body a moment before she twisted free of his grasp.

As Angèle stared at him, half accusing, half bewildered by the way they reacted to each other, he knew that it was more than the disaster that had befallen the army that was gnawing at him. It was fear of failing her, as he had so nearly done with the wolves. Damn it! He swore beneath his breath. Why did she have to look at him like that? Didn't she realise he could not save her from cannonshot, or dying of starvation or cold? He would be as powerless as the men all about them. He had to get her back to the Russian lines, even if he had to tie her to a saddle. André or no André, at least that way she would live. And you will not have to watch her die. A mocking voice in his mind told him what he was most afraid of.

The decision made, he relaxed a little; it no longer seemed so vital to keep a distance between them. He bent and picked up the whip, holding it out to her.

'A peace-offering,' he said drily. 'Or do you still want to horsewhip me for that last remark?'

'You deserve it!' she said icily.

'I know,' he confessed. 'I did not mean it nor half the things I have said lately. Forgive me?'

She nodded, disarmed by his unexpected admission and apology.

'Thank you.'

He inclined his head in acknowledgement of her generosity. He doubted she would forgive him so easily for what he was going to arrange as soon as he reached the regiment.

'How's your head? Is it still aching?' he asked.

'It's much better.' She exaggerated her reply a little, knowing how much he blamed himself for her injury.

'Then do you think you could drive from here? I had better ride Montespan in case we run into trouble.'

'Yes, of course.'

'You're sure? You look pale.'

'It is just that, having lived all my life at the dacha, I am not used to being among so many people. . .but I suppose I shall have to become used to it if I am to live in London.'

'Yes,' he responded tersely. He hated having to lie to

her, but now was not the time or place to tell her of his decision.

Angèle watched in silence as he saddled Montespan and threw his threadbare and near-useless campaign cloak over his Cossack coat.

He looked up and caught the question in her eyes.

'Rule number one: try to avoid being shot by your own side,' he said wryly. 'Speaking of shooting, I don't suppose you have ever used a pistol?'

'Several times,' she answered, enjoying the surprise that flashed across his face. 'My stepfather insisted that all the household knew how to handle a pistol in case the serfs should ever rise.'

'Good,' he said after a moment, expertly loading and priming one of the hunting pistols they had taken from the lodge. 'Then take this one. But be careful, it has a hair trigger.'

'I know,' she said, more than a little stung by his assumptions about female incompetence.

His eyebrows rose as he handed over the pistol and an ammunition pouch, but he was silent as he mounted the black mare and loaded the other pistol.

'Ready?' he asked, glancing at her.

'Yes.' Again her voice quavered, and she saw anxiety in his eyes.

'Don't stop for anyone; shoot if necessary. Such a situation can bring out the worst in even the best of men, you understand?'

'How could I forget?' She made an attempt at humour, not wanting him to see just how afraid she was of what lay ahead. She did not want him to think her more of an encumbrance than he did already.

'With some difficulty, I presume.' He smiled. The first she had seen him smile since the night he had saved her from the wolves.

'No.' She shook her head gravely. 'With a great deal.'

'I suppose I asked for that.' He laughed. 'I am

beginning to think it was a mistake to let you have a pistol—your tongue is quite dangerous enough.'

Before she could think of a suitable reply he was already riding on and she had no choice but to follow.

'Captain! Captain Beaumaris!'

Angèle jolted as a man, some thirty paces to her left, shouted and waved. She was exhausted from the effort of steering the sleigh through the tangle of men, wagons and guns and had nearly dozed off.

The man was stocky, and his face was burned almost as dark as his brown eyes by the wind and cold, except where it was covered with grizzled grey stubble and a luxuriant if unkempt moustache. An incongruously feminine silk scarf, obviously looted from Moscow, was wound about his head, giving him a distinctly buccaneer-ish appearance, as did the two pistols stuck into his belt. And even as she stared at him he drew one of them and raised it, apparently pointing it at Tristan. There was no time for questions. She snatched up her own pistol, took aim and fired.

The recoil almost knocked her out of the driver's seat, but it was a perfect shot. The buccaneer's pistol went spinning out of his hand, and he stood open-mouthed with shock.

'What in the name of. . .?' Tristan broke off as he brought Montespan around on her haunches and looked at Angèle's smoking pistol. 'I told you to be careful with that trigger!'

'It wasn't an accident! I thought he was going to shoot you,' she retorted crossly, realising that the brief truce between them was over.

'Who?'

'Him!' She pointed to the tattered figure with the cerise silk scarf around his head.

'Him?' The tension on Tristan's face dissolved suddenly as the man came trudging towards them through the slush.

'It was my fault, Captain,' the buccaneer said a little breathlessly as he reached them. 'I was about to fire in the air to get your attention. . .when the young lady here shot at me.'

'Thank the gods she missed you, Sergeant Leclerc!' Tristan said, scowling at Angèle.

'I didn't miss! I was aiming for the pistol!'

For the briefest of moments she had the satisfaction of seeing astonishment on Tristan's face, and a flicker of admiration in his eyes, before they became unreadable again.

'*Sacrebleu!*' The sergeant made no attempt to hide his surprise. 'A woman who can shoot as straight as you, Captain!'

'Mademoiselle Kerenski has many unusual attributes,' Tristan said sardonically. 'As I am beginning to discover.'

'Any more as useful as that and I'd ask her to join the regiment,' the sergeant said, grinning at Angèle.

'Thank you.' She smiled back, liking the sergeant instantly. 'I'm sorry about your pistol.'

'Don't mention it.'

'Speaking of the regiment,' Tristan cut in, 'why aren't you with them?'

'I stopped to pick up the young 'un after the last skirmish,' Sergeant Leclerc replied laconically, gesturing to what Angèle had taken to be a bundle of rags lying on the ground near where the sergeant had been standing. 'Then my horse gave up.' He shrugged. 'So here we are, among the flatfoots.'

Before either man could say any more Angèle sent the sleigh closer to the pathetic figure. What she saw twisted in her heart like a knife. This was not a soldier—it was a child! Someone, the sergeant presumably, had wrapped him in a blue satin and fox-fur coat that had

obviously graced some Moscow lady's boudoir, and made
him a makeshift hood of grimy velvet. The ludicrous
clothes only served to emphasise his youth, and beneath
the hood she glimpsed straw-yellow hair that reminded
her unbearably of Yashi. . . She had to do something,
no matter how futile the effort.

'Sous-Lieutenant Bourdon,' Sergeant Leclerc said in
response to Tristan's glance at the still figure as they
followed.

'Is he badly wounded?' Tristan asked curtly,
frowning.

'Got knocked out when his horse went down. Nothing
that warmth, food and rest wouldn't take care of. . .
but. . .' Sergeant Leclerc shrugged with the detachment
of an old soldier '. . . I don't think he'll last long here.'

'Put him in the sleigh! We can take him!' Angèle cut
into their conversation.

A girl giving the captain orders. The sergeant's bushy
grey brows lifted in astonishment.

'It is a long story, Sergeant,' Tristan grated as he saw
the question in the older man's eyes. 'I'll tell it to you
over a bottle of wine in Paris.' Then he turned to Angèle.
'You cannot take him,' he said harshly, his voice rough
with regret. 'It makes sense for the sergeant to come
with us, since he is still fit enough to fight. But the sous-
lieutenant will be nothing but a dead weight.'

'But he is one of your own men! And you are asking
me to leave him here to die!' She stared at him in
disbelief. 'How can you be so callous?'

'You explain to her, Sergeant,' Tristan snapped, averting his gaze from her face before the contempt in her
eyes destroyed his judgement completely. 'Perhaps she'll
listen to you. I am running out of patience.'

'The captain is right, *mademoiselle*,' Sergeant Leclerc
said after one startled glance at his superior's face,
knowing it wasn't the decision the captain would have
made if it had been only his own skin at stake. 'We are

between three armies. Speed may make the difference between life and death. The thaw has made the snow soft—the runners are sinking in already. The more weight in the sleigh, the more difficult it will be for your ponies and the quicker they will tire. Sous-Lieutenant Bourdon will have to take his chances like the rest of the wounded; he would make the same decision if he were in the captain's shoes.'

'I don't care. Put him in the sleigh now!' Angèle spat the words out, hating men, hating war and hating Tristan in particular. 'Have you no pity? How old is he? Eighteen?'

She looked from Tristan's shuttered face to the sergeant. Neither man would meet her eyes.

'Very well. If you won't, I will.' She began to scramble down.

'You stubborn little fool, don't you realise you could be signing your own death warrant?' Tristan growled at her.

'I would rather die than have to live with a conscience like yours!' she hissed, glaring up at him, certain that right was on her side.

'All right, have it your way.' He gave in wearily, and nodded to the sergeant, his temper not improved by the barely concealed amusement in Leclerc's eyes. 'Put him in the sleigh, Leclerc.'

'Yes, sir!' The sergeant bent and lifted the boy into the sleigh.

'You had best take Montespan. I will walk for a while,' Tristan added when the sergeant re-emerged. 'That way this foolishness may not cost us the ponies.'

'It is I who will walk. I would not have *my* foolishness inconvenience you, Captain,' Angèle retorted acidly. 'Since the sergeant is in need of rest, he can take a turn at driving the sleigh.'

'*Non*. . . I could not let you do that, *mademoiselle*,'

Sergeant Leclerc protested instinctively, glancing up at his captain.

'I should not waste your breath, Leclerc,' Tristan said, deciding that it would give him an opportunity to discreetly enlist the sergeant's help in getting Angèle to safety. 'If she wants to be a damn fool, let her!'

The sergeant wisely made no further objections. But his curiosity increased a hundredfold. Whoever would have thought it? Ice-cool Captain Beaumaris at sixes and sevens over a girl who was all eyes and mouth!

Tristan grimaced as he read his sergeant's expression. He did not need reminding that he was in severe danger of making a fool of himself over Angèle Kerenski. And then, as he looked back over his shoulder at the slim, stubborn figure wading determinedly through the knee-deep slush, it occurred to him that, had circumstances been different, it would almost be worth it.

Damn. . .fool. . . Damn. . .fool. . . The words echoed in Angèle's skull like a hammer, in painful rhythm with the rise and fall of her feet. She had never dreamt that walking could be so difficult. Within minutes the icy slush had gone over the top of her boots and numbed her feet so that she could not feel them. To make matters worse, the ice and snow clogged on the soles, so that at every step it felt as if she were lifting a block of lead. They had travelled just over a mile and it felt like a hundred. She had stumbled clumsily and fallen more times than she could count, but each time pride had brought her to her feet and she had ploughed doggedly on in the wake of the sleigh.

'No!' she groaned in protest as she fell headlong in the freezing morass of snow and ice for the third time in as many minutes. She lifted her head; the distance between herself and the sleigh was increasing all the time—she must get up. Slowly she dragged herself up; there was no pain in her muscles any more, just a numbness.

One. . .two. . .three. . .four. . . She made herself take the faltering steps, and then she fell again. This time she just lay there. She was going to die and she didn't care.

'Come on, up you get.'

Strong, all too familiar arms were pulling her to her feet and lifting her into a saddle.

'I don't need. . .' She began to make a feeble protest.

'Forget your damned pride and stop pretending. I've been half a dozen paces behind you for the last half-mile.'

'Oh. I didn't see you.'

'I know,' Tristan said coldly. 'I took care to stay out of sight until I was sure you wouldn't have sufficient strength left to argue.'

'You'd have been safe enough half an hour ago,' she admitted ruefully as he began to lead Montespan towards the sleigh.

'But you might not have been,' he replied caustically. 'You seemed to have studied the art of making me lose my temper with you as assiduously as most young ladies study the latest fashion plates!'

'Study wasn't necessary!' she snapped. 'You find fault with everything I do or say! You have done nothing but carp at me for the last two days! I wish you would go away and leave me alone! I do not want the company of someone who would rather leave a boy to die in the snow than have to share his supplies!'

'*Sacre nom de Dieu*!' he roared furiously. 'If it weren't for your sex I'd make you answer for that!'

'For what? Speaking the truth?'

'You would not recognise the truth if it was written in the snow!' he scathed as he brought Montespan to a halt beside the sleigh.

'Hah!' she fired back at him, using the only weapon she had. 'At least I know the difference between a King and a self-seeking impostor who would rather watch his men die than sacrifice his pride and surrender!'

'If I hear you say anything like that again within earshot of these men I'll have you shot as a traitor! Don't doubt it!'

'I don't!' she flared. 'After all, you serve a murderer! For that is what the Duc d'Enghien's death was—murder!'

'*Mon Dieu*! You go too far!' He reached up and dragged her down from Montespan's back and dumped her unceremoniously on her feet. 'I am sick to death of your royalist cant! You know nothing of France or what Napoleon has done for her people! You vilify an honourable man who has done great good for his country for one mistake, made at a time when his own life was under constant threat from the intrigues of the Bourbon princes. If Napoleon is a murderer then so is every last one of your precious Kings! What of those people they consigned to a long, slow death in the Bastille without as much as the semblance of a trail? And I am not so convinced that d'Enghien was quite the innocent he is painted. He fought with the armies of our enemies for nine years. And why do you think the English paid him four thousand guineas a year? Out of the kindness of their hearts?'

'I did not know he was in the pay of the English,' she said stiltedly. 'But——'

'You know nothing of anything except how to be a damned nuisance!' he rapped, his eyes blazing pure silver fire. 'And now, if you have a shred of sense in your skull, get in the sleigh before I forget I am a gentleman and administer the punishment your nurse should have given years ago.'

'You wouldn't dare,' she said, paling, but standing her ground.

'Wouldn't I?' he roared.

'*Mademoiselle*. . .' suddenly Sergeant Leclerc was beside her, propelling her into the sleigh '. . .best to do as he says; don't worry about the ponies, I'll lead them

for a bit,' he said, giving her a sympathetic smile. 'There
are always times when it is best to retreat,' he whispered
with a grin as he closed the flap.

Some two hours later they reached the Chasseurs'
encampment near the banks of the river.

'It's all right, *mademoiselle*,' Sergeant Leclerc told her
with a conspiratorial smile when Angèle finally got up
the courage to step out of the sleigh and face Tristan.
'He's gone to report to the general.'

'Did he say how long he would be?'

'An hour or two at least.'

'Good,' she said with feeling.

Sergeant Leclerc laughed as he added a handful of
wood fragments to the fire he had kindled. 'Don't be too
hard on him; he is a southerner—from Provence—they
cannot help their tempers. They eat too many peppers,'
he added with true Parisien disdain.

A southerner. She should have known it from the
blackness of his hair, the deep bronze of his skin and the
fire that lurked just beneath the surface of those ice-grey
eyes. . .but she did not know him. She had thought she
knew the important things about him, that he was
humane, generous and brave. But his attitude to Sous-
Lieutenant Bourdon had shaken her belief in her own
judgement. . .and yet in some ways she was glad to find
he was flawed. It made it easier to convince herself that
she was looking forward to the moment when she would
never have to see him again.

A dull booming wave of sound rather like thunder,
that made her ears sing and the ground beneath her feet
tremble, broke into her thoughts.

'What was that?' she asked shakily.

'What? Oh, you mean the guns,' the sergeant said
calmly, setting a billycan of snow on the fire.

'Russian guns?' She could not keep the quaver out of
her voice.

'Yes. Don't worry, they're miles away at Borisov; we're not in range here. They'll be firing to stop us trying to repair the bridge, and the longer they stay there the better.'

'Oh,' she said, swallowing hard. If that was what guns were like at a distance, the thought of being any closer to them made her stomach knot in terror.

The sergeant glanced at her pale face assessingly. Long experience with raw recruits had taught him that activity was by far the best cure for fear. 'The captain told me you have some skill with wounds; I wonder if you would consider tending some of the men—they would be grateful for your attentions. . .'

As he had hoped, she accepted his suggestion with alacrity and immediately fetched her medicines bag and began to lay out the things she would need.

A good 'un, thought the sergeant as he went off to spread the word to the wounded. He was beginning to understand why the captain was desperate to get her out of danger. He grinned to himself. Whoever would have thought it: Captain Beaumaris falling for a Bourbon lily? He could hardly wait to see his comrades' faces when they heard the news.

'Coffee, *mademoiselle?*' the sergeant asked when Angèle's last patient had thanked her profusely and limped away.

'Thank you.' She accepted the metal beaker gratefully and leant against the side of the sleigh. The coffee was pale brown, weak and flavourless, but it was hot, and did something to revive her spirits.

'You are tired,' the sergeant observed. 'Why didn't you tell me? I'd have sent some of them away.'

'I should have been angry if you had. I only wish I could have done more,' she answered wistfully. 'When I think of the still room at the dacha with its jars and bottles of ointments and lotions and the herbs hanging

from the racks. . . I would give every penny I own to
have those things here now.'

'You've done a good job with what little you had,' the
sergeant told her. 'And I've never seen a prettier piece
of bone-setting than you did for Corporal Martin.'

'It's such a waste.' She sighed, only half listening. All
too often she'd had to force a reassuring smile on to her
face as she'd uncovered blue-white flesh or smelt the
sickly sweet odour of gangrene. The perfume of
death. . .and as she looked about her it was not difficult
to imagine that it hung in the air, along with the smells
of woodsmoke, cooking, cordite and horses. Her
depression increased as she looked from the knots of
thin, hungry men huddled about meagre fires to a
pathetic row of horses, all of them dull-coated, ribs
showing and heads down disconsolately. With the excep-
tion of Montespan and her ponies, she had not set eyes
on a single horse that looked as if it would last another
week since they had joined the army. And how would
the army survive without cavalry to defend it from the
Cossacks or horses to pull what were left of its supply
wagons and guns? For the first time the full implications
of the catastrophe that had befallen Bonaparte's army
became clear in her mind. It was quite possible that
every one of these thousands of men was going to die. . .
die of cold, hunger, disease or at the hands of the
Cossacks, and so would she. . .

'Tired of war already?'

The dry, sardonic voice brought her eyes jerking back
to the fire. But instead of the sergeant there was only
Tristan, standing staring at her.

For a second the doubts that the incident with
Bourdon had raised were forgotten. Her heart leapt in a
fierce gladness at the sight of him. Dark, strong, indomitable. An anchor in this awful chaos. Just his presence
was enough to make her feel safer. Safer from everything
except him. . .

'Lost your tongue? You're usually quick enough to speak,' he drawled, holding her eyes with his.

'You startled me,' Angèle said stiffly, knowing that she had allowed herself to return his stare for just a moment too long.

'My apologies.' He made an ironic bow. 'I came to see how Bourdon is.'

'Do you care?' Her emotions were ragged from the last few hours and she could not disguise her bitterness.

'Of course I do!' he snarled. 'But I gave my word to try and ensure your safety, and that means trying to ensure that you don't exhaust your ponies and supplies before you reach. . .safety. If I did not have a duty to protect you, do you think I would have made the same decision?'

Duty. Another cold word to go with obligation and honour. Didn't he care for her at all?

'I'm sorry,' she apologised stiffly, her voice flat with disappointment. 'I should not have doubted your motives. . .'

'No, you shouldn't have,' he agreed tersely. 'I had hoped you knew me better than that. But while we're on the subject of Sous-Lieutenant Bourdon I should appreciate it if you would refrain from contradicting my orders in front of the non-commissioned officers and enlisted men. It is difficult enough to keep any sort of discipline in such a situation without you behaving like a prima donna!'

'Prima donna!' Her brief sense of contrition vanished in a flood of anger. 'At least I am not a bigoted, arrogant oaf who threatens to shoot people for convictions different from his own!'

'Such a short acquaintance and you know my character so well!' he jeered sarcastically.

'I know all I wish to of you, Captain Beaumaris,' Angèle retorted, her head held high. 'And,' she added with a carefully disdainful glance at him, 'it is more than enough!'

Tristan would have laughed if he had not been so angry. There she was with a smudge on her cheek, clad in a tattered coat that a beggar from the sewers of Paris would have turned his nose up at, and she had the gall to look down her straight little aristocratic nose! By heaven, he would teach her to play the *grande dame* with him!

'You are sure of that?' he asked with a mildness that every man beneath his command had long since learned to fear more than most officers' rantings. 'That was not the impression you gave a day or two ago.'

'I was distraught then!' she snapped contemptuously. 'You know I did not mean what I said!'

His eyes drifted with insolent slowness from her face to the too rapid rise and fall of her breasts, and then he smiled derisively.

'Your friend was right. You are a terrible liar.'

'It is you who deludes yourself!' she spat back at him. 'Do you really think I want to know more of one of the Corsican's lackeys?'

'Shall we find out?'

She saw her danger too late. Before she could move he placed his hands against the sleigh on either side of her, trapping her between his body and the stiff leather canopy.

She froze; there was scarcely room to pass a knife blade between their bodies. Every inch of her flesh had become taut, expectant, fearful. Her own heart-beat threatened to deafen her, and she could not draw breath.

'What do you want of me?' She tried to sound cool, unconcerned, but the naked desire in his eyes made her voice quaver. Her body was betraying her by the second. His nearness, his eyes were draining her life-blood, leaving in its place a sweet, unfamiliar, unbearable ache. An ache that was transmuted by some alchemy she did

not understand into an all-consuming desire to be
touched, kissed, caressed by him. . .

'This.' His eyes flared like a diamond held to the light
as his head came down to hers.

'No!'

In a futile attempt to escape she jerked her head aside,
shutting her eyes, trying to blot out the impact he had
on her senses. Deprived of her mouth, his lips brushed
the soft white skin of her neck. The whole of her body
became tight, unbearably sensitive in a split-second. Her
breath dragged from her throat in a low moan as his
hands dropped to her shoulders and drew her tense,
trembling body against his.

He laughed triumphantly, his breath warm against her
skin as he trailed his lips along her throat and brushed
over her mouth before lifting his head.

'Look at me. . .' he said, his voice low and compelling.
His hands came up to the sides of her head, turning her
face back to his.

Look at him. She dared not. She could not.

'Look at me! he repeated.

Slowly, reluctantly, her dark lashes lifted from her
white cheeks. His eyes sliced into hers like a surgeon's
scalpel, peeling away all her defences. She had lost. She
could lie with her lips but not with her eyes.

'Now tell me you don't want me,' he drawled.

'I. . .' she began, but the lie stuck in her throat and
would not be spoken.

'Well?' His black brows lifted mockingly.

'All right! I can't!' His arrogance, combined with the
unbearable tension in her body, was too much for her
temper. She punched at the wall of his chest with her
hands in sheer frustration. 'I am not used to such games!
I've never felt like this before, and when you touch
me. . . I can think of nothing except I want to be kissed
by you, held by you! Now are you satisfied?'

For a second he was stiller than stone. Then he smiled. A slow, lazy smile.

'No.'

The word hung between them like a naked blade. Fear uncoiled itself in her stomach: what had she done. . . what had she unleashed? But then there was no time for coherent thought. His head bent and his mouth took possession of hers, storming her senses, destroying the last vestige of her pride.

Her hands slid up around his neck and she clung to him, filled with a sweet, wild relief as his arms wrapped around her, crushing her against his scratchy green wool cloak. She was safe. Safe. While his arms were around her nothing mattered, nothing could harm her. The cold, the danger, Blanche, André ceased to exist. There was only his warmth, his strength. Safe. . . The illusion shattered as his kiss deepened and his hands, which had somehow freed themselves from their gloves, slipped between the fastenings of her coat, finding the curve of her hips, her waist. . .exploring, learning the lines of her body. And she had no desire to stop him. The growing, unfamiliar heavy ache inside her told her only that she wanted to be closer to Tristan, to touch him as he was touching her. She ran her hands over his chest, resentful of the layers of fur and cloth that separated their flesh. All too clearly she could remember the beauty of his naked body, the leanness, the strength. . .

She juddered and gasped aloud as his hands grazed over the tips of her breasts beneath their covering of wool and silk, turning her body to flame.

'Angèle. . .' He murmured her name as he felt her mouth melt beneath his in complete surrender.

She opened wondering eyes to his burning charcoal gaze. She no longer cared if today was all they had. She was his, she belonged to him; she had never been more certain of anything in her life.

Tristan lifted his head and stilled, breathing raggedly

and cursing himself for not having realised the truth before. She was falling in love with him; it was written in the blue-green depths of her eyes.

He swore and released her so abruptly that she almost fell.

'We have to stop this now.' His voice was jerky, angry.

'Why?' she breathed as she slumped back against the cold damp leather of the sleigh. She didn't want to return to reality; while he was holding her she could blot out the horrors that surrounded them. 'Don't you want me?'

He went ashen as if she had run him through with his own sabre. Then he exploded. 'Dammit, Angèle! Have you no care for your reputation? No sense of propriety?'

'Propriety? Reputation?' she repeated blankly as she stared at his tall, stern, disapproving figure, and then something inside her snapped. A bubble of irresistible laughter escaped her lips. She had see-sawed between elation and despair so often in the last few days that she could no longer control her emotions. She had to laugh, because if she did not laugh she would break into a thousand pieces.

'Angèle, this is not amusing.' Tristan was grim; grim as the reaper himself.

'It is,' she hiccuped. 'You standing here, in the midst of this,' she gestured to the chaos around them, 'lecturing me on propriety!' Laughter overtook her, until she was shaking helplessly.

'Angèle!' He caught her shoulders and shook her so sharply that she bit her tongue.

The pain and the salt taste of blood in her mouth acted like a bucket of cold water on her euphoria.

'I'm sorry,' he said as she stilled beneath his hands. 'But you were losing control.'

'Yes,' she said after taking several gulping breaths of the cold air. 'And you are losing your sense of humour.'

'I see little to laugh at. My behaviour was inexcusable, I treated you as if you were a. . .coquette.'

'The blame is not all yours—I behaved little better,' she said, remembering how she had clung to him, touched him.

'True,' he said with the faintest curve of his mouth. 'Shouldn't you have slapped my face or something?'

'I have never been very good at doing the correct thing,' she said ruefully as their eyes met and held.

'Nor I,' he answered tightly, dragging his hands away from her, putting a distance between them. 'But I am going to break the habit of a lifetime. I'm not going to kiss you again, much as I want to. It wouldn't be right.'

'No. . .' she said dully, tearing her eyes away from his, before she made a complete fool of herself. 'I had forgotten Blanche. . .'

'Blanche?' He was startled. Blanche had been the last thing on his mind. He had been thinking only that in a few hours he had to send her away, that he would never see her again.

'Is she. . .is she very beautiful?' Angèle hated herself for asking but could not prevent the words leaving her lips.

'Blanche?' Tristan dragged his attention back to what she was saying. 'She is petite, helpless-looking, with a cloud of soft brown hair, light blue eyes that tilt up at the corners and a distinctly feline mouth. I suppose "kittenish" would be the best description.'

'Do you love her?'

His face stiffened into a mask and then he gave a half-laugh. 'I thought I was used to your directness, but you can still surprise me. . .'

'I'm sorry,' she apologised, deeply ashamed. 'I have no right to pry. . .'

'No. . .' he said slowly. He was going to hurt her anyway. Perhaps this was the quickest, the kindest way to kill her feelings for him, to let her leave without regrets. . . 'But the answer is yes, I fell in love with Blanche a long time ago.'

'Then why did you kiss me. . .how could you make me feel like that?' Her voice was small, disbelieving, like that of a child who was about to be punished for a misdemeanour it had not committed.

'If you were more experienced you would know that there is a difference between lust and. . .love.'

'I see.' She went whiter for a moment than she had been when he had picked her up off the snow after the wolf attack. 'You're saying that what there is between us is. . .lust.' She stumbled over the word. 'Nothing more?'

'Yes,' he grated and then jerked his gaze away from her face, unable to bear the pain in her eyes. He was as ashamed as if he had hit her. By God, he hoped it was worth it, that it would be enough to make her agree. He cleared his throat. He couldn't put it off any longer. Briefly, without looking at her, he explained that men had been raiding Cossack camps regularly to get fodder for their horses, and that he had arranged for her to be escorted to a camp that night. 'It should not be too dangerous for you,' he finished awkwardly, unnerved by her silence and absolute stillness. 'Just say that I took you hostage and forced you to drive me to the army. Judging by that Platov fellow's reaction, your step-father's name should be enough to protect you. . .'

'I told you I am not going back,' she said with deadly quietness. She felt numb. How could he hold her, kiss her, and then send her back to André?

'You have to!' he said desperately. 'Surely the last few hours have shown you why! At least at the dacha you would have food, warmth, safety——'

'And my cousin André,' she cut in bitterly. 'Don't leave him off your list of advantages. I wonder what sort of welcome he will give me when he returns. A cousinly kiss, do you think?'

'What the hell are you trying to do to me?' Tristan rapped back at her, folding his arms across his chest to prevent himself from reaching out and shaking her.

'Don't you think I feel badly enough about this already? You have to go back; I gave my word to your friend. . . How do you think I'm going to feel if you're killed while under my protection?'

'Relieved, probably!' Angèle retorted. 'You'd be rid of a royalist nuisance, would you not?'

'In the name of Liberty!' he snarled, white to the lips. 'If you were a man I'd call you out!'

'How unfortunate for you I am not! Think of the time it would save if you were to kill me now!'

'Don't tempt me!' he thundered, and then as two soldiers passing stopped to look at them curiously he dropped his voice to an icy murmur. 'Go back, for my sake if not yours.'

'For your sake!' She gave a brittle laugh. 'Now we come to the truth of the matter! I might be inexperienced but I am not a complete fool. Do you think I don't know why you are so eager to send me away? It is because you want me and you hate yourself for it! You love Blanche, but it does not stop you wanting me, one of the Bourbonist aristocrats you detest!'

'Blanche and politics have nothing to do with it!' His voice rose again. 'It's self-preservation! How long do you think I'm going to last in battle if I'm constantly looking over my shoulder to see that you're safe?'

'I am such a burden to you.' The fight went out of her eyes and face, leaving her deathly pale again. It had never occurred to her that her presence might endanger his chances of survival.

'Oh, hell! I did not mean it like that!' He groaned. 'It's just that I cannot fight and protect you at the same time. . .and if something happened to me. . .you'd be on your own in this hell-hole. . .' He paused and rubbed a hand over his stubbled face. 'Please, Angèle, let me take you back to the Russian lines. I'm not ordering you, I'm begging you. . .'

'You! Begging!' She laughed harshly, hating him for

having found where she was most vulnerable. 'I would do anything for you. . .but not that. . .' she blurted, not even noticing his intake of breath at her unconscious admission. 'Don't you see? The way André looks at me makes me sick to the stomach, and when he touches me. . .' Her voice tailed off as she beseeched him with her eyes to understand. 'Don't make me go——'

'I have to,' he rasped brutally. This was pure torture. He could not look at her for fear his resolve would fail. 'There's no alternative, at least you'd be alive——'

'Alive!' Her voice splintered as tears began to stream down her face. 'I'd rather be dead. . .' Ducking past him, she ran blindly, slipping and sliding on the treacherous ground, her bright hair tumbling loose down her back.

'Angèle!' He ground out her name as he made a lunge to stop her. But she was too quick for him. With an oath Tristan sped in pursuit, only to collide with a burly trooper. By the time he had treated the trooper to a choice selection of oaths and regained his feet, she had vanished among the sea of men, wagons and horses.

CHAPTER SEVEN

THE slight thaw had turned the Berezina from a modest river into a raging torrent. Angèle stood on the edge of the bank, mesmerised by the freezing black water and the massive ice floes sent crashing and tumbling along by the current.

Black water. Black as the despair in her heart. Black as André's savage and cruel eyes. She shuddered, remembering his sneering face as he had told her in vulgar language exactly what he was going to do to her when he returned from hunting the French.

'No!' She made her decision aloud. She could not go back, but how could she go on without the sleigh or supplies? And if she went back Tristan might do as he had threatened—force her to return. The guns boomed again from Borisov, reminding her that she did not have the courage to face a battle alone among all these strangers.

Her stomach lurched as snow cascaded suddenly from under her feet and a segment of the bank to her left broke and fell into the foaming water. The ground beneath her trembled; she should move, she thought dully, but perhaps this was the easiest solution. The water was freezing; it would not take long, a minute at the most, then no more André, no more dead and dying men and no more Tristan Beaumaris. . .

'*Mademoiselle!*' A hand caught her arm, dragging her back as the ice beneath her feet broke away and splashed into the water, sending icy spray on to her cheeks.

'That is not a good place to stand,' her rescuer said, releasing her arm after an assessing look at her reddened eyes and ashen face.

'Isn't it?' She looked at him blankly, not sure if she
resented or was grateful for his intervention. 'At least it
would have been quick.' She paled as another thunder-
ous roar of guns shook the winter air. 'The Cossacks
might not be so kind.'

'Do not despair, *mademoiselle*.' The man tapped her
frozen cheek with his gloved fingers. 'You are not in the
hands of the Cossacks yet! Chitchagov is well and truly
duped! We are not beaten yet. You have my word on it.'

His word. She had an irrational desire to laugh. What
difference was this little man, who was not as tall as she
was, going to make? The assurance and arrogance with
which he spoke made Tristan seem positively modest by
comparison. Who was he? A quartermaster or a clerk,
she guessed, taking in the intelligent, almost scholarly
face with its deep brow and rather large, compelling pale
eyes. Yes, a clerk, she decided, noticing for the first time
the exactness of the fit of his plain grey greatcoat and
boots. Yet he spoke like a warrior, as if he were going to
outwit three Russian armies single-handed.

'I wish I could share your optimism,' she answered
politely. In a way he had saved her life, and there was
something about his confidence that rekindled her own
spirit. 'You sound so certain. . .'

'Ah!' He laughed. 'I have the advantage over you in
that, *mademoiselle*. You see, I have infinite faith in
Napoleon Bonaparte.'

'Not you as well,' she muttered half to herself. 'That
is something I will never understand. . .'

'Understand what, *mademoiselle*?'

'Why you all admire him so,' she sighed. 'I tended the
wounds of more than a dozen men this morning, half of
them dying, and not one had a word of criticism for the
man who has brought them to this. . .' She gestured to
the chaos around them.

The stranger's brows rose a fraction. 'And what is
your opinion of Napoleon Bonaparte?'

'I don't know any more,' she confessed. 'He is a usurping tyrant, and yet he can inspire such loyalty, such blind faith in intelligent and brave men. . .'

His pale eyes were distinctly distant for a moment and she knew that, like Tristan, he resented the slightest criticism of the Emperor. Then to her astonishment his face relaxed suddenly and he laughed out loud.

'Are you always so truthful, *mademoiselle*?'

'Tactless, you mean.' She smiled at him wrily. 'I fear so.'

'It's not such a bad trait. I wish more of my associates would emulate it. To make good decisions you must be aware of the truth, not simply what people think you wish to hear. . .otherwise you find yourself in this sort of mess.' He frowned as he looked at the river and the nearly completed bridges, fragile as grubby strips of lace against the dark water.

Momentarily his assurance had vanished. He looked haunted, lonely. But a moment later he turned to her again, his wide and rather appealing smile back in place even if it did not quite reach his eyes. 'But one thing I must correct you on: Napoleon is not a usurper. The Bourbons had left the crown in the gutter; he simply picked it up with his sword.'

'That's what Tristan says——' she began to argue, but he interrupted.

'Tristan?'

'Captain Beaumaris of the Chasseurs. Do you know him?'

'Very well.' His smile broadened, lending an attractiveness to his rather sombre features. 'Don't tell me you are the Captain's Angel I have heard so much about. Mademoiselle. . .Kerenski?'

'Yes, how did you know?' She was astonished that he knew her name, and embarrassed by the sobriquet she seemed to have acquired.

'The Chasseurs are like a family. News travels faster

than a cannon ball from the mouth of a barrel. I was told earlier of your kindness to the wounded. . .and your beauty. I understand Captain Beaumaris is particularly in your debt.'

'He has already repaid any kindness I have done him,' she answered hastily, taken aback by his compliment. 'Are you a Chasseur?' she asked, wanting to change the subject; talking about Tristan was too painful.

'Among other things.' There was a flash of amusement in his heavy-lidded eyes. 'Enough of one to be surprised that any Chasseur would let a lady wander about here alone, particularly one of Beaumaris's stamp.'

'The captain doesn't know where I am.' She found herself defending him. 'We had a. . .disagreement.'

'I see,' he said gravely, offering her his arm. 'Since you are without an escort, will you not join me at my fire for some refreshment? I am sure a little cognac would do much for your spirits. . .'

'Thank you.' Utterly weary, she accepted the offer. She had nowhere else to go.

'Sit down,' he invited a few minutes later, pointing to a couple of empty ammunition boxes near a large fire. 'You will excuse me for a moment. . .'

'Of course.' She watched him curiously as he walked towards a knot of officers, standing around a smaller fire a few yards away. They all sprang to attention as he approached and treated him with some deference; he must be more senior than he looked, she thought. A minute or two later one of the officers broke away from the group and mounted a thin bay horse tethered near by. A Chasseur. If she got out of this alive, how long would it be before the glimpse of a green uniform and a dark head ceased to freeze her heart with pain? Too long, she decided bleakly as her rescuer returned and offered her a beaker of brandy.

* * *

'Damnation! Is there no one else who can do it?' Tristan swore as the young trooper hailed him and passed on his instructions.

'The order is specific, sir. It must be you.'

'Very well! How far is it?'

'About five minutes that way, sir!'

Five minutes! Tristan swore again beneath his breath. Five priceless minutes in which anything might happen to her, if it had not already. But orders were orders and he could not disobey them. He set his heels into Montespan's sides, and rode on, searching the mass of humanity with his eyes all the time. She had to be here somewhere, if she wasn't at the bottom of the river by now. . .

'Cordier!' He roared at the Chasseur who saluted him as he came up to the Emperor's escort troop. 'There's a despatch for me to collect—where the hell is it?'

The grin that had begun on the trooper's face faded instantly as he met the captain's eyes. Leclerc had been right. Captain Beaumaris's legendary composure appeared to have deserted him.

'Over there, sir!'

Tristan was down from the saddle before he had finished. He strode towards the fire, halted, and saluted the man who turned away from the blaze as he approached. And then a flash of gold-bronze hair on the far side of the fire caught his eye. Hardly daring to hope that his eyes had told him the truth, he looked again. Angèle! Here! He could not begin to make sense of it. But it did not matter. She was safe. *She was safe*!

'You called the Emperor *what*?' Tristan said in disbelief as he lifted Angèle down from Montespan's saddle and threw the reins to the sergeant, who was trying hard not to smile.

'A usurping tyrant,' she admitted hesitantly. Apart from the occasional question he had barked at her, he had been morose and silent as he had led Montespan back to the sleigh.

'What were you trying to do? Get yourself shot instead of drowning yourself in the river?' he scathed.

'I didn't know he was Gen. . .the Emperor,' she corrected her further gaffe hastily as he glared at her. 'I thought he was just a soldier——'

'Just a soldier!' he sneered. 'He just happens to be the most famous soldier in Europe. Any child would have recognised him, but not Angèle Kerenski.'

'Why should I?' she snapped back. 'Do you think my mother hung his portrait on the salon wall?'

'No,' he retorted nastily. 'She obviously had about as much taste and sense as you! What the devil possessed you to run off like that anyway? Don't you realise men are murdering each other for a crust of bread and a warm coat?'

'You know perfectly well why!' she spat back at him.

'So you will not take the Emperor's advice either?'

'No. And if you try to force me I will make so much noise that every Cossack for a hundred miles will hear us coming and you'll be sending your men to their deaths!'

'You wouldn't,' he said flatly.

'Wouldn't I?'

After one look at her stubbornly defiant face he turned away. Wrapping his cloak about him, he slumped down beside the fire the sergeant had lit in the lee of the sleigh, his face in his hands.

The silence lasted while she and the sergeant prepared a simple meal. The sergeant made himself scarce the moment he had drained his wooden bowl of soup, and Angèle did not blame him. The atmosphere around the fire was like that just before a thunderstorm when everyone was on edge, waiting for the first bolt of lightning to strike.

'I will not be a nuisance to you for much longer. I'll take the sleigh and half the supplies for myself and the sous-lieutenant,' she said, unable to bear the tension any longer. 'You and the sergeant can have the rest.'

'Don't be a fool,' he growled dismissively. 'Bourdon has about as much idea of war as you. The pair of you wouldn't last five minutes on your own.'

'Then what do you want me to do?' she said, exasperated.

'Go back,' he said curtly and was silent again.

There was no point in answering. Defeated, she gave up and rummaged in her valise for her hairbrush. Taking it out, she gave all her concentration to the task of brushing out her tangled hair.

The routine task did nothing to alleviate the tension that she could feel winding tighter and tighter inside her. The crackle of the fire, the rhythmic crunching of the horses eating their hay, and the angry silken swish of the brush through her hair all seemed abnormally loud. Her skin prickled, and without looking she knew Tristan was watching her. The realisation distracted her and she moved the brush carelessly, flinching as it touched the graze on her temple.

His sharp intake of breath made her risk a sideways glance at him from beneath her thick lashes. It wasn't your fault. She almost spoke aloud as she saw the raw guilt in his eyes. But then the guilt was gone, replaced by something darker and more dangerous as his eyes followed the path of the brush through the soft gold waves of her hair. From the crown of her head, down over her breasts to her hips. Her mouth went dry as his eyes snapped upwards suddenly, searing across her face like molten steel. The brush tumbled from her suddenly clumsy fingers and skidded on its silver back across the snowy ground that separated them. She reached for it, only for her hand to be imprisoned in his iron grip. As she looked up questioningly the torment in his eyes sent a wave of guilt through her.

'Go back,' he said softly, 'or I'll end up insane. I've

seen you die a thousand times in the last hour, of the
cold, hunger, a Cossack lance or a bayonet in the dark,
and each time I can't reach you quickly enough. . .'

'I've told you! I cannot.' Her refusal was almost a sob
as she jerked her hand out of his grasp. 'I do not
understand! You don't care for me—why does it matter
so much to you if I live or die? We are nothing more
than travelling companions, and unwilling ones at
that. . .'

The corners of his mouth lifted in a bitter, mocking
smile. 'Travelling companions! Are you telling me there
is nothing more between us than that?'

'If there is it is no more than lust,' she retaliated, 'as
you so kindly pointed out!' Throwing her hair back over
her shoulders, she twisted it into a coil with sharp angry
movements.

'And you believe me?'

'You have given me no reason to doubt it,' she said,
bewildered by the mixture of bitterness and laughter in
his eyes.

'Haven't I?'

Before she could answer, or even begin to make sense
of what he was saying, there was a loud cough behind
them.

'Yes, Sergeant?' Tristan asked impatiently.

'Time's getting on, sir; shall I round up the lads for
the raid?'

'Shall he?' Tristan turned to look at her.

'You know the answer to that.'

'Yes.' He sighed. 'There will be no raid, Sergeant.
Mademoiselle Kerenski is not going back.'

'Ah. . . I see,' said the sergeant.

'What raid is this, Beaumaris?' another voice thundered from just behind Angèle's shoulder. 'Can't you
wait until tomorrow to get yourself skewered with a
Cossack lance again?'

Tristan was halfway on to his feet before the man had

finished speaking, and the sergeant was standing to attention.

Angèle looked over her shoulder in time to see a burly, ragged-looking man with an untidy red beard dismounting from a rather cow-hocked grey with rolling eyes.

'At ease, Tristan, sit yourself down again; we're not at the bloody Tuileries now.' He grinned, showing white teeth against his leathery skin. 'See to my horse, can you?' he added carelessly to Leclerc as he sat himself down without waiting for an invitation after giving Angèle the most cursory of nods. 'What's the soup? Horse?' he asked, peering dubiously into the iron pot on the fire.

'Ham,' Tristan answered. 'Want some?'

'Ham!' The shaggy ginger brows rose as he leant forward and took up a wooden bowl eagerly, scooping some of the steaming broth from the pot. 'I won't ask where you got it, you lucky bastard. You always did have the devil's own luck.'

Angèle tried not to be shocked. He was obviously a friend of Tristan's, and if she was going to stay with the army she was undoubtedly going to hear worse language, but nevertheless she felt her cheeks growing hot, and she dared not meet Tristan's eyes, which she could feel on her face.

'Michel. . .I think you should——' Tristan began uneasily, but his guest was not easily silenced.

'What's this fairy story I hear about your being rescued after that skirmish by some Russian bit of fluff who shot a pistol out of your sergeant's hand at twenty paces?'

'Thirty paces,' Angèle cut in icily. Being ignored and sworn in front of were things she could put up with in the circumstances. But to be referred to as a bit of fluff was too much to bear in silence. 'And I am not Russian; I am French.'

'In the name of France!' The stranger swivelled to stare at her, his bowl of soup poised halfway to his mouth. 'Damn me!' he said as his eyes travelled rudely from her Cossack cap to her grimy coat. 'You're a woman! And a damned pretty one under that lot. Who'd have thought it?'

What did he expect? A ball-gown? She glared back at him, treating his own ragged and battered clothing to an equally disparaging scrutiny.

'And what are you, sir?' she said with acid sweetness, ignoring Tristan's shaking head. 'A soldier or a tramp?'

For a moment he looked dumbstruck, and then, quaking with laughter, he turned to Tristan, who was having difficulty in keeping a straight face.

'D'you hear that? She asked *me* if I was a soldier!'

'That's nothing,' Tristan said, trying to look censorious and failing. 'She told the Emperor to his face that he was a usurping tyrant.'

Both men dissolved into helpless laughter, leaving Angèle utterly bewildered.

'I don't see what is so funny,' she said to Sergeant Leclerc, who had come back from tethering the grey horse.

'You have just asked Michel Ney, Marshal of France, if he is a soldier, *mademoiselle*,' the sergeant explained carefully, straight-faced.

Angèle groaned and put her face in her hands. No wonder Tristan found her an embarrassment. But when she raised her head she found he was looking at her with a mixture of affection and humour.

'I am sorry, I should have introduced you at once,' he said when he had caught his breath. 'Marshal Ney, this is Mademoiselle Angèle Kerenski.'

'Delighted, *mademoiselle*.' Marshal Ney smiled at her with no trace of ill-will. 'I have heard much about you. Only Beaumaris would be lucky enough to find himself such a guardian angel. Beautiful as well as brave—what more could a man want?'

'A piece of fluff perhaps,' she could not help retorting.

'Any woman who can shoot as straight as you has my unreserved apology for that remark.' The marshal grinned engagingly. 'Am I forgiven, *mademoiselle?*'

'It is forgotten, Monsieur le Maréchal,' she answered formally, still a little uncertain as to what to make of this man whom Tristan held in such esteem.

'Thank you.' He inclined his head and then turned his attention back to Tristan. 'How would you like a chance to hit back at our Russian friends on the other side of the river? The bridge is ready. We are to cross in an hour or so to back up Oudinot. And I need an *aide de camp* with a brain and a horse that still has four legs! I spoke to your general a little while ago; he has no objection.'

Tristan's face lit up. The prospect of being able to take some constructive action made him look ten years younger, thought Angèle, realising just how impotent he must have felt during the last few days, watching men die of cold and starvation and not being able to retaliate against the constant attacks made by the Cossacks on the stragglers.

'I should be honoured, Marshal,' he began eagerly, but then as his eyes touched on Angèle's face his expression became shuttered again, 'but are you asking or ordering me?'

'I'm asking you as a friend, Tristan; I need a man I can rely on.'

'Then I cannot,' Tristan said, set-lipped. 'I am sorry——'

'Can't? Why the devil not?' Marshal Ney scowled. 'Is your wound troubling you?'

'No.'

Angèle opened her mouth to argue but was silenced by a glare from Tristan.

'Your horse is fit, isn't she?' the marshal continued.

'Yes, better than most,' Tristan grated. 'But I have other obligations. . .on which my honour rests. I gave

my word that I would do my best to ensure Mademoiselle
Kerenski's safety; I cannot do that and act as your *aide
de camp*.'

'I could order you,' growled the marshal.

'You would be forcing me to break my word,' Tristan
said, looking as if he were being racked.

'Damn!' the marshal swore and drained the last of his
soup in one swallow before getting to his feet. 'Then I'd
better look for someone else.'

Angèle could hardly bear to look at Tristan's face. It
was obvious he longed to go with the marshal, and that
he had just been forced to put her in front of his pride
and friendship. Her presence and Irina's ridiculous
bargain were humiliating him. She had to find a way of
releasing him from his word or he would end up
despising her more than he did already, and she could
not bear that. The answer was so simple that she
wondered that she had not thought of it before.

'Monsieur le Maréchal, please wait!' she called out as
Ney put his foot into his stirrup and prepared to mount.
'Captain Beaumaris may feel differently when he hears
what I have to say.'

Ney looked at Tristan and shrugged, but he took his
foot out of the stirrup and leant against the grey, one
hand drumming impatiently on his saddle.

'Well?' Tristan snapped. 'What is it?'

'I've changed my mind,' she said simply, lying as she
had never lied in her life before. 'I do not have the
courage to face the guns if there is a battle tomorrow.'

'You will go back!' The joy and relief in his eyes and
voice sliced into her painfully. He might desire her, but
it did not make him any the less eager to be rid of her.

'Yes.' She hesitated as she came to the crucial part of
her performance. 'You might as well go with the marshal
now; I'm sure Sergeant Leclerc and the men he spoke of
will be able to get me back to the Russian lines safely.'

'No,' he protested instinctively, 'you are my responsibility.'

'Please.' She lowered her voice. 'I should rather say goodbye to you here, not in the midst of a raid, with strangers all about us. Sergeant Leclerc will look after me, will you not, Sergeant?'

'Of course, *mademoiselle*,' the sergeant answered after a momentary hesitation, his shrewd hazel eyes scanning Angèle's face. 'I'll saddle up for you, Captain,' he added, turning towards Montespan.

Tristan looked at Angèle. 'You are sure?'

'Yes. Quite,' she said abruptly, not daring to meet his eyes. 'You help the sergeant. I'll find you some food to take and oats for Montespan.' And then, before she betrayed herself, she almost ran to the sleigh.

'A minute, Marshal?' Tristan asked when everything was ready, inclining his head towards where Angèle stood, pale and uncertain beside the sleigh.

'Of course!' Ney grinned as he mounted his grey. 'But no more.'

'Thank you.' Tristan nodded and then looked at Angèle. Without a word she followed him away from the fire until they were screened from the marshal and Leclerc by the sleigh.

They halted as if by mutual consent and stood in an awkward silence like complete strangers. Angèle found herself mesmerised by the way the clouds of their breath merged in the cold air. She could not speak. A numbness was growing inside her, blotting out everything. A minute and she was never likely to see him again. A minute—no, less now. Her mind had turned into an inner clock, marking off each second.

'Angèle. . .' He said her name raggedly, his voice thick with longing, regret. . .

Her eyes came to his slowly, hardly daring to believe that the anger that had been such a barrier between them had gone as if it had never been. Involuntarily her hands reached out to him, a tentative, helpless gesture.

A breath later and his arms were around her, holding her against him so tightly that she could scarcely breathe, while he stared down into her upturned face, as if imprinting it on his memory. And then his head bent to hers in a hungry kiss that neither of them wanted to end. And when he withdrew from her at last, kiss by reluctant kiss, the sense of loss was so acute that she wanted to cry out. Her body was clamouring to belong to him totally, completely, but she would never know what it was to be loved by him. The pain of that knowledge was piercing, as if someone had pushed a blade into her heart and then cut it out.

'I wish. . .' she murmured brokenly as he lifted his head and she opened her eyes to his burning silver stare. 'I wish. . .we'd. . .'

'You think that now. . .but later you will see it is better that we didn't. It will be hard enough to forget as it is. . .' His voice was raw, as anguished as her eyes.

'*Forget?*' She made a sound that was somewhere between a sob and a laugh.

'You must.' He wrenched the words out. 'I told you before that you must learn to live for today. Life is too short to waste on dreams of what might have been or what might be.'

'It's all right for you!' Her despair spilled over, out of her control. 'You have Blanche to go back to, whereas I. . .!' She stopped, having so nearly given herself away.

'Whereas you are returning to a man you despise,' he said grimly. 'If there was any other way, Angèle, do you think I should send you away? All I want is for you to be safe. . .you know that, don't you?'

'And what of you? Will you be safe?' Her voice cracked into shards like broken glass.

'I can take care of myself,' he tried to reassure her. What point was there in telling her that Michel Ney did not know the meaning of fear or the word caution, and where the marshal went he was honour-bound to follow? He forced his mouth into a smile. 'Don't you know only the good die young? Have you forgotten I'm a Bonapartist? According to your royalist friends, that alone should qualify me for a wicked old age and a short descent into hell!'

From somewhere, for his sake, she tried to dredge up a smile, but her mouth trembled dangerously.

'It's not knowing that will be the worst,' she said huskily, beyond caring about her pride. 'How can I live the rest of my life not knowing if you are alive or dead?'

'You'll know.' He sighed, stroking her silky hair as she buried her face on his shoulder. 'It is like that between us. . .'

'And Blanche?' she asked, lifting her face to meet his gaze again. 'Is it like this between you and Blanche?'

'No.' He exhaled on the word. It would be kinder to lie in the long run, but his resolution had been destroyed by her brimming turquoise eyes. 'It was never like this with Blanche. I lied to you. Blanche has not meant anything to me for years.'

'Why?' she breathed, her heart jolting with a ridiculous, bitter-sweet joy. *He didn't love Blanche.* 'Why did you lie?'

'Because I thought it would make it easier for you to go back if you thought I did not. . .feel anything apart from desire for you. . .'

'Do you?' Her eyes flew to his, glittering with unshed tears and hope.

'Hasn't it been obvious?' His brows tilted up, half mocking her, as he lifted a hand and brushed an errant strand of gold-red hair away from her mouth. Then he shook his head as he read her expression. 'No, I suppose not; I forget what an innocent you are——'

'Beaumaris! What the hell are you doing? How long does it take to say goodbye? Come on, man!' Marshal

Ney bellowed from behind the sleigh before she had a chance to take in what he was saying.

'I have to go. . .'

'I know,' she whispered. Part of her was singing with joy, and part dying. He cared for her, and she might never see him again. She could not let him go without telling him how she felt.

'Tristan, I——'

'Don't!' he said almost savagely, putting a finger to her lips. 'Don't say it! We have no future. . . It will only make it more difficult.'

'Beaumaris!' Ney's shout was closer this time.

Tristan stepped back, and looked at her for a long moment. 'Goodbye, Angèle Kerenski,' he said almost tersely as he turned abruptly on his heel and walked towards the impatiently gesturing marshal, who was riding towards them, leading Montespan by the reins.

'*Au revoir*, Captain Beaumaris,' she called after him as he swung lithely into the saddle.

He lifted a hand in acknowledgement but didn't look back.

'God keep you safe,' she added beneath her breath as the two mounted figures disappeared among the tangle of men, wagons and stacked pyramids of muskets. It was only when he was out of sight that she allowed the first hot tears to spill down her cheeks.

CHAPTER EIGHT

'THAT was a fine performance, *mademoiselle*,' Sergeant Leclerc said when Angèle returned to the fire.

'You know I lied?' she said in surprise.

The sergeant nodded his head. 'I was not as eager as the captain to believe that you would go back. He has been worried to death about you since he saw the condition of the army. He cares about you a great deal, *mademoiselle*.'

'You really think so?'

The sergeant smiled at her eagerness and nodded. 'Before he left with the marshal he told me he'd have me shot if I didn't make sure you are safe with your stepfather's people before the battle begins.'

'I'm sorry, it hadn't occurred to me that I might get you into trouble,' she apologised, fighting down a wave of panic. 'If you'd prefer me to go on alone——'

'*Non, mademoiselle*.' The sergeant laughed and shook his head. 'So far as I can see, there is little difference between a Russian bullet and a French one. And besides which I do not think the captain will be so displeased to find I have disobeyed orders if we all survive. And,' he added after a look at her tear-stained face, 'don't you worry too much about him. I've known the captain get himself out of a dozen impossible situations where other men would have died. Some of the men swear he must have a pact with the devil to be so lucky. But it's not luck, *mademoiselle*. It's cool judgement, quick thinking and sharp reactions. That is why the marshal went to such trouble to get him as an *aide de camp*. If anyone survives this débâcle it will be Captain Beaumaris, I promise you.'

137

'He's right,' put in a young and rather shaky voice. Angèle and the sergeant looked up at the same moment to see the wan-faced Sous-Lieutenant Bourdon standing behind them.

'Sous-Lieutenant Bourdon!' Angèle smiled at him, her heart a thousand times lighter because of what the sergeant had said about Tristan. 'You have recovered far quicker than I had hoped, but please sit down; you should not be on your feet yet.'

Sous-Lieutenant Bourdon's cornflower-blue eyes looked puzzled. 'You have the advantage of me, *mademoiselle*; I do not know you, or how I came to be in that sleigh.'

'This is Mademoiselle Kerenski, a friend of Captain Beaumaris's, sir,' Sergeant Leclerc said. 'If she hadn't given you a lift in her sleigh you probably wouldn't be alive now.'

'She saved my life!'

Astonishment, closely followed by dumb adoration, passed across the sous-lieutenant's face as he stared at Angèle. 'I cannot think of anyone to whom I would rather be indebted. To be rescued by a girl like you. . . my friend Parceaux will be green with envy,' he added so ingenuously that Angèle almost laughed. Then his face lit up with delight. 'The captain is alive, then?'

'Very much so,' said Leclerc drily. 'So I should stop looking at Mademoiselle Kerenski like that unless you want to end up on the wrong end of Beaumaris's sabre.'

'It would be a small price to pay,' the sous-lieutenant said, making a flourishing bow, the effect of which was rather ruined by his voluminous satin coat. Then he drew himelf up in what was so obvious an attempt to imitate Tristan's natural authority that Angèle had to turn a laugh into a cough. 'I owe you my life, *mademoiselle*. From now on my sabre is at your command.'

'Thank you, but the sergeant is too modest,' she said gravely, ignoring Sergeant Leclerc's shaking head and facial contortions. 'It was the sergeant who really saved you—he went back for you after the skirmish.'

'He did?' The sous-lieutenant was astounded. 'But Sergeant, you told me that there was only one person you looked after on campaign and that was yourself. And I remember you told me just before I went down that I was as much use as a——'

'Everyone makes mistakes from time to time,' Sergeant Leclerc interrupted curtly. 'Coming back for you was probably mine. The Cossacks were withdrawing! What the devil made you go after the officer? You'd seen him kill three of ours already!'

'The captain would have——' the sous-lieutenant began defensively.

'The captain would never have done something so stupid!' the sergeant snapped. 'And besides which he is one of the best *sabreurs* in the regiment, something which you are not, sir.'

'Yes, I know. . .' Sous-Lieutenant Bourdon sighed and sat down, looking crestfallen.

Angèle glanced from him to the sergeant curiously. There did not seem to be the division between the ranks that she was used to in the Russian army. None of her cousin André's men would have dared address a superior officer in such a way. . .but on the other hand she doubted they would have risked their lives to go back for an officer. For the first time it occurred to her that perhaps the revolution had not been all bad, and that there was much to be said for equality and treating people on their merits rather than their position. Suddenly she felt ashamed of some of the remarks she had made to Tristan.

She looked at the two men again. The sous-lieutenant was staring gloomily into the fire. Wanting to cheer him, she offered him what was left of the soup, which he accepted with alacrity.

'But I am getting better, aren't I, Sergeant?' he asked

eagerly a moment or two later between mouthfuls of the hot broth. 'In the last practice bout with the captain before we left Paris I almost got beneath his guard.'

'Only because he let him to give him some confidence,' Sergeant Leclerc muttered to Angèle so that the lieutenant could not hear. 'He's a generous man in more ways than one, your captain.'

'I know,' she answered softly. Her captain. The thought sent a warm glow through her body. Suddenly she was filled with a certainty that she would see him again, that everything would be all right.

'*Pardon?*' said the sous-lieutenant, looking up from his soup.

Angèle bit back a smile. 'The sergeant was just telling me how much your swordsmanship has improved,' she said gravely, 'weren't you, Sergeant?'

'Yes,' said the sergeant heavily. 'You're getting much better, sir.'

'I think,' Angèle said later when she had persuaded the sous-lieutenant to go and rest again, 'that your bark is worse than your bite, Sergeant.'

'Perhaps, but don't tell anyone.' The sergeant laughed. 'Now you had better get some rest, *mademoiselle*; it will be a long day tomorrow.' And a hard one, he added to himself. He hadn't heard or seen the flashes from the Russian guns at Borisov for over an hour now. That meant they were on the move; if they got within range before Napoleon had enough men over to hold them off he doubted that half the soldiers around them would see tomorrow night.

The sergeant shook his head as he left the group of men huddled motionless about the black ashes of a fire and climbed back on to the sleigh.

'Dead. Every one of them. Damn fools, don't they know that to sleep on the ground for half an hour in this

cold is to die?' His face was grim as he took up the reins
and sent the sleigh forward again across the frozen snow.

Angèle said nothing, knowing that his harshness arose
from grief and guilt that they had the sleigh, ponies and
food when others had nothing.

In the nine days since Napoleon had fooled Chitchagov
and slipped out of the trap set for him at the Berezina
more than half the men who had crossed the river had
died. A few had been killed by the Cossacks who harried
the retreating army mercilessly, but by far the greatest
number had died of cold and starvation, against which
they had no defence. The temperature had plummeted.
Often it had been too cold even to snow. But there had
been no respite from the blizzards. The wind had
whipped up the snow on the ground, lashing the icy
particles until they scoured a man's flesh, leaving it as
white and fragile as porcelain. Yet somehow men had
dragged themselves on, lured by the promise of supplies
and rest at Vilna. But by the time they had reached Vilna
the Russians were so close that there had been no time
to organise the distribution of food; the first there had
simply grabbed everything they could get their hands on
and left the rest to their fate.

A wave of depression swept over Angèle as she huddled deeper into her furs. Ney was commanding the rear
guard now; there would have been nothing left in Vilna
by the time they reached it. How long would the supplies
she had given Tristan last. . .? Please let him live, she
prayed silently as she stared out into the whiteness, and
then she jerked upright, every sense alert as her ears
caught a sound, mingling with the wind.

'*Houra, houra*!' The Cossack war-cry. From a distance
it sounded like the wind whistling through the pines,
but she knew it instantly. So far they had been lucky,
they had outdistanced the Cossacks, since a horse pulling
a sleigh over snow was faster than a horse carrying a

man, but the ponies had eaten poorly during the last few days and they were tired.

'Cossacks!' She shouted a warning to the sergeant above the howl of the wind. 'Coming this way!'

'Get us up to those Grenadiers ahead, quickly! Bourdon, wake up!' He thrust the reins into her hands, shook Etienne, who had been dozing, and began to load the pistols he had scavenged from dead comrades, cursing and swearing at the numbness of his fingers as he did so.

She did as he asked, sending the whip cracking above the ponies' heads until they were speeding across the bumpy ground at a dangerous rate. As the sleigh lifted and crashed down after each hump she half expected the runners to break, but they held. They reached the Grenadiers just as the first Cossack appeared from nowhere and hurled his lance.

'Form up!' the sergeant yelled. 'Around the sleigh. Don't fire until you can see them!'

The Grenadiers bunched around the sleigh, raising their muskets, and then everything seemed to happen at once. There was the crackle of muskets, the dull thuds of lances striking flesh, smoke, the smell of gunpowder and the Cossacks darting in and out of the eddies of snow like a shoal of deadly fish.

She saw a Cossack fall, then another. Then a Grenadier inches away from Angèle's foot groaned and crumpled, a Cossack lance in his chest. Nauseated, for a moment she could do nothing but watch as the Cossack struggled to jerk his lance clear and control his raw-boned chestnut horse that screamed and plunged as a musket ball grazed its quarters. There was a horrible sucking sound and the lance came clear.

Etienne pushed a pistol into her hand and instinct took over. She raised it, preparing to fire. Then she gasped in sheer terror as her eyes registered the blaze that ran like forked lightning down the horse's Roman nose. She knew only one horse with a marking like that. It couldn't be! But, as the Cossack straightened, lifted his bloodstained lance and looked directly at her, she knew she was right.

'André!' She whispered his name stupidly, frozen with shock.

'Don't just look at him! Fire!' the sergeant bellowed as he took aim at another rider.

André threw back his head and laughed maliciously, his teeth yellow like a wolf's beneath his heavy ginger moustache.

'Shoot, you French whore! Why don't you?'

The brief hope that he would not recognise her died as he taunted her in Russian.

Hatred boiled over inside her. She squeezed the trigger. But her shot went wild—her hand had been trembling too much.

'Dragoons!' At that moment there was a shout from one of the Grenadiers as a handful of French horsemen, some riding draught animals, suddenly appeared in the midst of the mêlée, wielding their sabres.

André glanced towards them and raised his lance, shouting a command to the Cossacks to retire. And then he twisted to look back over his shoulder at Angèle. 'I'll be back for you, Cousin, I promise.'

Her stomach lurched in pure fear. André's threats were never idle; she knew that from bitter experience. 'You know him?' the sergeant asked, seeing the haunted expression on her face as she stared after the retreating Cossacks.

'Yes,' she said woodenly. 'He is my stepcousin.'

'The one you're running away from?'

'Yes. Now he knows where I am, he will come back for me.'

'A pity you missed, then, *mademoiselle*,' the sergeant said laconically. 'Next time don't hesitate before you shoot.' Then he patted her affectionately on the shoulder. 'Don't worry, *mademoiselle*, we'll have a reception committee for him if he does. We'll stop with these lads from the Guard until we reach Kovno. We'll be slower, but there's safety in numbers.'

'Yes.' She strove to sound calm as she got down from the sleigh to see if there was anything she could do for those who had been wounded. But inside she was terrified. She knew she dared not relax for a moment now until they were out of Russia.

Her fears were confirmed during the next five days. Time and time again she glimpsed the same Cossack group shadowing them, flitting in and out of the pines, always just out of range. But not too far for her to see the distinctive bright chestnut horse.

'What is happening, Sergeant?' Angèle asked as she fought to calm the ponies as blue-uniformed men streamed past them, running from the Vilna gate out of Kovno, discarding their muskets as they went.

'The damned Prussians are deserting!' the sergeant replied. 'Their officer was hit and he shot himself, useless bastard! One Frenchman is worth a thousand of them! Look!'

Angèle looked in the direction in which he was pointing. One scruffy, belligerent figure had stood his ground and was hurling oaths she had never heard before at the fleeing men, and while he was doing so was bending to pick up a discarded musket and fire at the Russian army, which was at the gate. Bend, pick up, aim, fire. He behaved as if he were at a practice, apparently oblivious to the cannon-shot that whistled around him. A musket against cannon, one man against an army. 'Is it courage or madness. . .?' she breathed in disbelief as a handful of other ragged French soldiers came running to join him.

'If it were any other man I should have said the latter,' the sergeant muttered thickly. 'Take a good look,

mademoiselle. You will not see his like again. He is truly
the bravest of the brave.'

'You mean that is Marshal Ney?' Her heart stopped.
If Ney was here, Tristan might be close. . .

'It could be no one else, *mademoiselle*,' the sergeant
answered simply, and the part of her mind that was not
focused on Tristan registered that there were tears
running down his grimy face.

'I am going to help him,' Etienne announced from
beside them.

'No!' the sergeant barked, his usual brisk self again as
he climbed on to the driving seat of the sleigh. 'We are
getting out of here; if something should happen to me
you will have to see *mademoiselle* safe to the border. Get
into the sleigh, *mademoiselle*! Now!'

Angèle moved reluctantly to obey him. She could
think only that Tristan might be near. . .she looked
from one man to the next, hoping against hope to see
one tall familiar figure.

'*Mademoiselle*, get in!' the sergeant shouted as he
began to turn the ponies in the narrow lane.

'Angèle, come on!' Etienne added his voice to the
sergeant's as he climbed up beside him. 'There are
Russians inside the town already!'

Still she hesitated, and then out of a smoke-filled side-
street came a group of French soldiers, pushing and
pulling two light cannon towards the gate, where Ney
was still standing firm with a handful of men. A mounted
officer was with them, leaning across from his saddle to
drag the teamleader of an ammunition wagon into
position behind the guns. An eddy of smoke from the
Russian cannon obscured him for a moment, but it made
no difference—she knew him immediately. Tristan. *He
was alive.* Joy drove all sense of caution out of her head.
She began to run forward, not noticing that the sleigh was
already moving away, the sergeant and Etienne having
assumed she was already inside. She saw only Tristan.

'Angèle. . .'

A voice came from the shadows, halting her. She caught a blur of movement, but it was too late. The pistol butt rose and fell. There was a flash of pain and a deep, overwhelming blackness.

CHAPTER NINE

AWARENESS returned piece by piece. Angèle was on a horse, every step it took jolting her aching skull. An arm was clamped around her waist, a body, legs were behind hers, crushing her against the high pommel of the saddle. She recoiled, a wave of nausea sweeping over her as her senses told her what her mind had not had time to register. André. She knew it even before he spoke.

'We'll be closer than this before the night is out, my little French whore,' he sneered, pressing against her as he felt her tense. One of his hands moved up, and thrust inside her coat. She cried out as his hand closed cruelly on her breast. 'Won't we, brothers?'

There was a ripple of lewd laughter. And as her eyes focused in the orange glare of burning buildings she realised she was in the midst of a small group of Cossacks. Her eyes flitted from one face to another, hoping against hope to see Nicolai, her old riding master, or Yuri, whose wife and child she had saved with her healing skills. But with a sinking heart she recognised them all as André's particular friends. They were all young, wild and, she knew from past experience, sadistic to a degree that shocked even their hardened village elders.

A chill of pure elemental fear went down her spine, and panic took over. She had to get away. Driving her elbow back hard into André's stomach, she tried to break free from his grasp.

He gasped but his hold on her did not slacken. 'Do that again, Cousin, and I'll hand you over to my brothers,' he grated. 'Do you know what they do to traitors? Especially beautiful ones? First they have their pleasure, and then. . .' He drew his hand across her throat.

'The Count will punish you all for this!' Angèle shouted in desperation at the grinning men around her.

'He'll never know,' André sneered. 'He's gone to St Petersburg to be with the Tsar. So, my dear coz, you are under my protection. . .and I do not intend to let you out of my sight, day. . .' he paused significantly, dropping his hand to her thigh and caressing it blatantly '. . .or night. You're trembling, Cousin; does the thought excite you? Damn you! What's wrong with you?' He swore and snatched his hand away as she slumped forward and retched painfully.

'I'm going. . .to be sick. . . Let me down. . .'

'Very well! But don't get any ideas!' he warned as he swung down and hauled her from the saddle.

She landed awkwardly, falling on to her hands and knees. She retched again in vain. Her stomach was empty; they had eaten the last of their food the previous day.

'Come on! Get up!' André wound his hand into her hair and yanked upwards.

She started to obey, but then the world seemed to explode into white light, and a rush of air pressed her flat against the ground again. A ball had hit an ammunition store in a nearby warehouse. What had been a street of wooden houses was now an avenue of flame. André let go of her hair as he struggled to hold on to his rearing and plunging horse. Two other horses had gone down in their panic, and three of the Cossacks had been unseated. For a moment she was too bemused to do anything. Then, scrabbling to her feet, she began to run, not knowing or caring where, as long as it was away from André.

The road was rutted and slippery, but desperation kept Angèle on her feet. Acrid smoke filled her lungs as she ran, making her cough and choke. She glanced back over her shoulder and saw André fighting to mount his circling horse and shouting orders to his men. In seconds they would be after her. She ducked into the first turning she came to, steeling herself to run through a gap in the flames that licked out from both sides of the street. She was through. And then she recognised the horseman at the far end of the street, silhouetted against a flaming house. She tripped, and went sprawling on the ice. He was riding away. With the last ounce of her strength she scrabbled to her feet and shouted with all the force she could muster.

'Tristan!' She shouted again as she stumbled on in his wake. He must hear her. He must.

Relief swamped her as she saw him jolt and twist in the saddle as if struck by a musket-ball. Then he had turned Montespan on her haunches and was riding towards her at full pace, shouting and gesturing with his sword.

'Behind you!'

She caught the warning a moment after she registered the hoofbeats coming from behind. It was too late. André stooped from his saddle, caught her up and dragged her across his knees, turning his horse and riding back towards his men, who were hidden in the shadow of a large house.

Screaming, Angèle kicked and struggled until his fist thudded into her ribs, winding her, so that she could do nothing but gasp for breath as he hauled her astride, pinioning her with his arm, cursing her all the time.

She heard Tristan's roar of rage from behind and Montespan's hoofbeats coming nearer.

'No!' She tried to warn him. 'Go back! There are too many!' But her voice was nothing more than a sob.

André shouted an order and six Cossacks came forward, arrogant and confident as they lifted their swords. 'He'll not be so keen now,' he laughed, wrenching her arms behind her and binding her wrists with a leather thong that bit into her flesh.

But then as he looked up again he sobered.

'Are they all mad?' he muttered. 'First, one against the army, now this one. . . Do they all want to die?'

Horrified, she could do nothing but watch as Tristan came on, shouting a challenge, his sabre held high. Her heart ceased to beat. One against so many. What chance did he have? You idiot! You fool! she wanted to cry out. But, even if she had, she doubted if he would have heard her. Man and horse were moving as a single unit with a single purpose. Tristan's face was that of a stranger, a savage mask. Montespan's head was high, her ears back, her teeth bared as she half reared, snapping and striking at the nearest Cossack pony with her forefeet as Tristan sliced at its rider. It was like watching a whirlwind of steel and muscle as they scythed through the Cossacks—one, two, three went down in seconds. The remaining Cossacks backed off a little, wary now that they knew they were dealing with a master swordsman.

'Sons of wolfbitches!' André roared at them. 'Kill him! Or must I do it myself?' He raised his pistol and took aim.

'No!' Angèle screamed and twisted and kicked wildly, throwing his aim off. 'Please don't! Let him go! I will do anything you ask, anything. . .'

'You know him?' André was momentarily startled as he raised his pistol again. 'What is he? Another of your paramours? Then I will take even more pleasure in blowing his brains out! Sit still, you damned French whore!' he cursed volubly as the chestnut threw its head up and danced skittishly in response to Angèle's frantic struggles. Then he spat out another foul oath as a horse approached at speed from their right.

Angèle sobbed with relief. Riding straight towards them was another cavalry officer.

'Captain Beaumaris! Help him!' she shouted at the top of her voice. 'Please!'

The officer glanced from her and André to where Tristan was fending off the three Cossacks who had launched a simultaneous attack on him. The newcomer swerved towards the mêlée just as André fired.

She sobbed with relief as the bullet smashed harmlessly into the wall of a house.

'You treacherous witch!' André cursed her as another of his men went down, and the odds evened to one against one as the newcomer entered the fray. Shoving his pistol back into his belt, he wheeled his horse away from the skirmish, hauling Angèle back into the saddle as she tried to throw herself off the horse. 'Don't think you're getting away, Cousin!' he snarled at her, crashing his fist into her ribs again.

'No. . .' she moaned helplessly, sick and dizzy from pain, as André's horse leapt forward, carrying them out of sight and sound of the fight, into the maze of burning and smouldering ruins. To have been so close to Tristan and now to be back in André's hands was more than she could stand. As she made one last despairing effort to get away the shift of her weight made the chestnut lose its footing on the ice and go down heavily, pitching them both forward over its head.

'Sorry, Heymès, you'll have to get that last cannon up. . .' Tristan panted raggedly as the last Cossack fell, blood spurting from his shoulder. 'Tell Ney I'll be back as soon as I can. I've got to find her. . .'

'But. . .' Heymès was about to argue but, after a glance at Tristan's face, thought better of it. 'Bon chance, mon ami!' he said resignedly as Tristan brought Montespan around and took off at a gallop.

André shoved Angèle roughly through the wooden door hanging drunkenly from one hinge. She went sprawling helplessly on the wooden floor, unable to use her hands to save herself. Instinctively she rolled, dragging herself awkwardly up on to her knees and then her feet. André was staring at her, his face ugly in the hellish light from a blazing house opposite that spilled in through the flapping open door.

'Are you going to kill me?' she forced herself to ask coolly, though she wanted to scream. To scream for Tristan, even though she knew it was pointless.

'Later.' André laughed unpleasantly.

Then, even before the heavy clunk and chink of metal as he dropped his belt and pistol on to the damp and musty floor, she knew what he intended.

'Oh, no. . .please. . .don't. . .' she begged him, backing away, her pride disintegrating amid fear and revulsion.

His only response was to laugh as the wall brought her retreat to an abrupt halt.

She saw his knife blade glint evilly in his hand, and in one swift movement he stepped forward and sliced through the fastenings of her coat, her tunic, her shirt.

She screamed, hunching into the wall, trying to hide her exposed breasts.

'Scream as loud as you want.' He laughed harshly, reaching out and shoving her on to the floor. 'Who do you think is going to pay any attention in the midst of a battle? Your precious Frenchman? Do you think he's going to have time to look for you?'

'You're mad!' she said despairingly, fearing that what he said was true. 'Why don't you just kill me. . .and go——?'

'Later, later,' he sneered. 'First I'm going to have what you gave that tow-headed peasant. . .'

'No. . .you're wrong; you were always wrong about Yashi. . .' She kicked at him wildly with her feet. But it was futile; he was too strong for her, pinning her easily by sitting astride her hips.

She cried out at the agonising pain in her arms trapped beneath her body, and tried to roll sideways. But he caught her shoulders and slammed them against the floor, the hilt of the knife he still held digging into her white flesh.

'Enjoying it already, Cousin!' he mocked her, bending his head close to hers. 'It'll get better, I promise you. . .'

'Why are you doing this?' She gagged, turning her head aside to avoid his foul breath. 'What harm have I ever done you?'

'You know!' he snarled. 'Your mother made an impotent dolt of the Count for years, but you will not do it to me! I know what you want beneath those cool little airs and graces! You're a wanton little witch like your mother! Year after year you've taunted me. Swinging your hips every time you crossed a room, all those pretty gestures as you tossed your hair, promising everything with your eyes and delivering nothing! Now's the time to pay, Cousin. . .'

The depths of his madness destroyed the last of her hope that she might reason with him. Never by word or action had she encouraged him, *never*.

She shuddered as he drew the flat of his knife down her cheek, her throat and on to her breasts.

He smiled as she went rigid beneath him. 'That's a good girl, I'd hate to mar that pretty flesh before I've had my fill of it. Be nice to your cousin André. . .I might decide not to kill you after all——'

'Never!' she answered raggedly, coming to an instantaneous decision. 'If you think I'd ever willingly let you touch me. . . You're insane. . . I hate you, you revolt me. . . I'd rather die. . . Why don't you kill me now. . . you enjoy killing, don't you? That's probably the only way you can get your pleasure. I doubt you've ever had a woman——'

'Bitch!' His face contorted and he slapped her face and she knew she had stumbled on something close to the truth. As he raised his knife she felt a crazy relief; he would kill her and it would be over. . .no more pain, no more humiliation. . . But the knife thudded down into the floor, not her flesh. He was laughing, his hands on her breasts, greedy and cruel. She shut her eyes, beyond fighting him. She just wanted it to be over, wanted him to stop hurting her.

'It was a good try, Cousin,' he gloated. 'But I'm going to have you first——'

'No, you die first, *canaille*!' The voice was low, deadly. Colder by a hundred degrees than the freezing night air.

'She comes with me!' André lunged for the knife again, but before his hand closed around the hilt he gave a surprised grunt and fell sideways. He rolled, and stared up at his attacker. 'You. . .' He laughed, a ghastly gurgling sound. 'I wish you joy of her, Frenchman. . . may you burn for her as I have. She's a witch, like her mother. . .once she's hooked you no other women will do. . .she'll suck you dry. . .' There was another rattling breath and then there was silence.

Tristan. Angèle tried to say his name, but her voice died in her throat as she opened her eyes and saw a stranger. A man she had never seen before. Tall and terrible in the flickering light, his sabre stained with blood. Several days' growth of beard covered the lower half of his gaunt, shadowed face. He seemed almost unaware of her presence for a moment as he stared at André's body with an expression on his face that she never wanted to see again.

'Tristan. . .' This time she managed his name in an uncertain whisper.

His eyes came to her blankly, then hardened as they touched her bare flesh.

Without a word he bent, severed her bonds and scooped her up into his arms. Kicking aside a connecting door, he carried her into the shell of another room and set her down before sheathing his sword and dropping to his knees and staring at her, his face set and grim.

'Don't be angry with me. . .please. . .' she begged him brokenly. 'Just hold me. . .please, Tristan. . .'

His breath left his lungs in a juddering sigh and she felt his hands tremble as he reached out and lifted her into his arms.

'Angry with you. . .' he said huskily. 'Is that what you think?'

She didn't reply; it was enough to be in his arms, to hear his thudding heartbeat, to feel his lips against her hair. The terror of the last hour or so had given way to a deep numb calm. She did not even wish to weep.

'I've been such a fool!' he went on fiercely, rocking her in his arms. 'For asking you to go back to that. . . You tried to tell me what he was like. . .I didn't listen. . .I didn't want to because I thought the alternative was worse. . . Can you forgive me?'

'Of course I do,' she murmured, realising that he needed reassurance as desperately as she did.

'Thank God. . .' He sighed and she felt some of the tautness leave his body as he let his cheek rest against her head. The stranger had vanished. It was the Tristan she knew and loved who was holding her. Tender, kind, loving. . .

Involuntarily she lifted her hand to his cheek, stroking the silken beard.

'And you. . .you are not angry with me for lying to you about going back?'

'I stopped being angry days ago.'

'You knew. . .'

'I realised the day after we parted that you had said *au revoir*, not goodbye. . . I've been looking for you ever since. The only thing that stopped me going mad was knowing the sergeant would never abandon you. I couldn't believe it when I saw you standing there alone. . . How the devil did you come to be there?'

'André snatched me when the sergeant and Etienne weren't looking. They probably think I'm still in the sleigh. I got away. . .but he came after me. . .then I saw you. . . I thought you weren't going to find me. . .' she blurted out, her false calm disintegrating as the recollection of André's face, his hands on her flesh, seared back into her mind. 'I was going to give in; I couldn't make him stop——'

'Hush, hush. . .' He pressed his lips to her forehead, her cheeks, her mouth in light soft kisses, soothing her. 'He can't harm you any more. . . I'm here now. I'd have stopped him sooner, but I dared not move until he'd put the knife down.'

'You heard what he said?'

'And saw from the window. I found the dead horse, and then I heard you. . .' he rasped. 'Dear God! When he hit you. . .and the things he was saying. . .'

'I didn't encourage him.' Her voice broke as André's taunts echoed through her mind. Suddenly she found that she dared not meet his gaze; if there was the slightest doubt in his eyes it would destroy her. 'And about Yashi. . .it is all nonsense. . .'

'Do you think I don't know that?' he scolded her with rough tenderness. 'I am not that much of a fool, even where you are concerned.'

'No,' she said as she brought her eyes slowly up to his, relief flooding her veins as she saw only compassion in their smoke-dark depths. Then she gasped as a wave of excruciating pain swept through her arms and shoulders.

'You are hurt? Where?' he asked fiercely, cursing himself for not having realised at once.

'No. . .my arms. . .cramp. . .' Tears came to her eyes as she jerked the words out. The flow of blood was returning to her arms, and the pain was unbearable.

With an oath he stripped off her sheepskin coat and began to chafe and rub first one arm and then the other.

It was only as his hand accidentally brushed against her breast that Angèle remembered the state of her clothes. Ashamed of her nakedness, she flinched, clutching at the gaping edges of her tunic with clumsy, half-numbed fingers. 'I must look awful.'

'No,' he said, his straight black brows lifting the merest fraction as their eyes locked again. 'I wouldn't say that.' Then with a ghost of the grin she remembered from the lodge he put aside her hand gently. 'Let me.' With gentle, impersonal fingers he wrapped her tunic and shirt across her body and secured them with her belt, before continuing the massage of her arms. 'Better?' he asked several minutes later when her breathing had become more even and he felt her shoulders relax beneath his hands. 'We ought to be getting out of here.'

'Yes,' she said a little uncertainly as he helped her back into her coat. As the agony in her arms and hands faded she was becoming aware of the other tender places on her body. Her ribs, her jaw, her cheekbone all throbbed painfully.

'As bad a liar as ever I see.' Tristan shook his head, and then swore and threw them both flat as another volley of cannonfire thudded into the houses all around them. A rafter from the already damaged roof crashed to the ground a foot or two away, showering them with dust and snow.

She sat up slowly, her head reeling. It was the last straw. She was at the end of her physical and mental strength. At the moment she could not have moved if the entire Russian army had been a yard away.

'Come here.' Somehow he seemed to know as he reached out and drew her into his arms. 'Rest for a moment.' Gratefully she let her head rest on his shoulder.

He frowned as his fingers touched the already swelling bruises on her cheek and jaw.

'If I killed him a thousand times it would not be

enough,' he muttered. 'When I think how frightened you must have been. . .'

'Not half as frightened as I have been for you,' she admitted. 'The more the sergeant told me about Marshal Ney, the more convinced I was that I'd never see you again. Does he have no desire to live?'

'Oh, plenty of that. I do not know a man with a greater love of life.' He laughed softly. 'But nor do I know anyone with less fear of death. Michel Ney is unique. . .and every man who makes it over the Niemen into Prussia will owe their life to him. The rearguard would have collasped days ago and we'd have been overrun if it weren't for Ney. . .but the men were more afraid of his wrath than of the Russians—it kept them going—— Listen. . .'

There was the noise of men running along the street outside, and shouted orders.

'We'll have to go. It sounds as if we are falling back to the bridge. Come on!'

Tristan lifted her to her feet and half carried her out into the street; she shut her eyes as they passed André's still form. It would be a long time before she was completely free of her fear of him.

Montespan was waiting by the porch, pawing nervously and tossing her head as the cannon-balls flew around her, but she had not moved from the spot where her master had left her. As she saw them her ears pricked and she whickered a greeting.

'Look after her for me,' Tristan murmured as he lifted Angèle into the saddle and started to lead the horse forward. 'She's a good beast. . .'

'What do you mean?' She paled, horrified at the thought of being separated from him again.

'You've got to get out of here, Angèle. Khutuzov is driving us back from the Vilna gate, and Chitchagov is beginning to attack the bridge on the other side. All we have left is a battalion under General Marchand at the bridge, and Ney has about thirty men with him.'

'But what are you going to do?'

'I am staying here. I cannot abandon the marshal; it is a matter of honour. . .' He sought her eyes as he spoke, pleading with her to understand.

'Then I will stay with you.'

'No!' All trace of tenderness had left his face; it was a granite mask again, hard and unreadable.

'I will not go! I will not leave you!'

His breath caught and he jerked Montespan to an abrupt halt in the lee of a relatively complete building. She had no idea of just how desperate the situation was, he realised, how little chance he and the marshal had of surviving. Once again he had no choice but to send her away.

'I had hoped I did not need to say this,' he said flatly, being careful not to look her in the face. 'Whatever sentimental idea you have in your head, it's time you got rid of it! A few hours and you will be out of this nightmare and back in the real world, Angèle. You are going to England, and even if you were not, do you really think it would work? An officer of Napoleon's bodyguard and the daughter of a die-hard Bourbon *émigré* is hardly an ideal match, is it? A lot of good such an arrangement would do my career!'

'Your career. . .but. . .' She stared at him, aghast. 'At the Berezina you said——'

'A few pretty words! I did not expect to see you again. In such circumstances people often say what they do not mean.' He dragged the words out, avoiding her gaze. 'I told you before, all we have in common is a physical attraction; once we'd satisfied it, I wouldn't give us a week before we were at each other's throats! Now follow those men and get out of here!'

'No. I don't believe you!' She was stunned. Minutes

ago he had been so gentle, almost *loving*. . . 'Why are
you saying such things?'

'Because it is the truth!'

'No. . .' She shook her head, refusing to believe him.

'Yes!' he said roughly. 'Here! If you insist on sentiment, take this to remember me by!' He reached inside
his tunic, tore something out and pushed it into the cuff
of her glove. 'It should be an entertaining souvenir for
you to show your English friends.'

Before she could even think of a reply he had turned
away towards a knot of men, retreating at a run.

'Dragoon Roche of the Guard, isn't it?' he barked,
grabbing one of them by the arm, and almost lifting him
off his feet.

'Yes, sir!' said the startled dragoon.

'Good. Get up behind the young lady here and make
sure she gets across the border safely or I'll have you
shot! There are woods on the other side of the bridge.
Keep going through them until you are certain you're on
Prussian territory that we hold. Understood?'

Yes, sir!' Dragoon Roche needed no second invitation
and a second later was mounted behind Angèle and was
taking up the reins expertly.

'Get going, then, man!' Tristan roared, bringing his
hand down on Montespan's rump.

As the mare surged forward Angèle twisted in the
saddle to stare back at him. How could he send her away
like this, with only harsh words and contempt? Sheer,
unadulterated anger overwhelmed her.

'I'll never forgive you for this!' she yelled at him.
'Never!'

'I doubt you'll need to.' His voice drifted after her.
'Goodbye, Angèle.'

It wasn't until dawn, when Montespan came to an
exhausted halt just ouside of a Prussian village, that she
began to weep, helplessly, hopelessly. She slumped
forward on to Montespan's lathered neck, sobbing into

the black mane. Crying for Dragoon Roche, who had fallen to a Russian musket-ball as they crossed the bridge with other stragglers, crying for Tristan, and most of all crying for herself. And it was there, an hour later, that Sergeant Leclerc and Sous-Lieutenant Bourdon found her.

'We ought to be paid more, Beaumaris!' Ney panted at dusk the same day as he flung aside a jammed musket and picked up another. 'Five of us against two whole bloody armies.'

'True!' Tristan laughed carelessly, his teeth white against his smoke-blackened face. Angèle was gone. He had lied to her again, hurt her again, sent her away forever. He did not much care if he lived or died. 'Have we any more ammunition?'

'No.' Ney grinned, throwing the musket he had just fired into the river, where it went skidding across the frozen surface. 'Time we were going, my friends.'

The handful of men turned as one, running for the shelter of the nearest trees.

'Cossacks to the right!' Tristan shouted a warning to Ney.

'I said you were a bloody fool to give your horse away,' the marshal retorted, increasing his stride. 'Run, man, run!'

CHAPTER TEN

'You should try to eat a little more,' Sergeant Leclerc said, glancing at Angèle's barely touched plate of cabbage and bacon broth.

'I am not hungry,' Angèle replied, dropping her untouched piece of heavy black bread back on to her wooden platter as the door of the already crowded hostelry opened. Her heart lifted as she caught a glimpse of a faded green cloak, and then fell again as she saw that its owner was stocky and fair-haired.

'Try not to worry so,' the sergeant said, following her gaze across the smoky room and reading the expression on her face. 'The captain is a hard man to kill——'

'The captain is none of my concern any more!' she retorted sharply, angry with herself for being such a fool. Tristan had rebuffed her, insulted her, hurt her. . .and yet still she was sitting here, watching, waiting, longing for him to step through the door. 'I have no interest in what becomes of him. In a day or so I shall leave for England. . . I want to find my father. . .and begin a new life. . .' she said, trying to convince herself that she meant it.

There was a silence in which the sergeant simply looked at her and raised his bushy grey brows.

'*Mademoiselle*,' he said softly, 'I don't know what happened between you and the captain at Kovno, but I do know when I am being lied to.'

Before Angèle could reply he put his wooden tankard down on the old pine table with a thump and stood up. He nodded towards the newcomer and said, 'I'll go and ask him if he has any news of Ney and the men with him.'

'Thank you,' she said, not having the energy to pretend further. She slumped against the back of the painted wooden settle and turned the little enamel cross Tristan had given her at Kovno over and over in her fingers. The crowded room seemed suddenly twice as hot and airless as she watched the sergeant walk towards the man who had just entered and begin to speak. Then she had to look away for fear of what she might read on the sergeant's face. Tristan might be dead. He didn't love her, never had, never would. He might be dead. The same thoughts drummed through her head, over and over, in a bleak rhythm.

'*Mademoiselle?*' There was concern in the sergeant's voice as he sat down opposite her again a few minutes later.

'Well?' She kept her eyes fixed on the table and her voice quavered. It had taken the last shred of her courage to ask and she did not know if she could bear the answer.

'Nothing new, I am afraid,' the sergeant said quickly, compassion in his hazel eyes as he scanned her taut face. 'The corporal who just came in crossed the bridge around noon. The marshal and a few others were still holding off the Russians. He thinks he remembers a tall dark-haired man beside the marshal, but he cannot be sure.'

'Noon.' She exhaled the breath she had been holding, and her hand unclenched from the arm of the settle. 'What use is that? That was eight hours ago! Anything could have happened between now and then!'

'I'm sorry——'

'No, I am sorry. It is not your fault,' she apologised. 'I don't know what I am doing or saying.'

'Was the captain so very angry when he found you had not gone back?' the sergeant asked quietly, thinking that whatever had happened in Kovno had come near to breaking her spirit.

'No. . .' She shook her head. 'That is what I don't understand. When he rescued me from my cousin he was so kind. . .until I told him I would not leave Kovno without him, and then. . .' She shrugged her tense shoulders and gave a bitter laugh. 'I suppose I should have known better. He has told me often enough before that I am nothing more than a nuisance to him. . .but I had not realised that my royalist connections made me such an embarrassment to him. . .'

'He told you that?' The sergeant almost dropped his beer. 'And you believed him? *Mademoiselle*, the cold must have numbed your brain! Don't you see? There is only one thing worse for a soldier than watching your loved one die on a battlefield, and that is to die yourself, knowing they will be left without protection. He would have sworn black was white to get you out of Kovno—he said the first thing he could think of to make you go. . .'

'You mean he lied to protect me. . .?' A numbing horror sent the blood from her face, leaving her as white as the limewashed wall behind the settle. 'He thought he was going to die?'

'I am afraid so.'

'And I told him I would never forgive him. . .' Her voice died in her throat as the sergeant reached across the table and took her cold hand in his.

'Courage; if there was a way out he will have found it—— What the devil. . .?'

His exclamation broke through the black wall in her mind and she turned her head to see what he was looking at. She stared helplessly at the spectacle of Etienne, looking unaccountably grim, dragging a young girl with midnight-black hair and a face like an angry madonna towards their table.

'Angèle! Please, you must help me make her see sense!' he announced as he reached them. 'Tell her I am not a philanderer!'

'*Mademoiselle*!' The girl spoke at the same moment. 'Make him let go of me—he is importuning me!'

'Importuning! What do you think I am?' Etienne blazed.

'She hardly has cause to think you a gentleman!' Angèle broke in crisply, the girl's obvious distress making her momentarily forget her own misery. 'Let go of Mademoiselle. . .?'

'Dupuis,' supplied the girl.

'Let go of Mademoiselle Dupuis at once.'

Etienne looked at his hand as if surprised to find that it was clamped around the girl's wrist.

'I'm sorry,' he said, letting go instantly and scowling as the girl rubbed at the red imprint of his fingers.

'Jean Dupuis's daughter?' asked the sergeant, whose first reaction had been to move his tankard and the jug of beer to the centre of the table, out of harm's way.

'Yes. You are a friend of my father?' Some of the anger and suspicion left the girl's face.

'We served together in the Low Countries under Doumouriez as lads,' the sergeant said, 'then I joined the Chasseurs and he the Grenadiers. I have not seen him for years, but I remember him well. Where is he?'

'I do not know, Sergeant,' the girl answered. 'He told me to wait here for him when the army left in the summer. A comrade of his told me yesterday that he had been wounded three months ago and was sent back to Paris. But he must have gone by a different route. . . I have had no word from him yet. I think he must be very ill or he would have sent for me by now. . .'

'Jean was pretty tough. You get yourself back to Paris and I'm sure he'll be waiting for you,' the sergeant said confidently. Then, after an astute glance at the girl's thin face, he asked quietly, 'Have you the means to get home?'

'No, she hasn't!' Etienne interrupted. 'She ran out of money a week ago and has been scrubbing the scullery floor in exchange for a meal, which is why I've been trying to get her to take this. . .' He dumped a handful of coins on the table. 'But she's as stubborn and proud as you, Angèle!'

'Thank you,' Angèle said drily.

Etienne flushed brick-red. 'I didn't mean——'

'I know.' She smiled to reassure him, and against all her expectations found herself trying not to laugh as the girl's brown-gold eyes caught hers in a moment of female empathy.

'I'm sorry, Sous-Lieutenant, I thought you wanted. . .' The girl blushed as her eyes met Etienne's blue gaze.

'No! I wasn't trying to buy your favours!' Etienne said huffily.

'Oh.' Relief lit up the girl's heart-shaped face and she smiled at him. 'I am sorry. . .' she said again, the blood leaving her cheeks as fast as it had risen.

'Then you will take the money.'

'No.'

'Why not? Is there something wrong with it?'

'No, but I cannot take it because I do not know when I can repay you. Now if you will excuse me I have work to do. . .'

'Give me patience!' Etienne grabbed at the girl's arm as she tried to turn away.

'Etienne, let go of her!' Angèle spat at him furiously. It was obvious to her why charity was the last thing the girl wanted from Etienne. 'Mademoiselle Dupuis, don't go yet. . .please,' Angèle began quickly. 'I am in need of a female companion to travel with me to the coast, where I shall embark for England. I would not expect you to accompany me there, but I would pay you well enough for you to be able to return to France if you so wished.'

'I could work for you as a lady's maid?' the girl said eagerly, the defensiveness and strain vanishing from her pretty face. 'My grandmother worked for a *Duchesse*; she taught me to sew and to dress hair. . . I should be delighted, *mademoiselle*.'

'Angèle Kerenski,' Angèle said with a smile as she heard Etienne sigh with relief. 'It is settled, then. Now will you come and eat with us. . .?'

'Danielle,' the girl said, colouring a little as Etienne helped her to her seat.

As Angèle watched them snatch surreptitious glances at each other while they ate their supper she was reminded of the first meal she and Tristan had shared at the Perenskovs' lodge. . . She remembered his smile, his dancing silver eyes, the first time he kissed her. . . Her heart twisted. She could not lose him now, not before she could tell him how blind she had been, how much she loved him. . .

'This is the house?' Danielle asked uncertainly early the next morning as she and Angèle rang the doorbell of an imposing-looking town house.

'The sergeant said the marshal was here,' Angèle replied, clasping her hands together to try to stop their trembling. Tristan had to be here, he had to be. . .

A housekeeper opened the door and looked at them dubiously.

'I don't think she's going to let us in,' whispered Danielle as the housekeeper looked from Danielle's spotlessly clean but often-mended cloak, to Angèle's ill-fitting and unflattering mustard gown, which had been hastily purchased from the landlady's daughter.

'I don't care,' Angèle replied. As the door had opened she had heard Ney's unmistakable bellow.

With a hasty apology she pushed past the startled housekeeper and ran towards a door, from behind which she could hear Ney demanding a plate of soup. She flung it open.

The group of men seated around the table in the room looked up in surprise at the interruption. Disappointment hit her like a hammer blow. When she had heard Ney she had been so sure she would find Tristan here. . .but the only familiar face was that of the marshal. A moustached man in a morning coat who she assumed was the doctor got to his feet and launched into a tirade of German that she did not even bother to listen to.

'Marshal Ney!' she gasped as a young officer in the blue uniform of the Grenadier guards pushed back his chair and grabbed her arm, obviously deciding she was mad. 'Please, I just wanted to know if you knew anything of Captain Beaumaris!'

'Beaumaris!' The marshal's hand paused in the act of breaking off a fragment of bread from the piece on his plate. His eyes flicked over Angèle without recognition or much interest. 'Dead, as far as I know,' he said curtly.

'Dead!' The air seemed to be sucked from her lungs, and the floor was tilting crazily beneath her feet.

'*Mademoiselle!*'

The young guardsman relaxed his grip on her arm and put a steadying hand on her waist. But she was scarcely aware of him. Her attention was fixed on the marshal's voice, which seemed distant and far off. She wanted to scream at him to stop, she did not want to hear what he was saying, but her mouth would not move and the voice went on, cold, detached, inexorable.

'We got separated in the woods. There were Cossacks hounding us. I waited for him on the other side, but he didn't turn up, so they must have got him. Bloody fool!' He laughed savagely. 'He'd be here now if he hadn't given his horse to that Russian chit. . .'

'You are saying if it weren't for me. . . No. . .' She shook her head, refusing to believe him. Then a moment later she was running drunkenly from the room. Running because she felt that if she remained a moment longer she would go insane with rage, not grief but a black, black fury against Ney for being alive when

Tristan was dead and with herself for allowing him to make her take Montespan.

The young guardsman caught her at the foot of the stairs.

'It is just the marshal's way, *mademoiselle*. The more he cares, the more callous he tries to sound. Captain Beaumaris and the marshal were old friends. . .the captain and the marshal were the last off the bridge at Kovno. . .to die for France and the Emperor in such a way is a great honour——'

'I don't care about honour! I don't care if France, the Emperor and Marshal Ney sink without trace like Atlantis! I just want Tristan. . .don't you understand——?'

'He is dead, *mademoiselle*. . . I am sorry. . .'

'No!' She shook her head, backing away from him as if he were threatening her life. 'No, you're wrong. . . you're all wrong. . .if he was dead I would know. . .he told me. . .'

'*Mademoiselle*, I think it would be best if we left now. . .' Suddenly there was Danielle at her side, her face anxious, kind and infinitely older than her years. The rage drained from her, leaving only the lacerating grief that was tearing her heart and mind apart, strip by strip. Inside Angèle was screaming, but she could not shed a single tear. Gratefully she let Danielle take her arm and lead her past the indignant, disapproving housekeeper and out of the house.

Tristan was dead. Marshal Ney had said so. So what was she doing? Angèle asked herself late that afternoon as she let Montespan pick her way slowly through the narrow winding streets of half-timbered houses. She was chilled to the bone from the biting wind, exhausted from asking every weary straggler if they knew anything of Tristan Beaumaris, only to die a little more inside every time they shook their heads. The sergeant, Danielle and

Etienne all thought she was deluding herself—and she probably was. If she searched all night she would not find him, ever.

The pain of loss was physical. She slumped forward, resting her cheek against Montespan's warm neck as the mare turned into a deserted side-street, so narrow that the upper storeys of the houses that jutted out nearly touched each other. In the dusk the white walls of the houses seemed to be all shades of lavender and grey, and the shadows were darkest violet and black. Sombre, mournful colours that echoed her mood. This search was pointless, futile. . .like your life without him, a seductive voice in her mind whispered as her hand touched the butt of the pistol the sergeant had given her for protection. But that would be a betrayal. Tristan had risked his life to save her from André, and then given her Montespan, his chance of escape, so that she would live. How could she throw such a gift away?

'Come on, girl. . .' She straightened and whispered brokenly to the black mare, who had come to a halt as if sensing her anguish. 'Let's go back. . .'

But Montespan would not turn. Her neck was stiff, her ears pricked as she stared into the darkest shadows at the far end of the street.

'What is it?'

Then she understood as her eyes caught a flicker of movement at the far end of the lane. A figure, blurred and indistinct in the twilight, had stepped out from a doorway of a rather disreputable-looking tavern and was walking slowly away. Her heart raced and then seemed to stop beating altogether. She shut her eyes and opened them again, terrified that it had been a trick of the light or an illusion produced by the intensity of her longing to find him. No. She was not mistaken. It was him. He was alive! Dear God! *He was alive. . .*

'Tristan!'

Her shout was muffled by the overhanging buildings

and the wind that was blowing in her face. He hadn't
heard. She threw herself down from the saddle and ran
recklessly over the uneven compacted snow. The wind
threw back her hood and cloak, and pulled loose the
heavy, silken coils of her hair, flaring the thick tresses
out behind her as she ran.

A wave of dizziness forced Tristan to stop. He put out
a hand and leant against one of the rough plaster walls,
regretting having accepted the beaker of rough wine
pressed on him by a brother officer. His body was
screaming for rest, food, sleep. But his mind would not
let him stop looking. She had to be here somewhere. For
the last few hours he had dragged himself from inn to
tavern to lodging house, looking for her. Just to make
sure she was safe, he had told himself, then he would
have fulfilled his part of the bargain and she would go to
England and that would be an end to it. It would be a
relief. A weight off his mind. His life would be as it had
been before he had met her. . .*empty*. The word took
him unawares. But before he had time to think about the
implications of his own admission, the part of his mind
that was tuned into perpetual alertness after years of
soldiering registered the rapid footsteps behind him.

He turned, screwing up his eyes against the setting
sun, reaching instinctively for his pistol before remembering that it was empty. Warily he stared into the
shadows, trying to discern more of the fast-approaching
figure. A woman, he thought, relaxing as he made out
the flutter of her skirts and cloak. Some *Fräulein* in a
hurry to be home before dark. He was about to turn and
walk on when he heard her gasp and cry out as she
skided and fell on the ice.

Damnation! He swore beneath his breath as he began
to stride towards the patch of dense shadow where the
woman was lying. There was no one else around to offer
assistance—he'd have to help. More time would be lost.
Supposing Angèle left for England before he found her?

He didn't even know the name of her real father, and he'd have no way of tracing her. . .no way of knowing if she was safe. . .

A shaft of yellow light suddenly arrowed out into the shadows as someone placed a lighted lantern in their downstairs window, illuminating the woman who was struggling to get to her feet, hampered by her skirts.

'*Sacrebleu*!' Disbelief and anxiety made his voice rough as he broke into a run. A moment later Tristan was scooping her up angrily, glaring into her shining face.

'Can't you stay out of trouble for a moment? What the hell are you doing, racketing about the streets alone?' he growled, holding Angèle so tightly that she could scarcely breathe. 'Have you no sense? Are you hurt?'

'No. . .you can put me down,' she said breathlessly, her joy too great to be touched by his anger. 'I was looking. . .for you. . .'

'For me?' He exhaled a long, ragged breath as he met her iridescent eyes; perhaps it was not too late, perhaps. . . But he had to be sure; he had made a fool of himself over Blanche, and it was a mistake he had no intention of repeating.

'I said you can put me down,' she repeated.

Reluctantly he set her down on her feet, but his hands stayed on her waist of their own accord.

'Why?' he asked tightly. 'Why were you looking for me?'

'Because. . .' she lifted her eyes to his and found them veiled and unreadable in the half-light, and the words she so wanted to say stuck in her throat as all her doubts rushed back into her mind '. . .I thought you might need help. . .'

'So, despite what I said to you at Kovno, you're still set on being my guardian angel.' He shook his head. He was too tired to fight this any more. A part of him had conceded defeat the moment he had felt her yield to his kiss at the lodge. Not for the first time he wondered whom he had really been trying to protect when he had tried to make her go back at the Berezina—her or himself? All he knew was that her vulnerable eyes had cut through his carefully built defences like a rapier through silk. 'Tell me, Angèle Kerenski,' he sighed, mocking his own foolishness in believing he could simply let her walk away, 'are you going to haunt me for the rest of my life? I am beginning to fear I'll never be rid of you. Cossacks, cannons and the cold seem to have no effect. . .'

The blood drained from her face and the light left her eyes. The sergeant had been wrong. She had been clutching at straws, inventing every reason except the real one for why he had sent her away so cruelly at Kovno. *He did not want her.* But then why was he still holding her. . .looking at her like that? Suddenly the strain of the last few days finally proved too much. She felt heavy, lead-limbed, defeated, incapable of feeling anything except the desire to curl up in a dark corner and not to see, hear or think of him again.

'You will be rid of me soon enough,' she replied, wondering at the flat coolness of her voice when her heart was breaking into pieces. 'I will be leaving for England in a matter of days.'

'England!' The word exploded from his mouth like an oath and his hands clenched on her waist as if he wanted to shake her. 'Then why were you wandering about the streets looking for me? To wish me farewell?'

'Yes. . .and to. . .return your horse,' she lied desperately as his eyes seared across her face. She would rather die now than let him know the real reason.

'My horse? I see.' The taut lines of his face relaxed suddenly, and there was an unmistakable bubble of laughter in his voice that destroyed what was left of her pride.

'Yes,' she answered woodenly. 'I believe this is yours

as well.' She fumbled with her locket and held out the little enamelled medallion he had given her at Kovno.

He took it, the corners of his mouth lifting as he felt her fingers tremble as they touched his. 'That is all you have to say?'

'All but goodbye!' she said, jerking free of his grasp and turning away while she still had a fragment of pride left.

'Angèle!'

The way he said her name sliced across her raw nerves like a knout, halting her as surely as if he had caught hold of her.

'Don't you know yet when I am teasing you?'

'Teasing!' She wheeled back to face him, her emotions swinging from despair to fury as she saw the expression on his face. He had broken her heart and he was laughing at her! 'How could you?'

'You know me.' He shrugged. '"I make myself laugh at everything, for fear of having to weep."'

'You weep!' She tried to sound scathing. But there was something in his face that made her heart turn over with love for him. And she could not bear it. Why was he doing this to her? Why did he have to stop her from hating him? 'Oh! I could kill you, Beaumaris!' The words tore from her choked throat as she flew at him, hitting out with her clenched fists. 'I could kill you!'

'I seem to remember you saying something of the sort before. . .' The shadow had left his face and he was laughing, apparently oblivious to the blows she was raining on his chest. 'Before I kissed you. . .then you seemed to forget. . .'

'Oh!' she gasped, his unfairness fuelling her rage and making her turquoise eyes blaze. 'I mean it! You stand there, quoting Beaumarchais. . .laughing. . .at me. . .' Her voice broke suddenly as she began to cry, not prettily, but in great racking sobs that shook her whole body. 'Don't you understand? The marshal. . .he told. . .me about the Cossacks. . .he said you. . .were . . .dead. . .'

'Dead! My poor angel. . .' His laughter faded to a wry smile as he captured her flailing hands and drew her into his arms. 'Are you saying all these tears are for me? An irredeemable Bonapartist?'

She didn't answer, bowing her head so her hair fell forward, shielding her from the mockery that she dreaded seeing in his eyes.

'Angèle?' With infinite gentleness he smoothed the silky strands of gold hair away from her tear-wet face and looked at her searchingly.

'No! Yes. . .' She sobbed helplessly, burying her head on his chest. 'I. . .can't help it. . . I didn't want to. . . but. . . I love you. . .'

'I know, fool.' He laughed huskily as he wrapped her tighter in his arms and touched his lips to the crown of her bright head. 'I know. . .'

CHAPTER ELEVEN

'So am I forgiven after all?' Tristan asked softly some time later when Angèle's sobs had subsided into the occasional smothered hiccup.

'For what?'

'For lying to you as well as myself?'

She lifted her head from his chest and looked at him warily. 'What you said about your career. . .have I really been such an embarrassment to you?'

Her voice quivered as her blue-green eyes searched his face anxiously, and he felt her tense and shrink from him as if she half expected a blow.

'Of course not!' he breathed, his eyes dark with self-contempt as he scanned her too thin, too vulnerable face and saw the doubt in her tear-bright eyes. 'I lied to you because I wanted you out of Kovno before it was too late, and I knew you'd never go if I told you the truth. . .'

'So you do not hate me for being a royalist?'

Again there was a shake in her voice that twisted his insides into a knot.

'I could never hate you,' he said thickly, swearing to himself that he would never hurt her again. 'If you were Lucqueville's daughter it would not make a *sous* of difference to the way I feel about you. . .'

'It would not?' Her eyes lit with relief. 'You see, I——' She began to tell him, but he silenced her with a finger against her lips and a moment later it did not seem important.

'And what of you? Would a royalist deign to live in Paris with a captain of Bonaparte's guard?'

His tone was light but knife-edged, and for a moment

she thought he was mocking her again. Then she became aware of his unnatural stillness and the wariness in his charcoal-dark eyes as he scanned her face.

She had too much faith in his sense of honour for her to think he meant anything but marriage. Sheer, over-whelming joy held her speechless. He wanted to marry her and that meant he must love her. She wanted to shout it aloud from the roof-tops.

'Yes, I suppose it is a ridiculous idea,' he said harshly after a glance at her stunned face. 'I should not have asked you. No doubt you realise this campaign is just a beginning not an end to war. I can offer you nothing except more separations and uncertainty, whereas in England I am sure your father will find you a far more suitable match——'

'Stop!' she exploded, grabbing his shoulders and shaking him. 'Don't you dare say another word! Do you think I would choose security above you?'

He stared down into her upturned, half-angry half-glowing face. Slowly the tight lines around his eyes and his mouth smoothed out. She loved him more than herself—hadn't she already shown that when she had lied to let him go with Ney?

'I'm sorry,' he said softly as he held her sparkling gaze. 'I had forgotten that you are ruled by your heart, not your head. . .'

'I doubt I will change,' she warned him.

'I'll never forgive you if you do. I love you. . .just the way you are. . .'

'You do?' she breathed in joyous disbelief.

'Perhaps not just,' he added thickly with a lop-sided grin as his eyes dropped from her face to her second-hand raiments. 'Tears are very gratifying, but you might have run to sackcloth and a few ashes, my love—it would have been a distinct improvement on that gown. On balance I think I preferred you as a Cossack.'

'I see that now I have agreed to go to Paris you have

reverted to insulting me again,' she countered with a
watery smile, understanding with sudden clarity that his
sardonic humour was a disguise he used when he felt
things most deeply.

'What do you expect from an unprincipled
Bonapartist?' he said with a provocative lift of his brows.
'That gown does have one saving grace, though.'

'What?' she asked warily, warned by the glint in his
eyes as they skimmed down from her face again and
came to rest on the *décolleté* neckline of the mustard
gown.

'It seems to be falling off you without any assistance.'

'Oh!' Instinctively she dropped her hands from his
shoulders and clutched at the gaping neckline of the
dress. Even at the best of times her curves had never
matched those of its former owner.

Laughing, he wrapped his arms around her and bent
his head to hers. He tasted of wine and smoke, and his
beard rasped against her skin, but the knowledge that he
loved her gave this kiss a sweetness all of its own, and
she never wanted it to stop.

'Since the captain is still asleep, I thought you might like
to take supper in your room,' Danielle announced two
days later as she came bustling into Angèle's room with
a tray covered with a linen cloth, which she put down on
a small table beside the fire. 'You still look tired yourself,
mademoiselle.'

'Yes. . .' Angèle agreed dreamily, staring out across
the courtyard to where a lantern shone in the tiny
window of the apple loft, where the landlord had put a
pallet for Tristan. 'Do you think we should wake the
captain? He has slept the clock round again and he has
not eaten since Frau Hesse took food to him in bed
yesterday.'

'No.' Danielle shook her head emphatically. 'He
will. . . I think you should let him sleep.'

'Yes, you're probably right,' Angèle said, remembering how, within minutes of finishing his meal when they had returned to the inn together two nights ago, Tristan had simply keeled over into the deep, deep sleep of exhaustion. 'What about you?' she asked, lifting the linen cloth that covered the tray. 'There is ample here for two. . .will you stay and eat with me?'

'I should like to, but. . .' Danielle suddenly looked embarrassed.

'Etienne is waiting for you?' Angèle guessed with a smile. 'Then I will not keep you. Run along. . .'

'If you're sure. . .' Danielle protested rather unconvincingly. 'That gown needs brushing out and there is your hair. . .and your bath. . .'

'I can manage,' Angèle said firmly. 'Now go. That's an order.'

'Thank you, *mademoiselle*!' Danielle smiled her thanks and almost ran from the room.

An hour later, after Frau Hesse the landlady had emptied the wooden bath-tub and removed it, Angèle changed into the new lace-trimmed nightgown and a rich blue shawl purchased that afternoon from a local seamstress.

She would eat in a little while, she thought, looking at the cold collation on the tray, after she had brushed out her hair. Wondering why Danielle had put two glasses on the tray, she poured some white wine from the pitcher into one of them and sat down in a well-upholstered wing chair beside the fire. She sipped her wine, toying idly with the fringes of the deep blue shawl with her other hand and luxuriating in the warmth of the fire. Heat, food and shelter were things that she would never take for granted again. She shut her eyes, and the scent of woodsmoke and the crackle of burning wood instantly filled her head with memories of Tristan. . .looking at her across a fire. . .at dawn. . .at dusk. . . Tristan walking, riding, holding her, kissing her. . .

A tap at the door jolted her out of her reverie.

'Come in, Danielle,' she called out without opening her eyes.

Tristan opened the door and then came to a halt, his hand still on the iron latch. The room was in darkness except for where she sat in a pool of soft yellow and amber light given off by a pair of candles on a side-table and the flickering log fire. His breath caught in his throat as he looked at her. Dressed in the white lace-trimmed gown, she looked utterly feminine and fragile. Her head was tilted back against the chair and her long lashes lay on her cheeks. Her hair was drawn up and back from her face, accentuating the upward slant of her cheek-bones. What was it the sergeant had said the men called her? The Captain's Angel. . . At this moment she looked as near to one as he could imagine. . .and then he smiled at the incongruity of the comparison as he remembered her in her Cossack garb, handling a pistol as deftly as a practised duellist and wading defiantly through the snow after rescuing Sous-Lieutenant Bourdon. . . She was like no other woman he had known, and in that moment he knew he would never want any other.

'Angèle. . .' He said her name gently.

'Tristan!' Her eyes flew open and wine splashed from her glass as she came to her feet and clutched at the edges of her shawl with her free hand. Her whole body jolted in shock at seeing him so unexpectedly. She had not been ready or prepared and she found herself staring at him helplessly. Against the reality her memories were pallid imitations. Clad in a robe of heavy black velvet and sable, he seemed taller, stronger, darker, more overtly sensual. Her skin prickled from head to toe as her eyes were drawn inexorably down from his freshly shaven face to the paler V of his chest with its sprinkling of crisp black hairs. And then lower to where the robe was fastened at the waist by a single heavy silver clasp.

'Danielle said you were still sleeping.' She found

herself babbling as her mind refused to focus on anything except his physical presence. 'That is why I didn't go down to supper——'

'It was a conspiracy. I enlisted her help to get past Frau Hesse,' he cut in softly. 'I am tired of sharing you with half the army. I want to be alone with you.'

'Danielle knew you were coming!'

'Why do you think there are two wine glasses on the tray?'

'But. . .but whatever will she think?'

'That we are lovers, of course.'

Lovers. Her heart thudded into a crazy gallop. He said it so easily, so confidently, while the word had sent her into a whirlpool of anticipation and panic.

'Now can I come in?' he asked with the slightest questioning lift of his brows.

'Yes,' she answered instantly, knowing that this had been inevitable since they had first met. Society's conventions had ceased to matter to her in the last three weeks. She loved him and he her, and they were alive, when so many had died; nothing else was important. No one would ever convince her that loving him was a sin, or something to be ashamed of. . .and yet as he stepped into the room she felt suddenly shy of him and dropped her eyes to the floor. Out on the wind-swept steppe they had both been fugitives, equals. But now she was overwhelmingly aware of the gulf between them in experience and sophistication; supposing she disappointed him. . .?

'If you'd rather wait. . .until we know each other a little better. . .' he said, halting as he sensed her uncertainty. 'I'll understand. Perhaps I had better go?'

'No. Don't,' she stammered as a rush of love for him for understanding swept over her. 'We know far more of each other than if we had met twenty times in a drawing-room; couples go to the altar knowing far less of each other than we do. I want to be with you tonight. . .'

'Honest as ever. . .' He laughed a little shakily as he
closed the door and slid the bolts home. 'Are you always
so shameless, Angèle Kerenski?'

'No.' She lifted her head; the way he was looking at
her made her breathing quick and shallow, but she
managed to answer in an almost steady voice. 'It must
be the company I am keeping. Are you in the habit of
visiting ladies' bedchambers in your dressing robe?'

'No.' He grinned as he saw the multitude of questions
in her eyes that nothing would induce her to ask. 'You'll
have to excuse my dress. It was given to our host's father
in lieu of payment by some impecunious Prussian noble-
man. It was all he had that would fit me.'

'All. . .' She took a step back and almost stumbled as
the edge of the chair caught the backs of her knees. Her
azure shawl slithered unnoticed from her shoulders as
she stared at him. So he was as naked beneath his robe
as she was beneath her thin white muslin.

'You have seen me in less,' he reminded her, halting
inches away and removing the dangerously tilting wine
glass from her nerveless fingers. He put it down on a
side-table and smiled wickedly as he reached out and
cupped her pale face between his weathered hands,
forcing her to meet his gaze. 'As I have you. . .though
not for far too long.' He bent his head and stole a swift,
light kiss before she could answer.

'That was different.' She blushed as he lifted his head
and smiled at her.

'Purely medicinal?' he teased. His eyes sparkled devilishly. 'If I said I was in danger of a severe relapse, would
you come to bed with me?'

'Bed?' Her mouth dried as her eyes went to the
intimidating carved and painted bed with its pristine
starched white covers, precisely placed pillows and cru-
cifix hung above. It looked daunting, formal. A bed for
the respectably married. 'I can't. . .'

'Because of what André did?' he asked, frowning

suddenly as his fingers feathered over the bruises on her cheekbone and jaw. 'I would never hurt you, Angèle. . . I swear it.'

'I know. It's not you.' She swallowed hard. 'It's the bed. It looks so. . .so disapproving.'

'Is that it?' His voice cracked with relief as he glanced towards the bed. 'Now you come to mention it, it does have an air of Frau Hesse about it. Wait there; don't move.'

She watched him in bewilderment as he swept an armful of the white feather quilts and pillows from the bed and spread them on the floor in front of the fire and extinguished the candles.

'No Cossacks or wolves, I'm pleased to say, but is snow and firelight more to your liking?' he asked, the corners of his mouth tilting upwards in a grin that melted her bones as he straightened and held his hands out to her.

'Yes,' she whispered shakily. Instinct told her that this would bind her to him forever, that there could be no going back from this, no forgetting. If she let him love her now, this more than any marriage vow would make her his for the rest of her life. . .

'Then come here.' He held his hands out to her.

Slowly she put her hands into his and let him pull her gently into the warm pool of firelight. Very carefully, without letting their bodies touch, he kissed her. First her lips, then her bruised cheek, her eyelids, her throat, the hollow at the base of her slender neck. Light soft kisses that kindled a dull, unnamed ache inside her that held her motionless even when his hands released hers and lifted to her hair.

There was the noise of the metal pins dropping on the hearth, a tug as the heavy coil snaked down her back. Out of habit she tilted her head back and shook it to free the shining waves.

A rasping breath left his throat and his hands buried

themselves in the scented silky mass, cupping her face and lifting it to his. His kiss was deeper, more urgent this time, intensifying the heavy, swelling ache inside her to touch, to be touched. Yet she recoiled instinctively as his fingers brushed the rising slope of her breasts and untied the ribbon that held the gathered neckline of her nightgown in place.

He lifted his head and looked down into her vulnerable face questioningly.

'If you want me to stop. . .'

'No. . .it's just I haven't. . .done this. . .felt like this before. . . I don't know. . .what to do. . .' Her fear and sense of inadequacy spilled from her lips as his eyes searched her face.

'I should think not!' he mocked tenderly, his eyes warm, more blue than grey as they captured and held her gaze. 'Trust me. Let me show you?'

'Yes,' she breathed as he caught her hands in his and placed them on his chest, inside the loose neck of his robe. His skin was hot beneath her palms and she could feel the thud of his heart beneath her palm, erratic as her own.

Touching him turned her knees to water, and she swayed. He steadied her, encircling her waist with his hands as he brought his lips back to her soft mouth, tasting, teasing until she forgot everything except the need to know more of him. Her hands began to move without restraint over his chest, delighting in the different textures of his skin and the crisp black hairs that arrowed down towards his flat stomach. Her body strained instinctively towards his. But his response was to hold her more tightly, an unbearable hair's breadth from contact as his mouth travelled downwards, nuzzling the loosened gown from her shoulders until it floated free to her waist, held up only by the sleeves.

Her fingers dug into his ribs, trying to pull him closer as his lips and tongue traced the most delicate of paths

across her naked breasts, circling but not touching their
erect pink tips.

'Patience. . .' he murmured, drawing her hands away
from him and easing the lace-trimmed sleeves of her
nightgown over her slender fingers and then letting it
drop to the floor. A moment later his robe joined it, and
for what seemed like forever they were both still, each
awed by the beauty of the other's body.

His leanness, his hardness both frightened and drew
her like a magnet. Imperceptibly she swayed. Their
bodies brushed, breast to chest, belly to belly, hip to
hip. Her body seemed to explode into fire and she felt all
restraint leave him as he gathered her into his arms and
plundered her eager mouth with his tongue, mimicking
the greater intimacy their bodies were clamouring for as
they fell on to the billowy quilts in a tangle of limbs.

'I must have been mad to think I could let you go,' he
murmured raggedly as his mouth moved from her swollen lips to the pink tips of her breasts in a series of
hungry kisses.

Her answer became an incoherent gasp as his lips
closed on her nipple, taking her into a new realm of
sensation, filling her with a desperate, unfamiliar need.
Then she gasped in shock as his hand travelled downwards and found the most secret and intimate place of
all. She buried her hands in his thick raven-black hair,
clutching at him helplessly as everything else seemed to
dissolve in a haze of pleasure.

'Please. . .' she moaned aloud, without being sure of
what she was begging him for, to stop this sweet,
torturous pleasure, or to ease the unbearable longing in
her body. But he was merciless, continuing the devastating, intimate caress until she juddered uncontrollably
beneath him. Then at last he moved over her, lifted her
hips and made her completely his.

Angèle cried out as he slid into her. Not from pain,
but from surprise that the pleasure could increase still

more. He stilled as he gazed down at her flushed face
and saw the wonder in her eyes. Lovingly he kissed her
soft mouth and began to move. Slowly at first, then
faster as he felt her hands rake and caress his arms, his
shoulders, his back, and she gave herself to him without
fear or restraint.

Afterwards when they had recovered their energies they
picnicked on cheese, cold meats and the wine in the
warm glow of the fire.

'Tell me,' Tristan said lazily as his eyes drifted over
her utterly feminine body, 'how did you get to be such a
good shot with a pistol?'

'Practice,' she replied, rolling on to her stomach and
resting her pointed chin in her cupped hands as she
looked at him. 'I was thirteen when my stepfather taught
me how to use a pistol. I had a natural eye, and he
praised me. It was the first and only word of praise I'd
ever had from him. I was young enough to still crave his
approval, so I practised for hours every day. . .there was
little enough else to do at the dacha. I was black and
blue for months,' she laughed as she remembered. 'The
recoil used to knock me off my feet more often than
not. . .and my wrists used to ache so much that I cried. . .'

'And was he pleased with you?' Tristan asked, his
heart twisting as a vivid picture of her as a girl wrestling
with a too heavy pistol filled his mind. He found himself
angry with the man who had so starved her of love that
she had been driven to such lengths to win his attention,
his approval.

'I don't know. He never said after that first time.'

'But you kept practising,' he said quietly, his eyes
grey and soft as mist as they met hers.

'Yes,' she admitted with a wry smile, turning back on
her side and breaking away from his gaze. 'I suppose I
could never quite give up hope. . .stubbornness is one
of my failings.'

'And one of your strengths,' he replied with a grin. 'After what I said to you at Kovno, any sensible female would have fled to England without a backward glance.' Then his expression sobered. 'Are you sure you will not regret coming to Paris with me now? I know how you feel about the Emperor. . .'

'I have changed my mind about Bon. . .the Emperor,' she began, picking the safer topic first, 'during these last few weeks; listening to the ordinary soldiers, I've heard how much they love and admire him. I can see now that he cannot be all bad. Is it true he saved France from bankruptcy and starvation when he became First Consul?'

'Yes,' Tristan said. 'He also salvaged the Church from the corruption that was destroying it, created a Code of Law that is envied everywhere, to say nothing of transforming an unfed, unpaid, unclothed army into the best in Europe. All that in a few years, in which we have been almost constantly at war. Think what the man could do if we have peace, Angèle. It is such a waste. . .'

'You think there will be another war soon?' Fear formed a hard lump in her chest as she looked at his long, lean body. Again she was reminded of the bronze of Mars. Except that he was not made of bronze, he was human. Vulnerable. As the scars that decorated his body from ankle to head showed all too clearly.

Involuntarily her hand went out to touch a silvery scar at the base of his throat. An inch the other way and he would have been dead.

'Where?' Her voice shook.

'Austerlitz.'

'And this one?' Her hand moved to the white scar across his ribs.

'Wagram.'

'This?'

'Marengo.' Sensing her growing panic, he caught her hand and drew her into his arms, reading her thoughts in her face. 'Yes, I will have to fight again, and probably soon.'

'But why? Surely Napoleon will not want another war now?'

'No. . .but the English will,' he replied wearily. 'I am afraid the failure of this campaign will be a beginning not an end to war. The English general Wellington is pushing us back to our frontier in Spain, and Austria, Prussia and Russia will fall into England's lap if they think we are no longer strong enough to resist them. France will be surrounded by her enemies. I cannot desert the Emperor and France now, not even for you, my love. . .'

'I am not asking you to——'

'I know. . .but I promise you, as soon as France's borders are secure I will leave the army.'

'Do you want to?' she asked in surprise.

'I've wanted to for years. . .but I didn't really realise just how much until I met you. Since then I have found myself thinking more and more of my father's vineyards in Provence, and how much I'd like simply to wake up every morning beside you, grow grapes, make wine and watch our children turn brown playing in the sun. . .'

'Children. . .' Her eyes widened at the thought and she knew an instant later that she wanted his children almost as badly as she wanted him.

'It could be a little late if you don't like the idea,' he laughed, brushing his fingers over her flat stomach.

'I love the idea.' She smiled into his eyes as she wriggled closer to him. 'Shall we practise?'

CHAPTER TWELVE

Two days later Angèle ran down the stairs of the inn. It was only an hour or two since she had last seen Tristan—he had left her room at dawn for her reputation's sake—but already she longed to see him again.

The public room was crowded, but she saw only one tall figure, leaning against the mantel, clad in his battered but freshly washed uniform. He was deep in conversation with Etienne and a major of the Chasseurs, but he turned and smiled the moment she entered the room as if sensing her eyes on him.

However, for some reason her heart sank; there was something distant in his eyes, something that he had put on with the uniform. For the last two days and nights he had been wholly hers. This morning she had to share him with Napoleon Bonaparte again, and she knew as he walked towards her that she was not going to like what he had to say.

'What is it?' she asked, already half guessing the answer as she heard the major call impatiently for his breakfast from the other side of the room.

'I have to leave for Paris within the hour.'

'I', not 'we', she noticed. Her heart plummeted. 'Why?' she asked leadenly.

'There has been an attempted *coup*. The Emperor needs loyal men around him,' he answered flatly. 'I'm sorry. . .'

'Can't I come with you?' she responded instinctively, feeling a physical jolt at the thought of being parted from him.

'No,' he said gently. 'The major over there has offered

Etienne and me a place in his sleigh, which has fresh horses. We will be travelling night and day——'

'That would be nothing new.'

He sighed and smiled at her tenderly. 'Angèle, we are not in the wilds of Russia now. We have to conform to society's normal rules of behaviour again. Half the officers who shared coffee with you around a camp-fire at the Berezina would tell their wives in Paris to cut you dead if you travelled with me in such a fashion across Europe. So don't ask me to expose you to such slights.'

'And what of last night and the night before? Was that conforming to society's standards?' she said mutinously.

His brows rose, but his eyes were soft as he touched her cheek with his fingers.

'I did warn you that life with a soldier would be like this,' he said quietly.

'I know and I'm sorry,' she apologised, turning her cheek into his palm and catching his hand in hers, not caring who saw them. 'I just didn't think the separations would begin so soon. . .'

'Do you think leaving you is any easier for me?'

'No,' she admitted with a half-smile as she saw the way he was looking at her.

'Good. Now listen to me,' he said, leading her to a table and pulling out a chair. 'You, Danielle and the sergeant can follow at a more civilised pace, and by the time you get to Paris everything should be. . .calm again.'

'This *coup*—is that why Napoleon left the army at Smorgoni to return to Paris in such haste?'

'Yes.'

'I did not think it was cowardice,' she said half to herself.

'No,' he said a little defensively. 'That is one allegation even the Bourbons dare not level at him.'

'I am glad the *coup* was not successful,' she said impulsively.

'I almost think you mean that,' he said, regarding her intently.

'I do.'

'You're beginning to sound like one of those dreadful revolutionaries.' He smiled at her. 'What would your mother say if she could hear you now?'

'That I had lost my head along with my heart.'

'Just as well; you have to be mad to love a soldier.' He grinned at her.

'Totally,' she agreed. 'But it is time you stopped talking and ordered some breakfast; your major is looking impatient.'

'This must be it, Danielle,' Angèle said, hanging out of the window of the *diligence* as they turned into a quiet street of elegant white houses with pillared porticoes, lined with cherry trees, bare now, but she could imagine what they would look like in the spring. Both the houses and the street were grander than she had been expecting. Without meaning to, she searched the street for a familiar figure. But that was silly; he was not expecting her for another day yet, and he was not to know that her patience had given out and they had travelled through the previous night.

'He must have another income,' Danielle said, shrewdly eyeing up the houses out of the other window. 'A captain's pay would never run to this. What is his background?'

'I understood his family have a small vineyard in Provence,' Angèle said slowly, realising suddenly that she only knew the barest details of his family. He had made his father sound like a simple grape-grower. . .but his speech, his manners, his bearing all spoke of a gentleman's upbringing. She frowned, remembering a remark from a lifetime ago at the lodge: 'I am flattered you think me your equal. . . I am simply a citizen of France, no better, no worse than any other.' But not quite like any other, she thought drily as the coachman brought the vehicle to halt outside one of the gleaming white houses with an impressive wrought-iron gate.

'This cannot be the right place,' she said to Danielle, and yet at the same time knew in the pit of her stomach that it was. Fishing in her valise, she brought out a crumpled letter, one of the many Tristan had left for her at inns along the route. It was precise and quite clear.

> Go to my house, 5, rue de la Lune. Madame Jeanne my housekeeper will be expecting you.

'There is another rue de la Lune,' Danielle said thoughtfully, 'but that is on the other side of the Seine. Shall I go and enquire, *mademoiselle*?'

'No. I'll go.'

A minute later Angèle was standing trembling at the top of a flight of shallow marble steps, her hand lifted to the bell pull. The door was flung open before she rang.

'Darling! Oh. . .' The exquisitely pretty young woman who stood in the doorway recovered herself quickly and her hands fluttered back to her sides. 'My apologies, *mademoiselle*, I thought you were. . .someone else. As I am sure you must have guessed.'

'It is I who should apologise for disturbing you, *madame*,' Angèle said, quickly concealing her own disappointment that it was not Tristan who had opened the door so eagerly. 'I am afraid I must have mistaken the address of a friend; I was looking for Tris. . .Captain Beaumaris.'

The woman's eyes widened and she looked at Angèle properly for the first time, taking in her oval face, now free of bruises, her bright hair, and her tall, slim figure.

'You are Mademoiselle Kerenski?' For a moment, no more, the girlish lisp vanished and her face set, and for the first time Angèle realised that she was probably thirty-something rather than the twenty she had first judged her from the frothy pink gown.

'Yes,' Angèle answered, wondering how the woman knew her name and who she was.

'We were expecting you tomorrow at the earliest.' The charming smile returned at full force. 'Madame Jeanne told me Tristan was expecting a little refugee from Russia.'

Angèle paled. A refugee. She could not believe Tristan would have described her so derisively. Be calm, she told herself, there will be an explanation for this. But in the base of her stomach a creeping doubt began to grow, numbing her heart and mind. Tristan. She used his name so familiarly.

'My maid. . .' she began, gesturing towards the hired carriage, deciding that she needed the reassurance of Danielle's common sense.

'Oh, I'll send Madame Jeanne to fetch her in a moment,' the woman said airily. 'Now do come in— Tristan would never forgive me if I kept you standing on the step in this cold wind.'

She took Angèle's arm and propelled her into the house. Beside her petite, doll-like form, Anglèle felt clumsy and gawky. And she was acutely conscious of the difference between the art of the *couturière* who had produced the woman's rustling confection of ribbed silk and the more homely skills of the Prussian seamstress who had produced her own eminently sensible blue wool and plain black travelling cloak.

A young maid came scurrying into the marble-floored hall and skidded to a startled halt as she looked at Angèle.

'Where have you been?' Angèle's companion snapped. 'Isn't it your duty to answer the door?'

'But *madame*, you said you wanted to surprise the——' the girl began uncertainly.

'Don't be insolent!' The woman's voice was as sharp as a whiplash. 'Take Mademoiselle Kerenski's cloak and bring some refreshments to the yellow salon. And be quick about it or you will find yourself out of work.'

Set-faced, the girl did as she was asked without meeting Angèle's eyes when she smiled and thanked her for taking her cloak.

'Tristan is far too lenient with his servants,' the woman said as the girl scurried away. 'They do need a firm hand, don't you think?'

'I have always found that kindness and respect wins the same in return.' Angèle found her voice and the courage to say what she thought. But her mind was spinning in confusion. This woman spoke as if she were mistress of this house. But that could not be. . .

'How very egalitarian.' Her hostess gave a tinkling laugh, somehow making the last word an insult.

But before Angèle could respond she found herself seated on a golden brocade sofa in a large salon hung with sunny yellow silk and carpeted with soft blue rugs. And for a second or two she forgot her anxieties as her eyes took in the paintings that adorned the walls. Her mother had often spoken longingly about the paintings and houses of the French aristocracy, but her descriptions had not prepared Angèle for the reality. She had never seen pictures like these, paintings that were full of colour, texture and movement.

'Fragonard, David, Gainsborough. Wonderful, aren't they?' her companion said, following her awed gaze. 'Tristan is quite a connoisseur, but of course you would know that. . .'

'No, I didn't,' Angèle admitted. In Prussia he had talked about the future, the places he wanted to show her in Paris. But he had not talked much about himself. There was so much she did not know about him, including who and what this woman was. There will be a perfectly sensible explanation, she told herself firmly. He loves you. He told you a dozen times that night at the inn, and in any number of letters since. But she could not dispel her growing sense of unease and inferiority as she looked at the kittenish woman sitting opposite. *Kittenish*. 'Blanche? I suppose "kittenish" would be the best description.' As if in a nightmare she heard Tristan's voice inside her head. Her heart turned to ice and she could only stare helplessly as the woman went on.

'I am so sorry Tristan is not at home to welcome you. He has been on duty at the Tuileries night and day this last week. He does not even know I am here yet. . . I thought I would surprise him. . .' She laughed and fluttered her long brown lashes. 'You know how Tristan adores surprises. . .' Then her little hand, heavy with an assortment of rings, flew to her mouth. 'I am so sorry I have not introduced myself; I am——'

'Blanche,' Angèle said flatly, hardly realising she had spoken aloud.

'Tristan told you. . .about me?' There was a sudden wariness in the pale, almond-shaped eyes.

'Very little.' Angèle managed a smile, trying to fight off panic. Tristan did not know Blanche was here. She had said so herself. But if everything had been over between them years ago, what was she doing here, moving in as if the house were her home? And there was no doubt that she was staking her claim to Tristan very clearly. 'Just that you had been. . .close. . .a very long time ago,' she added more firmly. Trisan had said it was over, and she believed him. She had to. The alternative was too awful to contemplate.

Blanche's smiling mouth set, revealing little lines at the corners.

'Is that what he told you?'

'He was quite clear,' Angèle replied with a confidence that she was far from feeling.

'My dear,' Blanche purred, 'when it comes to. . . getting what they want, men will say anything.'

'Tristan is not like that,' Angèle returned desperately,

quelling the thought that he had lied to her before about Blanche.

'*All* men are like that. You really are an innocent, aren't you?' Blanche smiled as her eggshell-blue eyes drifted derisively from Angèle's slightly untidy chignon to the travel-stained hem of her gown. 'No doubt you were a novelty in the wilds of Russia, but how long do you think you can hold his interest in Paris. . .a month. . .six weeks?'

'That is none of your concern!' Angèle answered furiously. 'We are going to be——'

She stopped, not realising how much she was revealing to the more experienced woman. Tristan had never actually mentioned the word marriage. She had simply assumed it was understood between them. It had not crossed her mind that he would offer her anything less.

As Blanche watched her expressive face, her smile widened and she adroitly changed her attack.

'I wonder where the girl has got to with the refreshments! I should have thought she would have been bursting to see you. We never know what Tristan will bring home next. Do you know, he brought a stray kitten all the way back from Italy, in Austria he rescued the ugliest hound you have ever seen when its master was killed, and now it seems he has taken to acquiring penniless Russian orphans.' Again there was that tinkling laugh.

Such venom, so prettily wrapped. Angèle took a deep breath, her confusion turning to anger.

'You are mistaken. I am not an orphan,' she replied, trying to keep the anger out of her voice. 'My mother is dead, but my father, the *Duc*, is alive and well in England.'

'You father is a *Duc*?' Blanche's eyebrows rose.

'Yes.' Angèle refused to be drawn further. There had not been time to tell Tristan her father's identity in Prussia, and instinct told her that Blanche was the last person she would want to confront him with the information that she was the Duc de Lucqueville's daughter.

'Then I suppose you'll be leaving for England very soon. What a pity. . .' Blanche sighed, taking Angèle off guard again. 'Half the neighbourhood are agog to hear about your journey, across the steppe with the French army. It sounds so romantic and exciting. But Madame Jeanne tells me Tristan is such a killjoy, mention Russia and he says he never wants to think about the place again.'

'Romantic and exciting are not the words anyone who had been on the retreat would use,' Angèle answered, trying not to sound shaken. Surely there were some things about Russia he wished to remember? 'And I have no immediate plans to go to England.'

'Oh. . . I had the impression from one of Tristan's comrades who called this morning that he had said. . . but obviously I was mistaken.'

'Obviously,' Angèle grated.

'Tell me, why did you think this was the wrong house?' Again Blanche changed her attack.

'It was. . .grander than I had expected.'

'You are not the first to be misled by Tristan's—what shall I call it?—egalitarianism.' Blanche's mouth curled disdainfully again. 'He can be so deceptive. It is so naughty of him. You know, he refuses to use his title or even the "de" before Beaumaris. His father was almost as bad, pampering his peasants even before the revolution. He and Tristan were forever quoting something about all men being born equal that had been written by some American, Franklin or some such name.'

'Title?' Angèle said blankly. Her mind was reeling. Surely Tristan could never have really loved this social butterfly, whose views were so different from his own.

'Surely you know his father was the Comte de Cavillon? Tristan inherited a quarter of Provence's finest vineyards.'

'I. . .I had forgotten,' she lied desperately, feeling an utter fool.

'Forgotten?' The older woman laughed. 'Really! Did he tell you nothing of his family? He must have at least mentioned his brother Henri——'

'No. I did not know he had a brother,' Angèle said thickly. There was a lump rising in her throat that threatened to choke her. She needed to see Tristan, to talk to him, for him to explain all of this to her.

'I see.' Blanche's finely plucked brows rose.

At that moment a dark-haired boy of about five years burst into the room. 'I saw the carriage. Is it our luggage? Have my soldiers arrived?'

'*Non, chéri.*' Blanche visibly shrank from the small, sticky hands that clutched at her skirts. 'Now say hello to our guest and then run along back to your nurse; you know I am busy in the mornings.'

'*Oui, Maman.*' The child's shoulders slumped, but he turned obediently to make his bow to Angèle. '*Bonjour, mademoiselle.*'

'*Bonjour.*' Somehow Angèle forced the word from her lips, and a smile to her mouth. She felt as if the breath had been squeezed from her lungs. He could only be Tristan's son. Black hair, silver eyes, that wide mouth, so easily identifiable even at this age. And if he was Tristan's son then. . . Her mind froze, refusing to go further.

'My son, Lucien de Beaumaris,' Blanche said, watching the blood drain from Angèle's face with a smile. 'He is so like his father. . .'

'You are Tristan's wife. . .that is his son?' The questions tumbled from Angèle's lips in a voice that she scarcely recognised as her own.

Blanche leant back against the sofa cushions and sighed wearily. 'You mean to say he didn't tell you?'

'No.' She was too hurt, too shocked to pretend even for her pride's sake. The realisation that he had lied to her made her feel physically sick. 'He said it was all over between you. . .'

'If it's any consolation, there is an element of truth in that,' Blanche conceded calmly. 'He ceased to love me long before we were wed—I was a little indiscreet with a brother officer. Tristan always was an idealist, and of course once they become disillusioned. . .' She shrugged and drew a finger across her throat. 'But I was carrying his child and, being Tristan, he did the *honourable* thing.'

Angèle stared at her, disgust momentarily over-shadowing her humiliation. 'You married him, knowing he did not love you?'

'Of course. Principles don't pay the bills, but a rich husband. . .' Blanche laughed unpleasantly. 'Don't look so shocked; I enjoy his money and give him freedom to enjoy his little "amusements" in return.'

'You don't care about his infidelity?' she asked, sickened to the stomach.

'Why should I?' Blanche was dismissive. 'They're no threat to me; he knows if asked for a divorce I'd never let him see his son again. So. . .' she smiled, more cat-like than ever '. . .don't raise your hopes too high, *mademoiselle*.'

'Etienne!'

Danielle's face lit up as she stepped out of the small inn in a fishing village near Bordeaux and found herself caught in an enormous hug.

'I did not think you would come.'

'I couldn't let you go without being sure that you will come back. You promise, Danielle?'

'Of course. As soon as Mademoiselle Angèle is settled and has a new maid. Her heart is breaking, Etienne. She scarcely eats or sleeps. I could not let her travel alone in this state. . .my father agreed with me. And you. . .you do understand.'

'Yes. But there is much else I don't,' Etienne said

gruffly. 'Like why she is leaving him if it makes her so unhappy.'

Danielle shrugged. 'Don't ask me. Since we went to Captain Beaumaris's house in Paris two weeks ago she has hardly mentioned his name, except to insist that I should not reveal her whereabouts to him.'

'She has been to his house! Why didn't you say so in your letter? He does not know she has been to Paris——'

'But I assumed she saw him there—she went in and when she came out she was crying. I thought they had argued. . .' She stopped. 'You mean the captain has not seen her?'

'No. All he got was a cold little note, apparently posted two days' journey away from Paris, saying she had mistaken her feelings of gratitude towards him for saving her from her cousin for something stronger. And that, realising her mistake, she had determined to go to England and he would not hear from her again. He's been striding about the Tuileries with a face and temper like thunder ever since. None of us has ever seen him like this before—he even put the sergeant on a charge for insolence.'

'It does not make sense.' Danielle frowned.

'Perhaps this might help—he asked me to deliver it,' Etienne said, taking a slender envelope out of his tunic.

'A letter for her!' Danielle's face lit up and then clouded. 'You did not tell him where she is? She made me promise a dozen times you would not——'

'Of course not,' Etienne said huffily.

'Thank you.' Danielle planted a kiss on his cheek. 'Now let's go and find her; perhaps this will make everything all right between them!'

'I wouldn't raise your hopes too high,' Etienne said doubtfully. 'You should have seen his face when he gave it to me.'

'Danielle?' Angèle called out as she stepped into the

public room of the inn. There were no sailors drinking at this time of day and the room was deserted. She was about to turn away and try outside when she noticed the scarlet pelisse and green cloak spread across the back of a chair. The blood left her head, leaving her momentarily dizzy and sick.

'Angèle?'

She spun to see Danielle and Etienne in the doorway behind her.

'Oh, it's you, Etienne,' she said stupidly. 'I thought. . . Oh, never mind what I thought, it's lovely to see you. Are you well? And the sergeant? I am sorry to take Danielle away from you like this, but she will insist. . .and it will not be for long, I promise you.'

She was talking too quickly but she could not stop herself. Etienne was looking at her pityingly and she could not bear it. He, the sergeant, Ney, all of them must have known he was married. What a fool they must have thought her.

Etienne exchanged a glance with Danielle before replying. 'We are all in perfect health, but what of you?'

'I am well, thank you.'

'You don't look it,' Etienne said, crossing the room and taking her hands. 'You're like ice. Sit down beside the fire while I find the landlord and get us some refreshment.'

'Yes, sit down, *mademoiselle*,' Danielle said, leading her to a settle. 'Etienne brought this for you; it is from the captain——'

'The captain?' She sank back on the settle, her face ivory-white against the russet of her gown as Danielle put the slim packet of paper into her hands. 'Then he can take it back unopened.'

'For heaven's sake, *mademoiselle*, open it!' Danielle's hazel eyes flashed with the first sign of impatience Angèle had ever seen in them. 'What harm can it do? Please. . .'

'I dare not,' Angèle said, bringing her eyes to

Danielle's and pleading silently with her to understand. 'You see, if he asked me to go back I am afraid that I would say yes. . .'

'*Mademoiselle*, you are not making sense!'

'It does not matter. It is over,' Angèle said flatly. 'I am sure Etienne will be able to explain. Please give him my apologies, I am not in the mood for conversation.'

'Did she read it?' Etienne asked when he returned.

'No.' Danielle shook her head, perplexed as ever. 'She said she dared not open it because if he asked her she would go back. . .and she said that you would be able to explain.'

'I wish I could.' Etienne groaned. 'If Beaumaris's temper doesn't improve soon I think I'll ask for a transfer.'

'There is nothing wrong with my temper. Where is she?'

Danielle and Etienne turned as one to see Tristan standing behind them

'Etienne!' Danielle groaned. 'You promised not to tell him——'

'He didn't,' Tristan snapped. 'I followed him without his knowledge. Now, where is she? I have to start back for Paris tonight, so I don't have much time.'

'You'd better tell him,' Etienne sighed.

'On the beach,' Danielle said unwillingly. 'Walking.'

'Thank you.' He tossed his plumed shako and sword belt into an empty chair, turned on his heel and strode out of the room, ducking his head to avoid the low lintel of the door.

The January wind wind was chill and tugged strands of Angèle's hair loose from its chignon as she sat on a low, flat rock and stared out over the choppy grey water, mesmerised by the constant movement of the waves as they broke, foaming and white on the shore, in never-ending succession. Since she had spent all her life inland,

the sea held a fascination for her that almost blotted out
her misery, but not quite. If she could have convinced
herself that Tristan had not loved her in the slightest, it
would have been easier. Then she could have hated him.
But she could not. She shut her eyes, knowing that if he
had met her at the door in Paris she would never have
walked away, not even if he had told her he was married.
She would have stayed, accepted anything to be near
him. That was why she had to leave for England while
she still had some pride and sanity left.

The crunch of footsteps on the shingle behind her
broke into her thoughts and she glanced sideways.

Her stomach lurched as her eyes focused on tasselled
and spurred boots, dusty from the road. Unwillingly she
let her gaze travel upwards over the new deep green wool
cloak, with its high gold-embroidered collar and to the
perfectly tailored uniform beneath that glinted with gold
thread and polished buttons. A major now, she thought
dully, noticing the new chevron on his sleeve. How had
she ever thought him anything but an aristocrat? she
wondered as she took in the familiar hawkish lines of his
face. Because love made you blind from the moment you
met him. . .she answered herself as he returned her
scrutiny with eyes that were colder than the winter sea.

'What do you want?' she said flatly. Somehow she had
known he would come, known he would find her.

'To hear what you said in that note from your lips. . .
damn it! Did you think I'd let you walk away like that?
For all I knew, you might be carrying my child!'

'Thankfully I am not.'

'Thankfully.' He gave a harsh laugh. 'I had not
realised you found it such a repugnant prospect.'

She was startled by the hurt in his eyes. He had a son.
She had not expected him still to care so much.

'Well, say it, then!' he rasped, breaking the seemingly
endless silence between them.

'Then you will go and leave me alone?'

'With pleasure.' He pulled the note she had written him out of his tunic and threw it into her lap. 'Here, just in case your memory needs refreshing. . .'

The wind caught the square of paper before her fingers closed on it, and sent it fluttering wildly across the beach like a winged bird. She kept her eyes fixed on it, not daring to look at him as she fought to control her emotions. Part of her wanted to rage at him for humiliating her, for not telling her that he had a wife and child. . .but perhaps he had tried to. What had he said in Russia? 'I cannot offer you a future', but she hadn't wanted to listen, any more than she wanted to leave him now.

'Well?' he said stonily.

'I said all there is to say in my letter.' She forced the words out, still staring at the scrap of paper that was now floating on the tide. 'What happened between us was a mistake——'

'And those nights in Prussia? Were they a *mistake* too?' he grated. 'Or is that how you express gratitude?'

'I think it would be better not to discuss that,' she answered tightly, shutting her eyes because she knew they would betray her.

'I don't agree!'

He lunged for her, dragging her into his arms and crushing her lips with his angry mouth.

Turning her head aside, she stood rigid and unmoving, though every inch of her body longed to melt against him, to be held, comforted. To have the tearing pain in her heart healed by his kisses.

Accepting defeat, he released her. 'At least look at me.'

The anguish in his voice almost broke her. Her lashes lifted and for a moment as their eyes met in mutual agony she came within a hair's breadth of throwing her arms around him, kissing him.

'For pity's sake,' he pleaded, 'don't go. I. . .need you,

Angèle, more than I've ever needed anyone. Until I met you my life was empty of everything except war and death——'

'Don't!' She didn't want to hear. She knew if he told her what she could guess only too well about his life with Blanche that she would never leave him. She would stay on any terms.

'If it's the army,' he went on raggedly, 'I'll resign. There is nothing I would not give up for you. . .'

Even your wife and child? she wanted to say. But she dared not, for fear he would say yes. He had lied to her about Blanche, but even in the darkest moments she knew he had not lied when he said he loved her. But how could she deprive a child of its father? And how long would it be before he began to hate her for making him choose? She shook her head, struggling to convince herself that she was making the right decision.

'Stay. . .please. . .' he breathed.

'I. . .can't. . .' The words crawled out of her mouth and she had to look away.

'Why not?'

Her only answer was to wrap her black cloak about her like a shield, shutting him out.

'Angèle. . .what can I do if you won't talk to me?' His voice cracked as he saw the slow, silent tears roll down her cheeks. 'Just tell me what happened!'

'Nothing,' she forced herself to reply. 'It was as you said in Russia. What happened between us was just physical attraction intensified by danger. I just came. . . to my senses. . .that is all.'

'You're lying. There is something else,' he said furiously. 'Tell me the truth!'

'Very well,' she invented wildly, knowing she had to make him go before her resolve broke. 'The truth is that, now I've time to think, I want to be on the winning side when the Bourbons are restored——'

'If!' he sneered.

'When! You only have to look at the new conscripts to see that Napoleon cannot perform miracles forever!' she flared back at him. 'And when the Bourbons come back I want the de la Rochère lands back—they were my mother's. And if I am associated with you——'

'Money!' He looked stunned as if she had struck him. Then he laughed harshly in a way that tore at her insides. 'The second oldest motive in the world. Do you know, it never occurred to me as far as you are concerned? Though heaven knows I of all people should have guessed. I thought. . .you were different. . . Oh, for God's sake, say something. . .don't just look at me like that.'

'There's nothing left to say,' she said ferociously. 'Now go; you have what you came for.'

'Do I?'

His bitterness burnt her like acid and Angèle could stand no more of it. Picking up her skirts, she began to run blindly along the shore, uncaring of the incoming waves that splashed over her shoes and soaked the hem of her skirt.

For a moment he stood and watched her retreating figure and took a pace after her. But then he stopped and, grim-faced, turned away. What the hell was he doing? Had he really been about to sacrifice his pride to buy her affections, to tell her that he had more money than she could ever spend, enough land to lose the de la Rochère estates five times over? His mouth curled bitterly; her cousin had been right about her after all: she sucked you dry, then left you like the burnt-out hulk at the end of the beach.

CHAPTER THIRTEEN

'OH, CHARLES. . .' Angèle twisted her beadwork reticule over and over in her hands as she sought for the right words. 'I am very honoured; you've been so kind since I came to England, but——'

'Your answer is no, you won't marry me.' The tall fair-haired man in an immaculately tailored grey coat sighed. 'I was afraid it would be. I've known for months really, but I kept hoping that I was wrong. Foolish of me, really. . .' He smiled wryly as he sat down in one of the library chairs beneath a portrait of a de Lucqueville in the dress of Louis XIV's reign, and stretched out his long legs. 'You see, I can't forget the first time I saw you. . .'

'At Lady Leadbetter's?' Angèle was puzzled.

'No, it was a February morning in the park. You cannot have been here long. It had snowed. You were standing beneath the trees by the river. It was only just light; everything was silver or black shadow, except for where the sun caught your hair. If it hadn't been for that I'd have run you down. . .'

'That was you?' she said, startled. 'The cavalry officer exercising the horse.'

'Yes.' He shook his head and a lock of corn-coloured hair fell across his forehead. 'The expression on your face when you turned and saw me—it only lasted for a second, but it took my breath away, not to mention my heart,' he added with studied carelessness. 'I was about to speak to you, but then you turned and ran into the trees as if I were the devil incarnate. . . It's always puzzled me, and I suppose I've always hoped you might look at me like that again. Do you know, I angled for invitations to every bash in town for a month after that, trying to find you?'

'Oh. . . I'm sorry. You see, I was thinking about the past. . .and for a moment I thought. . .'

'I was someone else,' he said quietly to save her embarrassment; he had guessed as much the previous night.

'Yes. If I have misled you. . .then I'm truly sorry, believe me.' Angèle was aghast at her own thoughtless-ness. She knew she should have seen this coming. But as the news of the war in Europe had become steadily worse for the French during the last few months her thoughts had been preoccupied with wondering if Tristan was alive or dead. A note from Danielle had reached her six months ago, telling her that she and Etienne were now married and that Tristan was in good health, but that was all.

'Don't worry. I do,' Charles Cavendish, Marquis of Stretton said without rancour, although his blue eyes were a little veiled as he did his best to hide his disappointment.

'I would not hurt you for the world,' Angèle said sincerely. 'If it were not for your kindness, I know I should have made a. . .*croissant* of myself on a hundred occasions since I have come to England.'

'A cake,' he corrected her with a grin that removed some of the lingering tension between them.

She grimaced. 'I don't think I will ever master the English language.'

'You do very well, and, besides, I wouldn't have missed that conversation at Lord Derwent's ball for a hundred pounds.'

'You could have stopped me from asking the Countess of Drinkwater if she liked the bit of muslin her husband had bought,' she said, colouring, 'I thought the Earl had purchased a scarf for his wife, not a. . .'

Charles laughed. 'I couldn't resist it, I am afraid. It

was done so innocently that no one could blame you. And that old trout the Countess deserved her come-uppance; she's been the terror of the circuit for years, and ruined more girls' confidence than I can count.'

'I am not surprised! I thought she would brain me with her fan before you appeared at my elbow and asked me to dance. . .'

'I'm quite sure you could have defended yourself, having seen you outshoot Moreton at that picnic in August.'

'Something else a young lady should not have done,' Angèle remembered ruefully. 'I must be a trial to you, Charles.'

'You could never be a trial to me,' he said softly, seeking her eyes.

Instinct told her that he was about to repeat his offer, and she hastily looked away. 'We can still be friends, can't we?' she said quickly before he could speak. 'I don't think I am brave enough to face the Countess at Almack's this evening without an ally. . .or am I being unfair in asking? I'll understand if you would rather we did not meet again. . .'

'I shall always be your friend,' he replied firmly. 'But I think it would be better if you did not go to Almack's this evening. I don't want to see you hurt.'

'What do you mean?'

'Last night I was at White's. It is all over town that you are the *Duc's* illegitimate daughter, not a distant relative, and, I am afraid, that you travelled incognito with a French cavalry officer during Boney's retreat across Russia.'

Angèle paled. Charles did not need to say any more. Eleven months in England had taught her enough of English society for her to know that such behaviour in an unmarried woman was completely beyond the pale. She would be ostracised.

'But my father is the only man in England who knows

all this. I felt it only fair to tell him before he took me into his house. He made me swear not to tell a soul. . . I don't understand. . .' Shock made her blurt her thoughts aloud.

'It is true, then?' Charles said quietly. 'Both tales?'

'Yes.' She could not and would not lie to Charles any more. She had hated the charade of pretending to be a long-lost cousin of the *Duc's*, and had often wished that she had never let him press her into moving into Mornington Square. She had never felt at home there. The *Duc* had been polite, but distant. And she had soon seen him for what he was. A weak, dissolute and selfish man, kept by his wife, who had guessed Angèle's true identity the moment she happened to stand beneath a portrait of her paternal grandmother. The *Duchesse* had scarcely spoken to her since and had encouraged her daughters to treat Angèle with disdain.

'I rather thought so.' Charles sighed. 'I remembered how you looked at that column of French prisoners we passed last month.'

She looked at his handsome worried face and felt a rush of affection for him.

'You knew all this and you came here this morning and offered for my hand? Wasn't that rather rash of you, Charles?' she said, striving to keep him from seeing the panic that was growing inside her. Her money was getting low and she could not possibly remain at Mornington Square now. But with her reputation smashed beyond repair she'd not even get a post as governess to the children of the most lowly country curate, let alone as a companion, on which she had been pinning her hopes. 'I might have accepted,' she added with an attempt at a laugh.

'I don't think it was in the least rash. On the contrary, it's the most sensible thing I've done in years,' he said with a seriousness she had never seen in him before. 'Take a risk and marry me, Angèle; no hostess will dare cut a future Marchioness of Stretton. Come to Almack's tonight as my fiancée and this rumour will be strangled at birth.'

'But it is not just a rumour.' She swallowed as she met his eyes. 'It is the truth, Charles. You can not want me for your wife, knowing that.'

'It makes no difference to me. I know you're no lightskirt. And you have just proved yourself utterly honest. And if you could forgive me my past, which is considerably more crowded with skeletons than yours, I could forget yours.'

'But your family——'

'My father would be delighted. He refused point-blank to listen to an ill word about you. As far as he is concerned, any girl who has as good a seat on a horse as you and can mix remedies to ease his gout is an eminently suitable addition to the family. I spoke to him this morning before coming here.'

For a moment she was tempted. It would be so easy and pleasant to be looked after and cosseted by this open-natured, golden-haired, craggy-faced Englishman who reminded her so painfully at times of Tristan. They were similar in so many ways, both cavalry officers, both superb horsemen and swordsmen. Both slim-hipped, broad-shouldered, with the athlete's grace of movement. But when Charles smiled at her her heart did not stop, nor her skin turn to fire when he touched her. And if Tristan were in the same room now she would not hesitate in her choice.

'No.' She shook her head. 'You deserve a woman who can give you her heart, Charles Cavendish.'

'And yours is already taken by this Frenchman?'

She nodded.

'Then why aren't you with him in France? I cannot believe the fellow was foolish enough not to want you.'

'Oh, he wanted me,' she said huskily, the various shocks of the morning suddenly too much for her. 'But

he. . .was married. I only found out when I reached
Paris. But I can't make myself stop loving him. . . I
know it's stupid, pointless. . .but it makes no
difference. . .'

It was the first time she had told anyone—not even
Danielle had known why she had fled from France—and
to her horror she found herself crying.

Charles muttered something incomprehensible and
very impolite as he came and sat beside her and offered
her a very large, immaculate white silk handkerchief.

'Here.' He mopped her tears and said nothing until
she was calm again. 'Now do you want to tell me about
it?'

She nodded; she had kept her hurt a secret for too
long. She needed to talk and she trusted his discretion
implicitly.

Charles listened in silence, and when she had finished
he leant back on the green silk sofa and ran his hands
through his thick slightly curly hair, something she had
noticed him do when he was puzzled.

'He does not sound like your run-of-the-mill philanderer, but then I don't suppose you'd have been so taken
with him if he was. What was his name?'

'Beaumaris.'

'Tristan Beaumaris! Of the Chasseurs of the Guard?'

'You know him!' Angèle was astonished.

'We encountered each other in Spain two years ago. I
kept a pack of hounds out there. We were hunting near
the lines, the hounds were in full cry and I could see the
fox. . .but the damned thing made straight for a French
cavalry squadron. The other fellows with me fell back,
but I went on. It's a family tradition never to abandon a
chase. . .'

'That was you!' Angèle gasped.

'He told you about it?'

'Yes; he said how much he liked you.'

'It was mutual. We had much in common, we were of

a similar age and in a similar profession. . .not to mention being the elder sons of landowners with all the responsibility that entails. . .' Charles frowned. 'But he was not married then. He was very bitter about some woman called Blanche. She'd jilted him years ago to marry his twin. . . Henri. . .that was his name. A real gold-digger, by the sound of it. Apparently his brother lied to this female and told her that he was the elder of the twins by an hour, and that he'd inherit the title and the bulk of the estate. The woman dropped Tristan like a hot cake. Then the brother was killed in Spain three years ago and she found she had been duped. . .and before this Henri was cold in his grave she began to toss her cap at Tristan again. . . Angèle, are you all right?' he added in alarm as he saw how white she had gone.

'Charles. . .' Somehow through the fog in her head she forced herself to think. The scandal that had broken about her head no longer seemed of the least importance. 'You are sure you have this right? You are saying that Blanche was his twin brother's wife. . .'

'Certain. Surely he told you that?'

'No, you see, it was Blanche whom I met at his house, and I never told him I had been there or that I had discovered he was married to her. . .'

'It was her you met at his house!' Charles's fair brows rose. 'I suppose his feelings towards her might have reverted, but, from the way he spoke that night, I would have wagered he would choose to die rather than wed her.' He glanced at her stricken face. 'It sounds as if she duped you, my sweet. Why on earth didn't you ask him for an explanation there and then?'

'Pride and fear. I should have been just angry with him. Hated him for deceiving me. But the idea of him chained to that. . .socialite. . . They were so different. I could see how awful his life with her must be. I was terrified that if he confirmed what I thought. . . I should not have been able to leave him. . .'

'You would have stayed as his mistress?'

'Yes,' she admitted candidly. 'You must think I am immoral.'

'No.' He shook his head. 'I think you must have been very much in love with him. You did the right thing, as soon as you thought he had a wife and child. You walked away——'

'The right thing!' She lifted her hands and let them drop into the lap of her violet gown. 'If you are right, Charles, and she lied to me, I've been more stupid than you can imagine. He came after me when I was at Bordeaux, waiting for a boat to England. He pressed me to give him a reason for my change of heart. I told him that I did not want to be associated with him for fear that it would prejudice the return of my mother's estates if the Emperor was defeated and the Bourbons were restored.'

'Ah. . .' Charles nodded sagely. 'After what this Blanche did to him that would have touched a nerve.'

'What am I going to do?' she groaned. 'I've been such an idiot, Charles; if I had trusted him, asked for an explanation. . .'

'The first thing you'd better do is open this letter you've never read and see what it says,' Charles said practically. 'Then you had better write to him.'

'It doesn't say anything,' she said in disappointment a few minutes later, having fetched the little packet. 'There is only this——'

'Only!' Charles whistled through his teeth as he picked up the little blue enamel cross embellished with oak and laurel leaves. 'Are you telling me you travelled across Russia with the Grande Armée and you don't know what this is?'

'I know it's a medal of some sort.'

'Angèle, it's a commander's cross of the Legion of Honour. There are generals in the army who have not received this grade. It's the greatest reward that any of

Napoleon's soldiers can win. Boney only gives it to the best and the bravest of his men. Beaumaris could not have given you anything he valued more except his life, and, from what you have told me, he was willing enough to risk that for you.'

'He gave it to me once before, to remember him by. . .at Kovno; he thought he was going to die. . .' she said, not sure whether she was in a dream or a nightmare. Two thoughts kept revolving through her mind: Blanche was not his wife, the boy was not his son. 'Charles,' she said, coming to an instant decision, 'I have to go back to France. I doubt he will forgive me, but I have to see him, to explain. Will you help me?'

'No,' he said gently. 'France is about to become a battlefield. And don't think this is self-interest. From what I know of him, I'm certain Beaumaris would say the same if our situations were reversed. We are pushing in from the south, the Russians from the north and the Austrians from the east. And, even if I could be persuaded,' he said less forcefully as he saw the despair on her face, 'there is not time. I am leaving for Spain tomorrow to rejoin the regiment. But I will willingly take a letter for you, and do my best to see it finds him. You see, it's in my interests to get this resolved one way or another. . .because until it is I won't give up the idea of marrying you.'

'Thank you for being so generous.' Angèle kissed him on the cheek as he took the letter from her half an hour later. 'Don't get yourself killed, Charles.'

'I don't intend to.' He grinned. 'I'll be back, Angèle, and if he wants you Beaumaris is going to have to be quick off the mark.'

'I want her out of this house by tomorrow morning! Or you'll find your last set of gambling debts aren't settled from my account!' the Duchesse de Lucqueville shouted at her husband later that December morning. 'Since she's been in the house, hardly a man who has come here has looked at our two girls! It's like putting a swan beside two brown ducklings. I thought Stretton would take her off our hands, but she's refused him. What does she think she is doing? Refusing the heir to a dukedom! If she'd accepted him I could have found an Earl apiece for the girls.'

'Calm yourself, my dear,' the Duc de Lucqueville drawled, leaning back in his green brocade chair and loosening a button of his over-tight embroidered waistcoat. He regarded his spouse with jaundiced eyes, thinking how closely she had come to resemble her father, the Manchester industrialist. But perhaps she always had, and it was simply his urgent need for her fortune that had blinded him to it before.

'Be calm? When she has created the biggest scandal of the season about our ears and not done the one thing that would have repaired the damage? What prospects will our Amelia and Sophia have now?'

'T'will all be forgotten once she is out of London and the next scandal takes its place. Amelia and Sophia will not be harmed. God knows, no one could confuse them with Angèle,' he added beneath his breath, flicking an imaginary speck of dust from his satin breeches with a heavily perfumed lace hankerchief. 'In fact, I'll wager their invitations will double—half of London will want to hear their accounts of our scandalous guest.'

'They had better or I will never forgive you for it! I don't know why you took the hussy in the first place!'

'You know I had to offer her a place here to stop her carrying out this scheme of becoming a governess and giving my name as a reference.' The *Duc* continued wearily, 'Can you imagine if it had come out that my daughter was working as a governess?' His drink-blurred features set momentarily into a haughty mask.

'I doubt it would have been believed!' his *Duchesse*

spat. 'A member of your family working for a living would stretch most people's imagination to the limit.'

'De Lucquevilles never work, *my dear*. We leave that to the common folk like your father. They're so much better at it,' the *Duc* replied with acid sweetness, ignoring his wife's gasp of rage. 'But, to return to our "problem", she is ideally qualified to carry out a small task for the organisation, for which the time is now right.'

'And what makes you think she'll want to help your cronies? Did you not hear her defending the Corsican's request for peace at the Urquharts' last week?' The *Duchesse* said bitterly, 'I did not know where to put myself.'

'She will. I shall ask her to take a letter to France. . .a letter containing news of his wife's grave illness to a returned émigré who is forced to live in hiding. . .' the *Duc* said thoughtfully. 'She's soft-hearted enough to accept. And, judging by what you overheard of her conversation with Stretton this morning, she'll leap at it. She's a romantic little fool like her mother. . .' His mouth curved cynically. 'And that will be the last you'll hear of her, my dear, I promise you.'

'So I suppose that'll mean more of my money wasted on these incompetent conspirators,' the *Duchesse* scathed, her reddened face and narrowed black eyes revealing that she was far from mollified by the solution. 'Do you think these Bourbon princes will repay your efforts when they have their fat backsides back in Paris? I can tell you what the answer to that will be! Royalty never pay their bills!'

'On the contrary,' the *Duc* winced at his wife's raucous tones and lowered puffy eyelids over his reddened eyes, 'I think this could make us a little profit. But now can we talk about something else? It is so vulgar to discuss money.'

'Except when you want some of mine,' was his wife's

reply before she stormed out of the study, shutting the door with such force that the sash window overlooking the garden in the centre of the square rattled.

The *Duc* sighed and took the stopper out of his crystal inkwell and then frowned as it rolled across the tooled leather surface of his desk. Still scowling, he sprinkled sand on the spilled ink, then took up his quill with his white and rather bloated hands and began to write the first of two letters. One to his royalist contact in Paris, the other to the chief of Napoleon Bonaparte's secret police.

CHAPTER FOURTEEN

'ANGÈLE, your carriage is here,' Danielle announced excitedly two days after Angèle had arrived in Paris.

'Do I look all right?' Angèle asked nervously.

Danielle smiled as her eyes went from Angèle's shining red-gold curls that spilled from her chignon on to one bare white shoulder, and then to the perfectly fitting gown of lilac voile with its high waist and fan-trained skirt. 'Look in your looking-glass.' She laughed. 'I wish I could be at the Tuileries to see Tristan's face when he sets eyes on you. He'll forgive you everything the moment he sees you. . .'

'I wish I could be so sure,' Angèle said uncertainly. She was growing less sure of the wisdom of surprising Tristan with her presence by the minute, and she knew there was no chance of his having received her letter so soon.

'He will be delighted, idiot,' Danielle said, ushering her down the stairs. 'Now come along, don't forget Etienne will meet you at the entrance and find someone to escort you into the reception.'

'No. . . I won't. Have you seen my reticule? Oh, no!'

'What is it?' Danielle asked as Angèle turned a shade paler than she was already.

'My reticule. I was kept waiting in the garden at the house where I delivered the letter yesterday. I must have left it on the garden seat. I have to get it back; it has something in it that Tristan gave me. . .'

'You have plenty of time; call on the way to the Tuileries. The coachman will not mind,' Danielle said easily. 'Now go or you will be late. And don't leave until you have made everything right between you.'

* * *

219

'It doesn't look as if there is anyone in,' said the coachman, dubiously viewing the house at which Angèle had asked him to stop.

'Oh, no. . .but perhaps it is still where I left in the walled garden at the back. Wait for a moment.'

The coachman shrugged as she gathered up her skirt over one arm to keep it off the ground and ran down a side-alley to where there was a door into the garden.

To her relief, it was open. She slipped in. The little silver bag was still there on the stone bench near the rear entrance of the house. She could see it glinting in the moonlight. She went forward eagerly and was about to pick it up when she heard voices from a dark but open window above.

'So we get him tomorrow at the review outside the Tuileries?'

'Yes; the rest of the details were all in the letter the English girl brought,' said an educated woman's voice. 'Once Napoleon is dead, the *Comte* will make his move.'

'And what about his brat—supposing the bomb misses him?'

'You will be there at a safe distance. If the bomb does not succeed you must shoot them both.' The woman's clear, cold voice drifted down to Angèle. 'There must be no focus for resistance left. Bonaparte's brat must die as well.'

Horror held Angèle transfixed for what seemed like hours but was in reality only seconds. She had long since accepted that she and the *Duc* would never be more than strangers, linked only by blood, not feeling. And she knew he was devoted to the Bourbon cause. But she had not dreamt he would use her in such a fashion. Her own father had duped her, made her party to the planned murder of a two-year-old child as well as a man who had shown her nothing but kindness. But there was no time to dwell on her own hurt. She must get away from here now. Warn Napoleon. Tomorrow. . .they had said tomorrow. Grabbing her reticule, she fled from the garden, her heart in her mouth as her silken heels seemed to make a sound like hammers on the flagstoned alley. But to her relief there was no sound behind her from the garden or the house as she threw herself back into her carriage and told the coachman to drive on.

'Well, Mademoiselle Kerenski, this is an unexpected pleasure. Though I did not think a woman of your taste would stay in England for long.'

'Thank you, sire,' Angèle said awkwardly as Caulaincourt closed the door of Napoleon's study and left her alone with the Emperor. Who had told him she had gone to England? Tristan? Had he talked about her to his master? But she could not think about such things now.

'So what was it you wished to see me about so urgently?' Napoleon asked, leaning forward and picking up a little red wooden block, more of which were dotted about on a vast map that was spread on the floor. 'Armies; they represent my friends and my. . .enemies,' he said, following her gaze as he turned the block in his fingers. 'Which are you, *mademoiselle*?'

'Your friend, sire,' she replied, a little startled by the question. 'That is why I requested this interview.' Then as briefly and clearly as she could she explained how she had been asked to deliver the letter, knowing nothing of its contents, and what she had overheard earlier that evening.

After she had finished Napoleon got to his feet and began to pace about the room. He looked older, heavier than he had in Russia, the white waistcoat of the undress uniform of a colonel of the Chasseurs unbuttoned for comfort. He looked just like any other harassed middle-aged man. But then as he turned back to her and she met his clear pale gaze he was the Emperor again.

'Why did you come to tell me this, *mademoiselle*? I understood your sympathies were with the royalists.'

'I have no sympathy with murderers of whatever persuasion. . .and I have not met a single Frenchman or Frenchwoman, except those in England, who desire to be ruled by anyone other than yourself. I think your fate should be in the hands of the French people, not assassins. I swear I knew nothing of the contents of that letter.'

Napoleon's face lit up and he beamed at her.

'Thank you, *mademoiselle*. I cannot tell you how pleased I am that you came here tonight. I should hate to have given the order to have an intelligent as well as beautiful young woman executed.'

'Executed?' Angèle blanched. 'You mean you knew of this plot already?'

'For several days. You have been watched from the moment you set foot in France.'

'But how?' she said in bewilderment.

Napoleon opened a blotter that lay on a shelf and handed her a letter. 'An informer in England very kindly sent this to my chief of police. . .'

Angèle scanned the sheets of paper. There were names, addresses, dates, including that of her arrival. And, at the end, a note of the price the informant expected to receive for his information. And then a signature. A signature she did not want to read.

'You are shocked; you knew the Duc de Lucqueville well, I believe—we received a report that you were living in his house in London.'

'He is my father,' she answered tonelessly as she put the letter down on the desk, and in an instinctive gesture wiped her hands on her skirt as if to wipe them clean.

'Your father!' Napoleon's famous composure momentarily disappeared. '*Sacre nom de Dieu*! He was prepared to send his own daughter to a firing squad in return for money?'

'Apparently.' The last lingering shred of a childhood dream splintered and broke into ugly fragments. She had never expected his love. . .but that he could send her so coldly and deliberately to her death, along with a dozen others who had been his friends. . .people who trusted him. . . And he had sold them all for money. Without knowing what she was doing, she unfastened from her neck the locket that contained his picture and let it drop on to the letter. The man who had been her childhood idol was so contemptible that it did not bear thinking about. She knew now with sick certainty who had spread the scandal in London. No doubt he had been looking for a way to be rid of her. He had used her without a shred of regard for her or her mother, who had ruined her life for love of him. She was too shocked to cry. She felt sick, dizzy.

'I am sorry, *mademoiselle*; if I had known I should not have broken the news in such a fashion,' Napoleon said grimly. 'Can I get you something. . .some cognac?'

'No. . .' She shook her head. 'If you will excuse me. . .'

'Of course. Chevreuse!'

'Sire?' A Chasseur major came in and snapped to attention.

'Mademoiselle Kerenski has had a shock. Take care of her, please. Perhaps you could escort her to the reception, or to her carriage if she wishes to go home—but I hope you will stay,' he added. 'There will be many who will be delighted to see you again.'

'Would you like me to take you to the reception?' Major Chevreuse asked as the doors of Napoleon's study shut behind them a moment or two later. 'I am certain Major Beaumaris will not forgive me if I do not. . .'

And he might not if you do. Desperate for reassurance, she wanted to blurt out her fear but instead managed to nod her thanks. Shock had left her vulnerable, utterly unsure of what she was doing here. She needed Tristan

now more than she had ever done, but supposing she
had meant no more to him than her mother had to her
father? Supposing Blanche had been right—supposing
she had never been anything more to him than an
amusement? She wanted to run away. Not to know
would be safer, because Tristan was all she had left to
believe in. If he no longer loved her. . . The fear was
overwhelming, crippling her mind and body. Her chest
was tight, she couldn't breathe, her legs were weak and
the marble floor seemed to have become spongy beneath
her feet. But it was too late to run now. The great double
doors of the ballroom were swinging open in front of
her. Warmth, light and noise swamped her taut nerves.
She halted, clinging to Chevreuse's arm as her eyes
searched for one face among the hundreds that filled the
mirror-lined room.

She blinked, dazzled by the light from the crystal
chandeliers that reflected in the tall gilt-framed mirrors.
An orchestra was playing a lively gavotte and everywhere
there were beautiful women in pale dresses, spinning
and turning in the arms of men wearing uniforms of red,
blue, green and white. The room was huge, yet to her it
seemed unbearably hot and stuffy. The air was thick
with perfume and the smell of hot wax from the
hundreds of burning candles. She shut her eyes momentarily and tried to steady her breathing, fighting off the
sense of faintness that threatened to overwhelm her. But
as she opened her eyes again the women's jewels and the
gold braid and fringing on the men's uniforms all seemed
to merge into a sparkling blur. She didn't even see one
figure turn towards them and freeze, utterly still against
the whorling mass of colour about him.

'Angèle!' Tristan said her name aloud in disbelief as
his hands fell away from his partner and he stood staring
helplessly. The pretty redhead with whom he had been
dancing took one look from his expression to the ashen-

faced girl swaying on the arm of another officer at the door and flounced off the floor.

Tristan did not even notice her leave. He only knew that he had been longing to see Angèle, to touch her, for months. He was halfway across the room before he even asked himself what he was doing. And then, as he saw Chevreuse put an arm about her waist, the anger came flooding back. She might be beautiful, but she was mercenary, fickle and an associate of murderers. . .and she was on a list of suspects to be arrested for treason. His heart stopped, and then beat furiously again. The fool! Didn't she have any idea of the danger she was in by coming here of all places? But then she had never lacked for courage, he remembered bitterly. It was one of the things he had loved about her.

'My dance, I believe, Chevreuse.'

'Tristan!' She felt nothing except overwhelming relief as she focused on his tall form, immovable in the dipping, swaying room. He was here. She would be safe now. Safe from hurt and betrayal. . . But his eyes were cold as they met hers. Cold as the stars above Kovno, and his hawkish mouth was set, hard. 'Please. . .' she began helplessly; she was not ready for this now, her mind was leaden, refusing to form the words of explanation. She needed his comfort and all he offered her was contempt. . .

What little strength she had left her and she almost fell as he caught her arm and pulled her roughly from Chevreuse's grasp.

'Beaumaris, what the devil do you think you're doing? She's in no state to dance——' Major Chevreuse protested angrily.

'If you want to dispute the issue I'll meet you tomorrow at dawn. It's your choice—sabres or pistols,' Tristan rasped.

'For heaven's sake, man, what's got into you?' Major

Chevreuse returned furiously. 'Release her now or I'll be happy to meet you——'

'No. . .don't!' Somehow she made her frozen tongue form the words. 'It's all right, Major. . . I should be happy to dance with Capt. . . Major Beaumaris.'

'Thank you,' Tristan spat sarcastically as he swept her on to the dance-floor, holding her in a grip of iron. 'But don't think this is a pleasure. I just want to know what the hell you're doing here.'

Her dizziness was increasing as he half carried her through the measures of the dance. And she could only look at his face helplessly.

'I came to see you,' she said only half audibly.

'Liar! Can't you bring yourself to admit the truth? But then planning the murder of a child isn't a particularly pleasant topic for conversation, is it?' he sneered, jerking her back into step as she stumbled.

'You know about that? How?'

He paid no heed to her muddled question and spun her so viciously as they reached the edge of the floor that her head snapped back. Her feet were floating now. The colours around her had merged to a swirl of red and black dots. 'Tristan. . .' She moaned his name as the darkness closed in and became complete.

'Angèle!' He shook her angrily as she crumpled in his arms. 'If you think to get around me with your games——'

'Can't you see she's fainted?' Blanche sighed wearily from behind him. 'Really, Tristan, you can be such a brute.'

'Stay out of this!' he replied furiously, sweeping Angèle's limp form up into his arms. 'It's none of your affair!'

'Tristan. . .' Blanche began, and then shrugged as he strode off through the dancers. The girl was back now; he'd know the truth soon enough, and then, she thought wrily, she had better take care not to be at home. She turned back to her escort with a smile; he wasn't Tristan, of course, but Lucien was very fond of him, and he was almost embarrassingly rich.

The chill night air brought Angèle back to consciousness. For a moment she was aware of nothing except that she was cold; then, realising that she was lying on one of a flight of stone steps that led from the palace to the gardens, she sat up. Slowly she let her eyes go to where Tristan sat a yard or two away in shadow, anger still evident in every taut line of his body.

'Shall I fetch you a drink?' he asked coldly.

Still feeling sick and muzzy, she shook her head as all the pain and hurt of the last hour came flooding back. 'The plot—how did you——?' she began.

'I have access to some of the police reports,' he cut in. 'I know, for instance, that you've been living in Lucqueville's house in London. Was that his price for using his influence with Artois to get your estates back? To share his bed?'

'No. He is my father,' she answered flatly without looking at him. How could he believe such things of her? After her father's betrayal she did not think she could be hurt more, but this was worse, this was the man she loved above all others, the man whose love she wanted in return.

'Your father!' He laughed raggedly and she felt his eyes sear across her face. 'De Lucqueville's daughter! I should have guessed—it certainly explains your mercenary streak. So you're just being a dutiful daughter, are you, assisting him in murder?'

'You cannot think I would do that!'

'Can't I? You forget I have had experience of your cruelty.'

'It is you who is cruel!' she defended herself desperately. 'I came here tonight to warn the Emperor.'

'Oh, and I thought it was me you came to see. If you have to lie at least stick to one story,' he scathed.

His contempt hurt her more than she had dreamt was possible. What point was there in trying to talk to him if he had come to believe her capable of murder? Misery overwhelmed her and she didn't bother to reply. The January night air was cold as his voice, making her shiver in her thin gown.

He frowned as he watched her draw up her knees and hug them for warmth, reminded suddenly of Russia. Without thinking he unfastened the gold cord that held his sheepskin-lined pelisse on his shoulders.

He tossed the garment over to her without a word. Tentatively she took it up and put it about her shoulders. It was the first sign of tenderness he had shown her. And she looked at him with a tiny flicker of hope, wondering if something might yet be salvaged. Trust, she found herself thinking dully as she scanned his face and found it too dark to read properly. Love and passion isn't enough; there has to be trust as well. And she had been as guilty of not trusting him as he her. If she hadn't believed Blanche. . .

'Tristan,' she began, 'please, you must listen to me, let me explain. . . I thought you were——'

'No! I don't want to hear any more lies. You listen to me,' he interrupted bitterly. 'I don't know what you're doing at the Tuileries, and on reflection I don't want to know. I don't think I have the stomach for it. I probably ought to put you under arrest right now. You're on a list of traitors to the state. . .and that means if you're caught you'll most likely be shot. But I'll give you twenty-four hours to get out of Paris. You can take this passport. . .' He threw a piece of pasteboard at her. 'It's signed by Napoleon himself, and it'll get you through any French border post. And you had better take this as well; I owe it you for those nights in Prussia.' There was a clink of coin as he pushed a purse along the step towards her. 'Now if I were you I'd get in your carriage and get going; once you're under arrest there will be nothing I can do

for you, even if I wished to.' Then he got to his feet and
began to walk away.

Disbelief held her immobile and speechless. That he
should insult her in such a way. . . And then sheer,
overpowering rage took over.

'You can keep your money and your passport!' She
flung the words at him along with the money and the
piece of pasteboard. 'And this!' she shouted, making a
bundle of the sheepskin cape and hurling it at his head.
It missed, but he halted and turned to look at her. 'I
hate you!' she shouted as he stared down at her, arrogant
and implacable in the golden light that streamed from
the tall windows behind him. 'I should not want help
from you if you were the last man on earth!'

'I should not be fool enough to offer it again!' he
snarled back, bending to retrieve the pelisse, and throwing it over his shoulder. 'Get yourself shot! But don't
expect me to stay in Paris to watch!'

'Where are you going?' There was something in his
voice that killed her rage instantly and replaced it with a
cold dread in the pit of her stomach.

'To hell probably. . .anywhere where I will not have
to set eyes on you again!'

'Tristan. . .please, don't go. . .' Her voice broke as
tears began to stream down her face. 'Please listen. . .'
But it was too late; he ignored her, striding back into the
palace and slamming a glass door behind him. She was
alone.

She slumped across the cold steps, feeling as if he had
cut out her heart with his sabre.

'Oh, dear, I rather hoped you might have sorted things
out,' Blanche said as she stepped out from the shadows
and looked at Angèle, hunched and shaking, her skirts
spread in a pool of pale silk about her.'But don't worry,
he'll cool down eventually.'

'You!' Angèle drew in a sharp breath as she recognised

the face beneath the short girlish curls and white ribbon. 'Just leave me alone! Haven't you done enough damage?'

'You are referring to our little misunderstanding,' the older woman said calmly, without a trace of the little-girl manner that had grated on Angèle before. 'I wondered what you'd do if you found out the truth. I confess, I was surprised to see you—I thought you'd be married to some eligible Englishman by now.'

'Misunderstanding!' Angèle almost choked. 'You *lied* to me. You let me think you were his wife!'

'All's fair in love and war,' Blanche went on, unperturbed. 'Not that I blame you for being angry. I did behave like a perfect. . .well, I shan't add hypocrisy to injury; it is not you I am concerned for. After all, we are scarcely acquainted, but I do care for Tristan. . .I always have. . .'

'More than Henri,' Angèle retorted acidly.

'Yes,' Blanche sighed and sat down on the step beside her, having first brushed it with her hand. 'I was a fool. I knew before I married Henri that the resemblance between him and Tristan was only skin deep. Everything Tristan is, Henri was not. . .in any sense,' she added meaningfully.

'Why are you telling me this?' Angèle said, swallowing back her tears.

'Because I want to help make things right before something happens to Tristan. Since you left he has been living too fast, drinking too much. Sooner or later in a duel or in battle he is going to make a mistake. His sergeant swears he was deliberately trying to get himself killed at Leipzig and Dresden.'

'But why?'

'Because he's still desperately in love with you,' Blanche said wryly. 'I found that out when he refused the comfort I offered him after you had turned the knife at Bordeaux. But you must know that——'

'In love with me! You must be mad!' Angèle half

sobbed, half laughed. 'If you had heard what he said to me just now. . .'

'Surely you don't think he meant what he said?' Blanche sighed. 'He would never have offered you that passport if he did not love you. Until today I did not think anything was more important to Tristan than his loyalty to Bonaparte and France, but it seems he will sacrifice even his honour for you. . .'

'You listened to our conversation,' Angèle groaned.

'Yes.' Blanche was unashamed. 'I discovered I have a conscience. A little late, I admit. From the way he was hauling you around the dance-floor, I thought you might need some assistance. . .'

'Then perhaps you can explain why he said those things if he loves me,' Angèle said bitterly.

'You hurt him very badly, and Tristan does not like to repeat mistakes; this nonsense about assassination allows him to keep you from getting too close again. He does not want to listen to reason because he is afraid of being hurt again. . . I know this from experience. But you must not give up while there is a chance——'

'Did he give you a second chance?' Angèle interrupted sharply.

'No. But he will you,' Blanche replied with a slight tightening of her mouth.

'Why should he? If he did not forgive you for Henri, why should he forgive me. . .?'

'Because he never looked at me quite the way he looked at you tonight when you first came into the ballroom. I was not the only one to see it; Suzanne Detrois was most put out.' Blanche laughed maliciously. 'She always did think rather highly of herself. Now I suggest you let me take you to where you are staying in my carriage before you catch your death of cold, and then in the morning we will go to see him together and I will confess all. Then perhaps he'll listen to you.'

'You want to help me?' Angèle was bewildered.

'Only for Tristan's sake,' Blanche said crisply. 'Don't start to think I like you. I don't. You have the heart of the one man I want above all others, and I am not sure I'll ever forgive you for it. And don't look at me like that. Guilt is an emotion I really don't wish to become accustomed to. . . I am sure it's terribly ageing. And if I'm to be ravaged by the English when they invade Paris I do so want to look my best. . .'

Angèle managed a smile. 'I begin to see what Tristan saw in you; before I never could.'

'*Touché.* Now you're beginning to learn.' Blanche smiled back at her and held out a hand to help Angèle to her feet. 'Shall we be best of enemies?'

CHAPTER FIFTEEN

'I SHALL not keep you long, Beaumaris,' Napoleon said. 'This will be finished in a moment or two, will it not, Caulaincourt?'

While Napoleon finished dictating the despatch to his secretary Tristan looked at the map spread out on the floor. Four nations against them, moving in from the north, east and south. And all they had to face them with were raw recruits and old men. . .

'You were thinking it is impossible?'

'Yes, sire,' Tristan answered as Napoleon turned back to him suddenly. 'I think you should make peace. . . even if the price is high. . .'

'You think I have not tried?' Napoleon's brows rose. 'They are determined to destroy me, Beaumaris. But I shall not make it easy for them. Blücher. . .I have beaten before and can again, and the Russians. . .they do not have a general worth the name or all of us would have died at the Berezina.'

'And Wellington, sire?' Silver eyes met pale blue-grey and held.

'Wellington!' Napoleon's expression became sombre. 'He is of a different calibre. . .a worthy opponent. . .' Then, as if not wishing to think of Wellington any more, he wheeled around. 'Read back that last, Caulaincourt.'

Tristan's eyes followed him, and then were caught by the locket lying on the desk. Angèle's locket. He would know it anywhere.

Unthinkingly he stepped forward and picked it up. He slid his thumb over its polished back, worn smooth by contact with her skin. An image of her lying naked in

233

his arms flooded his mind, making his stomach knot with longing.

'Mademoiselle Kerenski left it here this evening,' Napoleon said, jolting him out of his reverie.

'She *was* here. . .why?' He forgot himself utterly as he barked the question. Dear heaven, if she had been telling the truth. . .?

Napoleon's brows lifted, but he answered coolly enough. 'She came to warn me of the conspiracy. Can you imagine, Beaumaris, that a man could sink so low? Duping his own daughter to take part in murder and and then informing on her. . .'

What the Emperor was saying penetrated the haze in his head.

'Lucqueville was the informer?'

'Yes; if I had known he was her father I should not have told her. . .'

'She knows it was Lucqueville. . .' The blood left his face as he realised how badly that knowledge must have hurt her. The father she had dreamed of, idolised as a child, had betrayed her and knowingly sent her to her death for money. And he had not offered her a grain of comfort. He felt physically sick as he remembered the misery in her eyes and chalk-white face as he had dragged her around the dance-floor. Why hadn't he listened to her?

'The despatch is ready, sire.' Caulaincourt sanded the document and handed it to Napoleon to sign and seal.

'You realise you will have to cross enemy lines to reach Soult?' Napoleon said as Tristan tucked the paper into his tunic.

'Yes, sire,' he answered flatly, his mouth twisting into a grim smile at the irony of it. Since the day she had left him at Bordeaux he had not cared much if he lived or died. But now. . .he wanted life, he had to live long enough to find her, to beg her forgiveness, to tell her. . .

he still loved her. The admission shocked him into absolute stillness.

'Beaumaris!' Napoleon said impatiently for the second time. 'You'll leave at once. Every hour is vital. *Bon chance.*'

'Thank you, sire.' Tristan bowed and left. Honour forbade him to refuse to take the despatch now. While Napoleon was still prepared to fight he would serve him. An order was an order, and, even if he'd had more time, he had not the slightest idea where to find Angèle or how to reach her.

'He's not here,' Etienne said apologetically later that morning as he returned to where Blanche and Angèle were waiting in the Tuileries gardens. 'He left at dawn.'

'When will he be back?' Angèle said, her heart sinking to her shoes.

Etienne's normally open countenance clouded and he would not meet Angèle's eyes.

'Etienne, where has he gone?' she asked sharply, a cold fear clutching at her stomach again.

'He volunteered to take a despatch to Marshal Soult on the southern front; it will mean crossing enemy lines. He seems determined to get himself killed, heaven knows why. . .'

Because he loves me. He despises me, but he cannot stop loving me any more than I can him, and he cannot live with himself. Angèle almost spoke the words aloud as the truth exploded in her mind. Blanche had been right. He had been as close last night to betraying his principles, his honour, as she had been that day on the beach. Oh, what fools they had both been. . .and she could think of only one solution: she had to find him and make him listen to the truth.

'Etienne,' she said sharply, 'do you know if he took Montespan?'

'No, he has a new bay; he has rested the black since

the Russian campaign—he said she had earned her retirement.'

'Where does he keep her?'

'In the stables at his house. Sergeant Leclerc had to leave the army after he was wounded at Leipzig; he looks after the house and the horses while Tristan is away. . . but why do you want to know?'

'I am going after him,' she said simply. 'Give my love to Danielle.' And then she turned, picked up her skirts and began to run towards the carriage ranks.

Blanche cast one startled look at Etienne and then they both followed.

'You're as big a fool as he is, I suppose you know that?' Blanche said wearily an hour later as she helped Angèle change her clothes in a bedroom in Tristan's house.

Angèle nodded as she pulled on the uniform jacket she had borrowed from Etienne, guessing that Tristan's spare would be far too big.

'The whole country is at war; the Prussians and the Russians have nearly reached Brienne,' Blanche continued, handing Angèle a blue silk *aide de camp's* sash, to belt in the waist of a pair of Tristan's old breeches. 'Why don't you wait? We'll be forced to make peace soon, and he'll come back to Paris then. As soon as he cools down enough to think straight he'll know you had no part in this conspiracy. . .'

'He could be dead by then and he will not know I lied to him at Bordeaux,' Angèle said, picking up the black busby from the canopied bed and stuffing her hair inside it. It was still too big and slipped over her eyes.

Shaking her head, Blanche opened a drawer in a tallboy and rummaged. 'Here.' She gave Angèle a silk cravat to wrap around her hair.

The hat now securely lodged on her head, Angèle stood back and examined herself in the looking-glass. The uniform was more or less complete except that she had had to keep her own boots of soft black leather. But when she was on a horse her cloak would cover them. She'd never pass muster on a parade ground, but it should do to get her through most sentry posts. . .and prevent the unwelcome attention a woman travelling alone could attract.

'I only hope the idiot knows just how much you love him,' Blanche muttered crossly beneath her breath as she too stared at the glass, and thought how fragile and vulnerable the girl looked beneath the black fur hat. 'I'm not sure even Tristan is worth this. . .'

'I am,' Angèle said levelly.

'Yes, I suppose that is the difference between us,' said Blanche, 'I've never valued anyone's feelings as much as I do my own skin. . .'

'And you'll probably live to a ripe old age to laugh at my foolishness,' Angèle answered lightly as she buttoned the last of the copper buttons and caught up Tristan's old campaign cloak from the back of a chair. It was clean, but the scent of woodsmoke and his skin still clung to it, and for a moment she held it to her face, before throwing it around her shoulders and running from the room. She felt more alive than she had for months. Everything seemed so simple now. Somehow she knew that if she could find him before it was too late it would be all right, he would forgive her in time.

Sergeant Leclerc was waiting for her in the stable-yard.

'Always thought you'd make a Chasseur,' he greeted her cheerfully as he helped her into Montespan's saddle. 'But I wish I could come with you. If it weren't for this damn leg——'

'I know,' Angèle said softly, bending to place a kiss on his whiskery cheek. 'Thank you for everything. Montespan looks wonderful. . .' she said as she stroked the mare's glossy black neck.

'Yes, she's in top condition—she'll not let you down,' the sergeant said, going decidedly pink. 'You're sure you can manage her? She's full of oats now. . .not like in Russia.'

'I was taught to ride by a Cossack,' she pointed out.

'I know, but once a cavalry horse. . .always a cavalry horse. . .' the sergeant said a little doubtfully. Then he shrugged. 'You realise he'll have me shot for letting you do this,' he said gruffly.

'He forgave you last time,' she smiled, 'remember?'

'Only because you survived, *mademoiselle*.'

'And I will this time. *Au revoir*, Sergeant. Blanche.' She waved, and Montespan bounded forward at the first touch of her heels.

'The marshal and the cavalry? The devil knows! I wish to hell they were here!' the grenadier major shouted in response to Angèle's enquiry. 'Those Hussars are going to cut off our line of retreat if someone doesn't stop them.'

'They are English?' Angèle said in horror as she watched the line of blue-uniformed men and horses surge over a hedge two fields away.

'Of course they bloody are! *Sacrebleu*!' The major gave her smooth cheeks a scathing glance. 'What are they putting in the Chasseurs these days? Take my advice— get out of here and go home to your mother!'

Then he turned to bellow more orders at his men to fall back with all possible haste.

Angèle hesitated, wondering if she should follow them. Until now she had managed to skirt the battles that seemed to be raging all across France. She had been turned back from Bayonne by the news that it was encircled by fifteen thousand English troops. Then to her delight she had been told that Soult was not there but at Gave-de-Pau, the last river to bar the English advance into the southern plain of central France. It had taken her two days' riding to cover the sixty miles, and, having arrived, she found the French army under attack by Wellington himself.

She looked about her uncertainly. Clouds of smoke from the guns and muskets drifted across the battlefield like black fog, obscuring everything. The Grenadiers had already vanished. She ducked instinctively as she heard the whistle of a musket ball, passing her so close that she felt the rush of air on her cheek. She couldn't stay here, but which way should she go? She could make no sense of the noises around her; the crackle of muskets and boom of guns seemed to come from every direction.

She jumped as a bugle seemed to trumpet its call almost in her ear. Montespan began to dance restively, tossing her head and pulling against the bit. 'Easy. . .' Angèle leant forward to stroke her neck.

'Charge!' She heard the French command and another bugle call at the same moment as an assortment of French cavalry materialised out of the haze of smoke all around her, their sabres held out, points down as they took a direct line for the English Hussars. Montespan surged forward with them, the bit clamped between her teeth. Taken unawares, Angèle was almost unseated. The ground was rough. She bumped from side to side in the saddle as she struggled to regain her stirrups, which were thudding against Montespan's sides, making her increase her pace. She could do nothing except cling to the pommel as she fought to get her feet back into the flapping stirrups. Without stirrups for leverage she could not begin to pull the mare up. Then everything went black. The busby had slipped over her eyes. Now that she was sightless, her other senses became acute. Her head was filled with the smell of cordite, the thunder of hoofs, the snorting breath of horses, the rattle and clink of harness and the shouts of men. It seemed forever before she managed to push the busby back with one hand while holding on for dear life with the other.

Then, out of the smoke, came the English. No more
than ten yards away. She could see their faces, the sweat
on the necks of their horses, the polished steel of their
blades levelled at her. . .

But she couldn't die now. She hadn't found Tristan
yet. Please. She found herself screaming at the mare as
she hauled on the reins, begging her to turn.

But it was too late. The blue wave of English horsemen
seemed to break over and eddy all about her. Then there
was nothing but the clash of steel, men and horses
screaming, and the awful dull thud of metal biting into
flesh. No! Frozen with fear, she screamed silently as an
Englishman crashed into them, his face contorted, merciless. Montespan reared, twisting like a snake, defending them with hoofs and teeth, tearing the man's sleeve.
But the Hussar's horse turned with them. Angèle ceased
to breathe as his sabre flashed in an arc towards her. . .
and miraculously fell away as a fountain of blood spurted
from his neck, soaking her tunic. The French Dragoon
had come from nowhere and then vanished again, saving
her life without a thought or second glance.

The instinct to survive took over from incapacitating
horror. With an extreme effort she wrenched Montespan
to the right and kicked her forward, slapping the reins
on her neck to urge her on. To her surprise, the mare
seemed to think she had done her duty and acquiesced.
It was working; a few more yards and she would be
clear—— Tristan! Dear God! It was! Twisting in the
saddle, she looked back to be sure she was not mistaken.
She wasn't. He was fighting the way he had in Kovno,
cutting, thrusting with almost effortless grace.
Montespan balked, making her look forward hastily.
More Hussars bearing down on her, so close that she
could count the rows of silver braid on their blue pelisses.
Their leader was riding straight at her, sabre raised.

'Tristan!' she shouted, but her voice was thin with

terror, inaudible against the clash of weapons and roar of guns.

Tristan sent the sword spinning from his opponent's hand, wheeled his bay, and stared in the direction in which the black horse had vanished. Angèle on Mountespan! Here! For a split-second he had been utterly certain. He shook his head. Fatigue had to be playing tricks on his mind. Not that it was surprising that he should conjure up her image. He had thought of little else but Angèle ever since leaving Paris. And the letter she had written from England had reached him two days before, filling him with hope. But Montespan was in Paris, and Angèle if he was lucky. . .not that it made any difference. Once the fighting was over he'd search Europe if he had to. But this was not the time or place to dream. He began to turn his bay—they needed to regroup before they took on this new wave of Hussars—but something nagged at him, made him look again at the mass of English cavalry. Then he swore as his eyes caught the flash of green and gold in the midst of the silver and blue of the English. There *was* a Chasseur among them and one in urgent need of assistance. He hadn't imagined the whole thing. He sent his bay racing forward. While he was still a dozen yards away he saw the black horse rear up, its slight rider clinging to its neck. Sweet victory, no! *It was her*. Time slowed. His bay seemed to be galloping through treacle, the distance between them endless. With horrified eyes he saw the busby fall from her head and her bright hair flare out like flame just as a Hussar brought his sword up and began the downward stroke. He saw her flinch, lift her arms to her head in a futile effort to protect herself from the blade. He saw the flash of metal as the blade came inexorably downwards, then mercifully his vision was blocked by another rearing horse. And then there was nothing but Hussars and the riderless black mare breaking free and trotting towards the French lines, where a bugler was sounding the recall.

'No. . .!' Someone was screaming with a rage that equalled his own. He could hear him quite clearly as he spurred his bay onwards. Then he realised the scream was his. Silent now, he rode straight at the English, wanting their blood. He would kill every one of them to reach her, to hold her once more. . .to tell her how much he loved her. He would make them pay. . .

'*Vive l'Empereur*!' a sergeant of the Chasseurs shouted as he passed and then raised his own sabre and followed him.

'Crazy devils, these Chasseurs!' a captain of the Carbiniers swore aloud, before riding after them and crashing into the first rank of Hussars a few seconds after Tristan.

'Damnation!' Charles Cavendish also swore as he straightened up from bending over the slight blood-stained figure on the ground and flung himself back into his saddle, ready to repulse the renewed French attack. 'Beaumaris. . .I should have known,' he said grimly as he saw the man who was scything through his men like corn. He sent his chestnut forward, sabre at the ready and then swerved towards the sergeant at the last moment. Beaumaris might be his enemy. But damn it! He liked the man and owed him his freedom. And he could not bring himself to try to kill the man Angèle had told him she loved, and, judging by his face, there would be no other way to stop him.

'I don't think you should drink any more,' the Comtesse d'Aubois said with unusual force late the following afternoon, moving the bottle of red wine away from Tristan's hand as he reached out for it.

'Why not?' he grated.

'Because in a day or two you will have to fight again, and a monumental headache will not improve your chances of surviving,' his companion replied shortly, her hazel eyes full of anxiety as she regarded her husband's friend.

'Do you think I care if I survive or not, Charlotte?' he answered bitterly. 'Angèle is dead. The Empire is finished, and probably all the revolution gained with it. How much longer can Napoleon hope to hold out? A few days and the Bourbons and their crew will be back in Paris, and France will stagnate for another fifty years.'

'Regimes might die, but ideas do not!' the *Comtesse* retorted. 'France will need people like you.'

'Will she?' he said sarcastically. 'France will get the government she deserves, Napoleon gave them victories for years. . .but at the first defeat they panicked and started undermining him. . .'

'You know perfectly well he created the seeds of his own downfall, he overreached himself——'

'Don't! You sound like her. . .'

He stopped, and the *Comtesse* had to look away because she could not bear the pain in his eyes. She and Philippe had seen him hurt and angry when Blanche had jilted him for Henri. But that had been mostly his pride, whereas this. . .this was his heart and soul.

'I still don't understand what she was doing there,' she said at last, winding a black curl about one of her long slender fingers.

'Don't you?' He laughed harsly. 'I wish I could say the same. But one of the Grenadiers told me he'd seen her earlier; she was looking for me. If I'd listened to her in Paris, if I hadn't walked away. . .she'd be alive. I of all people should have known she'd never give up so easily, that she'd follow me. . .' He laughed hollowly. 'Any sensible woman would never have wanted to set eyes on me again after what I accused her of. . .but not Angèle. She is. . .was the stubbornest woman I've ever met. . .'

'She might not be dead,' the *Comtesse* said helplessly, wanting to offer him some comfort.

'I saw her!' He banged his fist on the table at which he was sitting. 'I got close enough to see her! She was lying on the ground, there was blood all over her tunic and mud in her hair. . . I couldn't reach her. . .'

'You can't blame yourself for failing to do the impossible. The others told me you were outnumbered ten to one. . .' And that they had to drag you away forcibly when your horse went down, she added to herself.

'How can I not blame myself when it was my fault that she was there? I loved her, Charlotte, and I killed her, just as surely as if I'd pushed the blade in myself,' he said bleakly, his grey eyes staring into space. Then he laughed and smiled at her. A parody of his charm that made her want to weep. 'So be a nice girl, give me the wine. . .then I might even sleep tonight.'

Reluctantly the *Comtesse* pushed the bottle back towards him and left, shutting the door behind her. There was nothing she could say that would reach him while he was in this mood. Nothing to lessen his pain. Halfway down the stairs she halted, and struck at an old shield that hung on the wall with her small fist. 'I hate war!' she spat with completely uncharacteristic venom. 'Hate it!'

At the foot of the stairs she was greeted by an excited maid.

'Madame la Comtesse, there is an English officer here, under a flag of truce. . .he is asking for Major Beaumaris.'

'Then show him in, Annette.'

'But *madame*, supposing he is. . .dangerous?'

'Annette,' said the *Comtesse* tersely, 'we have thirty or forty officers billeted here. That should be sufficient to defend our honour against one Englishman. Now show him in.'

'Tristan!' The *Comtesse* tapped on the door of the bedroom for the third time.

'What is it?' Tristan growled as he opened the door. 'Please, Charlotte. . . I'd just like to be left alone. . .'

'This is important. There is an English officer downstairs under a flag of truce; he wants to see you.'

'Does he, by God? I can think of no one I'd rather see right now than a murdering English bastard!'

'Tristan, wait!' In vain the *Comtesse* tried to explain, but he was already past her, taking the stairs three at a time, leaving her to follow in his wake.

'Cavendish!' Tristan halted, his anger dying a little as he recognised the man in the salon. 'What brings you here? I am afraid I am not much in the mood for company tonight. Particularly that of a English cavalryman. I didn't think your people made war on women.'

'Tristan. . . Colonel Cavendish is my guest,' the *Comtesse* began breathlessly as she came in, but was silenced by a staying gesture from Charles.

'We don't,' Charles said through set lips. 'No one realised Angèle was a woman until——'

'Angèle. . .you knew her?'

'We met in England. I intended to make her my wife and still do if you haven't got the sense to want——'

'You mean. . .she's alive?' For a moment he could not bring himself to believe it for fear they would tell him he had misheard.

'Yes.' Charles felt an unexpected surge of sympathy for his rival as he saw the expression on Tristan's face. He looked like a man who had just looked through the gates of hell and been offered a reprieve. 'I recognised her in time to knock the fellow's blade aside,' he went on hurriedly, wanting to put him out of his obvious misery. 'She was knocked out when she fell from the horse. I left her where she was because it was the safest place. . .'

'She was badly hurt?' The numbing joy that had held Tristan motionless evaporated. He grabbed the

Englishman by his silver epaulettes and almost lifted him off his feet.

'Tristan! Really!' the *Comtesse* began, but he ignored her, his eyes boring into Charles's face.

'Where is she? How do I get to her? You can have my sword and my parole now—just get me to her!'

'There is no need,' Angèle said quietly, stepping through the door of an ante-room. 'I am here.'

'Angèle!' Tristan released Charles abruptly and spun round. For a moment he stared at her in joyous disbelief. She was still clad in the muddied and besmirched uniform, her hair hanging loose and dishevelled about her shoulders, but to him she had never looked more beautiful.

A breath later and Angèle found herself lifted off her feet and spun through the air. And then he let her down and simply looked at her as if he could not believe she was real. A lump came into her throat as she saw that there were tears glistening in his silver eyes.

'I love you. . .' he breathed. 'Without you——'

'It's all right,' she said huskily, touching his stubbled cheek. 'I know. . .'

Their eyes met and merged, and they were both silent for a long moment, not needing words or to rush into explanations. They were alive. They were together. It was enough for the moment.

Charles cleared his throat noisily and they both turned reluctantly to look at him.

'I had better be getting back,' he said a little tightly. 'Wellington can be damned unpleasant when officers disappear without leave. You'll be staying, I take it?' he added, glancing at Angèle.

'Yes,' she answered without hesitation, and then, seeing his expression, she added softly, 'I am sorry, Charles. . .'

Tristan released her reluctantly and gave her a slight push towards Charles. 'I think you two should say your farewells alone,' he said in response to the question in her turquoise eyes. 'I'll see you at the door, Cavendish.'

'Win some, lose some. . .isn't that the saying, Beaumaris?' Charles said, breaking the silence as the two men stood on the steps of the *château*, enjoying the stillness and tranquillity of the *Comtesse's* gardens, which was marred only by the occasional faint boom of guns carrying through the evening air. 'It seems that we've won the battle, but you've got the prize. . .'

'It would seem so,' Tristan agreed with a wry grin. 'You're more generous than I would have been in the circumstances, Cavendish; I should never have brought her back. . .'

'Oh, you would if she had loved me better than you.' Charles laughed a little brittly. 'But don't be so careless as to lose her again—the English don't believe in second chances. . .as your Emperor is finding out.'

'Napoleon might change their minds,' Tristan said with a half-laugh. 'Don't write us off yet.'

'I'd never make that mistake in your case. But I do hope that we do not meet again before this is over.'

'So do I,' Tristan said, offering him his hand in the English fashion. 'And if anything should happen to me in these next few weeks. . .I should count it a great favour if you would look after her for me. . .'

'My word on it,' Charles said simply as he stepped forward and mounted his grey. '*Au revoir*, Beaumaris.'

'I should have strangled Blanche years ago,' Tristan sighed that evening, raising himself on one elbow to look down at Angèle, who lay beside him on the canopied bed, her skin glowing like ivory against the crimson silk coverlet.

'It wasn't. . .all her fault,' Angèle answered a little unevenly as he took a handful of her newly washed hair and let it trickle through his fingers, splashing on to her bare shoulders. She was too happy to hold grudges.

Tristan was beside her, and by tomorrow night she would be his wife. Nothing else seemed to matter.

'Very true,' he agreed lazily, tracing the line of her mouth with his fingertip. 'If you'd had a better opinion of my character, asked me for an explanation. . .'

'And what about you?' she said, pretending offence. 'Your reasoning wasn't exactly brilliant at the Tuileries, was it?'

'Reason. . .' he laughed, winding his hands in her hair and rolling so that she ended up lying across his chest '. . .has never had anything to do with the way I feel about you. From the moment I saw you lying among the furs at the lodge I wanted you so badly. . .'

'How badly?' she asked innocently, feathering her fingers across a sensitive spot she had discovered on his ribs.

'There is only one answer to that,' he growled, pulling her mouth down to his, and kissing her hungrily.

'What is it?' he questioned softly a minute or two later as he felt her go still in his arms, and saw her eyes darken.

'This. . .' Her voice went thin as she touched a new scar on his chest, an inch or so below his heart.

'Leipzig. A flesh wound—it was nothing,' he replied quietly, holding her gaze and reading her fear. 'Don't worry, the fighting will be over soon; even Napoleon can't hold out much longer. And then I'll leave the army and we will go to Provence. . . I promise.'

'Just stay alive,' she whispered, hugging him tightly, frightened that even to speak of the future would be to tempt fate.

'I will. You have my word on it.' He smiled at her. 'Have you ever known me break it?'

'No,' she admitted huskily, and then he kissed her again, driving the shadows from her mind.

★ ★ ★

Was it only just over a year they'd had together? Angèle sighed as she reached the small hollow on the stony hillside and leant against a smooth sun-warmed rock to catch her breath. The air was heady, so thick with the scent of wild rosemary, lavender and fennel that you could taste them on your tongue. Summer in Provence. It was everything Tristan had promised it would be, except that he was not here.

Trying to put the thought aside, she sat down on the rough, springy grass and took Irina's letter from the pocket of her sprigged muslin gown. A brief smile touched her face as she read it for the second time. Irina wrote as she talked, with breathless enthusiasm.

Vienna is wonderful, and I have met a marvellous Englishman. He knows you—his name is Charles Cavendish; we are to be married in three weeks. . .

Irina sounded so happy. But the letter had been posted months ago in Vienna, where Irina's father had been one of the Russian representatives at the Congress. The Congress that had been so rudely interrupted by Napoleon's escape from Elba. For a hundred and thirty-six days Napoleon had cast his spell again. The tricolour had reappeared in every town and village throughout France, and men had flocked to his standard in their thousands, sharing in one man's dream.

'It is not just a question of loyalty,' Tristan had said when the messenger had arrived. 'He saved my life in my first battle in Italy. If I don't go——'

'You will never forgive yourself,' she had said, knowing him better than he did himself.

'And you?' He had cupped her face in his hands, making her look at him. 'Will you forgive me for going?'

'I love you,' she had answered, using the last shred of her courage. 'But do you think I would want you any different?'

She knew it had been in her power to stop him, but

she had let him go and she had been praying ever since that she would not regret it for the rest of her life.

The kicking of the child in her belly broke into her thoughts, demanding her attention. With a half-smile she put her hand on her stomach; a boy, definitely. But would Tristan ever see him? Her smile died. Ney had led the French cavalry against English squares at Waterloo, and the losses had been horrendous. That much she had gleaned from the news-sheets. And where Ney went, Tristan would follow. And there was nothing she could do except wait and scan the casualty lists as they were issued. Danielle would be doing the same in Paris, and in London Irina would be going through the same agony. Charles would have been at Waterloo; supposing he and Tristan had fought each other? It did not bear thinking about. Restless, she got up and climbed on to a small outcrop of rock. From here she could see the turreted *château* that was now her home. Then, as so often in the last few days, her eyes wandered to the empty white ribbon of road that twisted along the floor of the valley. From Belgium to Provence? How long did it take to ride that distance? Days? Weeks? *Forever if you were dead.* The landscape became suddenly blurred. Stop it; crying will not help, she told herself crossly, trying to stem the sudden flow of tears down her cheeks with her fingers. But it was useless, and, giving up, she sat down on the rock, her head on her knees, and wept.

'Anyone would think you'd missed me.' The voice was dry, faintly mocking and unbelievably, wonderfully familiar.

She lifted her head, scared that she had imagined it. She hadn't. Tristan was there, stepping through a gap in the tangle of stunted trees that edged the hollow. Travel-stained, weary, but whole and unharmed, his wide hawkish mouth curving at the corners as he saw the joy transform her face.

'Missed. . .you?' Scrambling to her feet, she swallowed a sob and scrubbed at her tear-streaked face with the back of her hand, trying to match his tone. 'A little. . .perhaps.'

'Liar.' He grinned as he reached the foot of the rock and she tumbled into his arms, half crying, half laughing. She clung to him, shaking, unable for a moment to say anything else as the reaction to the weeks of uncertainty hit her like a hammer-blow.

'It's all right, I'm here now,' he soothed her, kissing the tears from her face and stroking her hair.

'I'm sorry,' she blurted, 'it's just I've been so frightened for you and. . .the others. The news was so awful. . . Was the battle as bad as they say?' She had not meant to ask so soon, but she could not help herself.

'Worse,' he said softly, 'but Etienne is safe.'

'And Charles. . .did you see him?'

'Only afterwards,' he answered quickly, guessing at what had gone through her mind. 'In Paris, when I was on my way home, he took a sword thrust in the arm, but nothing serious.'

'I'm glad,' she said, exhaling the breath she had been holding.

'So am I.' He smiled. 'And what about you? Was it wise to climb this hill every day to watch the road?'

'How did you——?'

'I met Sergeant Leclerc at the gatehouse. Not that you seem to be suffering any ill effects,' he added, letting his hand slide caressingly over her rounded stomach.

'You. . .mean I'm getting fat.' She scowled at him.

'Just rounder in places and more beautiful.' He laughed, bending his head to kiss her swiftly. 'I've spent the last three months asking myself if I was mad to leave you. . .and now I know I was. . .'

'I shall remind you of that next time you go away,' she said wryly.

'There won't be a next time, my love,' he said quietly. 'Napoleon is finished. He won't return this time.'

'At least the war is over,' she answered, knowing that some of his dreams as well as his comrades had died at Waterloo.

'Yes.' The far-away look vanished from his eyes and he smiled at her. 'I shall always fight to protect the liberties gained in the revolution, but not with the sword any longer. There has to be a better way.'

'Politics?' she questioned, happiness surging through her as she studied his face. Her greatest fear had been losing him, her second that the defeat at Waterloo would have changed him, diminished his spirit. But Angèle knew now that her anxieties were groundless. He was already looking forward, not back.

'Perhaps.' Tristan shrugged. 'But just now France will have to do without me: I intend to devote myself to my wife,' he said, folding her more tightly in his arms. 'Just think of it—no more fighting, no more separations. . .'

'I am,' she sighed, letting her head lie on his shoulder. 'There's only one thing that worries me.'

'What?'

'Well, without Napoleon Bonaparte, whatever shall we find to argue about?'

'What to call our son?' he suggested, deadpan. 'I thought Bonaparte Beaumaris had quite a ring to it.'

'If you think I'm going to call our——' she exploded, and then stopped as she saw the laughter in his silver eyes, and the tell-tale tilt of his black brows. Laughing, she shook her head. 'How could you even suggest it?'

'Easily.' His grin broadened. 'Don't you know you're irresistible when you're angry?'

'Prove it, Tristan Beaumaris. . .or I'll kill you,' she threatened, tilting her face up to his.

And he did.

An irresistible offer for you

Here at Reader Service we would love you to become a regular reader of Masquerade. And to welcome you, we'd like you to have 2 books, a cuddly teddy and a mystery gift - ABSOLUTELY FREE and without obligation.

Then, every 2 months you could look forward to receiving 4 more brand-new Masquerade historical romances for just £2.25 each, delivered to your door, postage and packing free. Plus our free Newsletter featuring special offers, author news, competitions with some great prizes, and lots more!

This invitation comes with no strings attached. You may cancel or suspend your subscription at any time, and still keep your free books and gifts.

It's so easy. Send no money now. Simply fill in the coupon below at once and post it to - Reader Service, FREEPOST, PO Box 236, Croydon, Surrey CR9 9EL.

----------- NO STAMP REQUIRED -----------

Yes! Please rush me 2 FREE Masquerade romances and 2 FREE gifts! Please als reserve me a Reader Service subscription. If I decide to subscribe, I can look forward to receiving 4 brand new Masquerade romances every 2 months for just £9.00, delivered direct to my door, postage and packing free. If I choose not to subscribe I shall write to you within 10 days - I can keep the books and gifts whatever I decide. I may cancel or suspend my subscription at any time. I am ove 18 years of age.

Mrs/Miss/Ms/Mr _____ EP30

Address _____

_____

Postcode _____ Signature _____

mps
MAILING
PREFERENCE
SERVICE